CW00516869

THE HUNT IN ELUSION

USA TODAY BESTSELLING AUTHOR

M.L. PHILPITT

Cover Designer: Cat Imb, TRC Designs
Editing and Proofreading: Rebecca Barney, Fairest Reviews Editing Services
Formatting: M.L. Philpitt

AUTHOR'S NOTE

This is probably the longest author's note I've ever written so bear with me here as I go all over the place. Please read, because there are important points scattered in here.

I'm Canadian. I write using Canadian/UK spelling, unless the book is based in the US. This book is based in Montreal, Quebec, Canada, therefore my spelling reflects. This means words will have Us in them, or double LLs. (colour, flavour, signalling, etc.) These are not typos.

As a continuation to that point, if you're from Montreal, enjoy!

Next: The Hunt in Elusion is book 1 in the Fractured Ever Afters series. If you've read my Captive Writings series, particularly Burning Notes, you'll know who this book is about because the events in this one are dated after that series. There *is* mention of Hawke in this book, the main character from Burning Notes, so I want to address the question you might have:

Is it mandatory to read Burning Notes before this one?
No. This series is written to be separate. Characters in this one give a clear image of what happened to Hawke and why he's not here, but if you want the story from Hawke himself, then I suggest you read Burning Notes, but Burning Notes is not a standalone. If you're in it just for his story, fine, but warning: the events in that book are a conclusion of the rest of the series. If you have questions or concerns, feel free to reach out.

Lastly, this book has content some people may find triggering. If you are concerned about triggers, please visit my website for a list or contact me.

PLAYLIST

"Big Bad Wolf" by Roses & Revelations
"Baby I'm Dead Inside" by KOPPS
"I Put A Spell On You" by Annie Lennox
"Devil in Her Eyes" by Bryce Savage
"A Little Wicked" by Valerie Broussard
"Devil in Disguise" by EMM
"Figure You Out" by VOILA
"Heaven" by Julia Michaels
"you should see me in a crown" by Billie Eilish
"Monsters" by Ruelle
"Wolves" by Sam Tinnesz & Silverberg
"Sucker for Pain" by Lil Wayne, Wiz Khalifa, Imagine Dragons,
X Ambassadors, Logic, TY Dolls $ign
"Down" by Simon & Trella
"Wicked as They Come" by CRMNL
"How Villains Are Made" by Madalen Duke
"I See Red" by Everyone Loves an Outlaw
"Inside Her Head" by Bryce Savage
"She Keeps Me Up" by Nickelback

"In Flames" by Digital Daggers
"I Did Something Bad" by Taylor Swift
"Till Our Last Day" by Bryce Savage
"Memories" by EarlyRise
"Angel" by Massive Attack
"Atlantic" by Sleep Token

For those who want to be chased.

1
NICO

ometimes, based on the other party and the circumstances, I have a feeling of knowing where a conversation will lead to, even before it starts. It's that exact sense of restless unease I feel when I push open my office door, spotting Father there, his expression pinched with fury.

He leaps to his feet, shoving my chair back a few inches. His hand lifts, his index finger projecting toward me as I tread through the room, keeping a slow, steady gait. My casual attitude opposes his burst of irate energy.

"Where the fuck have you been? Why was it that when I dropped by yesterday, it was your brother I found here instead? Who, I should note, did not have a definitive response regarding your whereabouts."

Keeping my unhurried steps, I come to the side of my desk. My presence causes my father to step back, making room for me to take back my chair. I make a production of dropping into the rich leather, letting my shoulders hunch, as my hands go slack in my lap.

"He couldn't say where I was because he doesn't know. I'm here now though." I lazily shrug one shoulder. "So, say what you need to."

The red that creeps past my father's collar and into his cheeks is comical at best, but more irritating than anything. It's been a long twelve hours and Father is the last person I wish to see right now.

He moves toward my desk and positions his hands on the edge, leaning on his arms, so he can better loom over me. It's a position of challenge, one Father should know better than to take. He's molded me to be as ruthless as him, ensuring I always get what I want. And right now, I want him to back the fuck off.

"Not funny, *boy*. Why are you disappearing for an entire day? You can't shirk your responsibilities whenever you want, you know. You've been my underboss for nearly a year, but my decision is still questioned, given your age. There's many who'd love your position, Nico."

My fingers drum along the edge, to ease the annoyance building in me. Father is the Corsetti family's Boss and he promoted me to Underboss last year, with every intention that I'll take his place after his death. Father may be loud when touting my abilities to others, but in private, he still acts like I can't do the role we both know I can.

"Does it fucking matter?" I snap. "I left. Deal with it."

Father opens his mouth, likely to refute me, when my office door opens again and my brother strides through, his gaze bouncing between our father and me.

"You're back," Rafael states. "Good. I have news." He stops two feet away from my desk, attempting to straighten his unbuttoned suit jacket, as if it does anything for the messy, school boy persona he insists on maintaining.

By the glare Father shoots toward Rafael's attire, he clearly feels the same. With my promotion, Rafael was made a capo, in charge of a regiment of soldiers. Something to keep him busy and show his leadership, so when I'm eventually Boss, Rafael can slide into the underboss position. The untidy appearance Rafael keeps is opposite of Father's ideal.

Of course, Rafael couldn't care less about the job. He much prefers his other business endeavours.

Father straightens, pushing off my desk, his lips pulled in a snarl. "This isn't over, Nico." Then he shifts his focus to my brother, both of us waiting for Rafael to speak.

"Well, okay then." Rafael's gaze finally stops moving between us, settling on me. "While you were gone, there was an attack downtown at one of the clubs."

"Fuck." The curse flies out of my mouth instantly. *Fuck.* Attacks on my clubs only draw the attention of local police forces, which are already bothersome as is. My arms flex as I reposition, a need for action compelling me to get up. "Anyone hurt?"

"Soldiers took the shooter down before he could injure anyone."

"Good."

Father opts to interrupt in that moment, slipping closer to my desk again. His smug expression is one I'm sure he was saving for this precise moment. "*This* is exactly the thing I came to discuss with you yesterday. Any moment could lead to our downfall."

My eyes cut to him; my teeth clamped together as the only physical reminder not to snap at my father again. "It was handled. The shooter was dealt with before he could harm anyone."

"What if they didn't, or what if you were there? What if you were hit? What would become of us then?"

Now it makes sense. This isn't the first time Father's

mentioned this topic. Every once in a while, he gets on my ass about it, but it's been occurring more frequently lately, ever since he made me Underboss. For as long as I can recall, he's been obsessed with continuing our family's bloodline, beginning when he initially took control after his own father's death.

"You're showing weakness," he continues, bringing me back to this pointless conversation. "Every day you don't have an heir is one day closer to someone potentially ending us. It ensures the family's future leadership. Being aligned with another prominent family will show the rest of ours, you're fit for your role."

My jaw juts. "I fucking dare them to question me." Focusing on Rafael, I ask, "Did you find who was behind the attack?" I can certainly guess, but I want the guarantee.

My brother rolls his lips together. "Based on the tattoo we found on the shooter's hand, he's one of De Falco's men."

I nod at hearing the very name I was expecting. Stefano De Falco has been a thorn in this family's side for quite some time. Lately, it feels like some old anger has reignited with the increase in attacks. Most times, the attacks are so half-assed that they're barely worth my time to end Stefano.

"This can't simply be a play for power," I muse, glancing at Father, waiting for him to give his opinion.

Instead, he changes the subject completely. "I've come to inform you that your mother is hosting a party on Friday. She stacked the guest list with daughters from trading partners, wealthy businessmen—Canadian and international—and other associates." He straightens, his chin lifting, confident that I'll fall in line with this inane plan. "You will dance with all of them. You will *pick* one. Nico, for fuck's sake, you're twenty-seven. The family will continue to question your position if you don't take a wife soon. Not having an heir is a weakness. Find

4

someone so we can announce an engagement in a few months."
He sighs, a serene peace momentarily breaking through his rage.
"I say this with care, son. When I was your age, I did what was
needed, and this is why the Corsettis are who we are. I *took* my
power. Got what was owed to me."

"You also almost began a fucking war with New York's
Famiglia. We're lucky it's never come back on this family. Now
of all times," I point out.

With a slice of his knife, he wrecked possible relations with
the *Famiglia* when he killed their heir—and the would-be Don
—to steal Mother for himself. They're a crime family too prominent to have as an enemy, which is why healing that relationship has been my priority.

"If you're talking about your arrangement with New York,
for Aurora and Erico Rossi, you already know how I feel about
that."

It's one of the few decisions I've made since becoming
Underboss that he's been pleased by. I think it's less to do with
the connection though and more with healing the bad blood
between the two crime families.

Aurora will need a worthy match upon returning to this
life, and linking her with New York will make us a North Amer-
ican powerhouse, ensuring a necessary allegiance between the
two families.

My twenty-year-old baby sister, who was sent away from us
when she was six-years-old, for her own safety has been a topic
of decision the last few years. My parents have gone back and
forth on deciding when Aurora should return, finally deter-
mining to wait until her schooling has been completed. I've
always felt she should be home with us, ensuring the Corsettis
are complete.

Aurora Corsetti has been an unspoken mystery to much of

society. They were aware of her and knew she left for her safety, but then she stopped being constantly mentioned, becoming a shadow of the past that people remembered but no longer spoke of. No one knows when she's set to return to us—if at all —except for the Rossi family.

Pre-arranging her engagement is simply smart business, which Father also believes, but Mother still hasn't spoken to me since I made the announcement a week ago. Perhaps that's why she's throwing this stupid party. Some sick payback for marrying her baby girl off so soon.

"The moment you become too comfortable is the second a snake slithers in," Father says, snapping me from my thoughts. "We can't let that happen. New York is one connection, yes, but that doesn't solidify *your* heir, which brings me back to my original point. This Friday, you will attend the party and I won't hear more about this."

Following through on his latest words, Father stomps away from my desk, leaving me and Rafael alone, who then drops into one of two chairs across from me and stretches his arms along the armrests' edging.

His shrill whistle pierces the air. "Fuck, man. Gonna tell your little bro where you've been? Your message yesterday about going away for the night was cryptic. You usually at least tell me where. Which means, it's somewhere good."

There's very few people I can completely lower my guard around. Not even Father makes the cut. Rafael though, he's been by my side since we were kids, never once causing me to question his loyalty. But this...the truth in what I'm about to admit will be hard on him, making it a truth I'd prefer to remain hidden.

"Swear you won't say anything."

Rafael breaks into an easy grin, rolling his eyes. "You know I won't."

"No." My mouth remains a flat line, my eyes conveying no humour. "*Swear it*, Rafael."

My emphasis on affirming his silence finally causes him to realize the gravity in what I'm asking, and his lips form a small O. He flicks his bangs off his forehead for a clear view when he looks at me, lifting his hand to his heart, over the script tattoo etched there many years ago alongside his induction to the family, and makes an X with his right index finger.

"*Unisciti a leale. Muori leale,*" he recites our Italian motto. Join loyal. Die loyal. "On the family, you have my word."

"Not a word to Mother or Father especially." My tongue skirts the inside of my mouth and I opt to go with a single word —a name—to begin: "Hawke."

Rafael stands, his presence becoming larger as though he can't contain himself. A few emotions pass over his face: surprise, shock, and finally, confusion.

"Did you find him?"

I'll admit, I rarely feel guilt concerning any aspect of my life, but this time, the dark, little emotion creeps up, creating a tightness in my chest, right around my heart. Hawke is Rafael's brother and deserves to know everything I do.

"Months ago," I finally divulge. "I've been working on tracking him for a while."

"What the fuck, Nico?" he explodes, a mix of rage and anguish emitting from him. His hands fly to his head, yanking on his hair. "You kept *my brother* from me *for months*?"

The tightness grows, and for once, I'm not even a bit irate at his show of anger. The moment I reached out to Hawke months ago, I debated telling Rafael, but Hawke had made it more than clear that he didn't wish to be found, let alone speak with any of us, and I know both my brothers. Hawke would take off again if he felt threatened, and Rafael wouldn't be able to resist reaching out.

"Upon his request, Raf." My tone softens slightly, using his nickname to trick him into settling down. "He was pissed when I found him. The single conversation I had with him was brief, and he didn't want anyone else to know about his whereabouts, let alone how to contact him."

Rafael stops moving for a moment, his hands rising to weave between strands of his hair. He turns to face me again, the skin around his eyes pinched.

"Man, still. He's *our* brother, and you had no right to keep him from me. I may be younger than you, but I remember him leaving. I remember crying for weeks after he left, with only a basic understanding of what the fuck happened. Of what *Father* left him to deal with. It's no wonder he's forsaken us; I would too! For years, I've wondered what it'd be like if he walked through those doors and came home."

"I know." I recall holding Rafael, letting him cry into my chest as we hid away from Father, worried he'd view our heartbreak as weakness rather than as love for our brother.

"How is he? Is he okay?"

Seeing Hawke in person after thirteen years took a lot of strength, even for me. He's so different than the kid I recall, but stronger too, somehow. Life away from us created a better version of him, and that alone is a hard pill to swallow.

"A couple months ago, he reached out to me for help. Needed our connections to the RCMP."

"Shit." Rafael brushes a hand over his face before lowering back into the chair, this time, sitting upright and tense. "What for?"

Wordlessly, I pull my phone from my pocket and find the news article I bookmarked before turning the device toward him. He takes it, and reads it. Minutes pass before his eyes lift from the device.

"That's fucked. Guy sounds like a psychopath."

"He is," I agreed. *Was.* "Guess big bro's been chasing him for a while now, and needed our help arresting him."

"Could have brought in the entire family. We could have wiped the fucker out." His lips twitch, but I spot the strain, the show of how much he wished that was how it happened.

"Considering his dislike for our life, I'm assuming that's the very reason he didn't." When Rafael slowly nods, hearing me, I continue, "That was months ago. The other day he phoned again. Said the guy was in federal prison down here and wanted our men to take him out."

"Interesting. What brought him to that?"

"A woman." A gorgeous one at that. I think of the girl standing on his front porch as Hawke and I spoke. She's beautiful, but looks too tame for my tastes. "He once referred to her as 'his' and based on what the news reported about this girl, pretty sure she's the guy's latest victim."

"Wow," is all Rafael says, nodding faster this time. "Good for Hawke."

"Yes. The sick fuck escaped prison before we could get to him. By the time I warned Hawke, it was too late."

"Shit."

I shrug. "Pictures app. First one." I pause, waiting for my brother to follow those instructions, and I spot the moment he sees the image of the mangled body. His eyes get brighter, his appreciation for violence causing him to shift in place. "Hawke did that," I explain. "He called yesterday, asking me to dispose of his body. I took some soldiers with me, and saw him this morning."

Rafael stabs his finger into my phone screen. "*Hawke* did that? Mister-left-this-life did *that*? Damn." He whistles and tosses my phone back to me. It lands on my desk with a *thump.* "He must really like the girl."

"Bit more than that, but yes. Anyway, that's where I was."

Still nodding as he takes it all in, Rafael asks, "Going to tell our parents?"

"With time," I lie. In truth, I have no fucking clue what I'll do, but if Rafael believes I'll be informing them, then he won't. The less people that know, the better. "For now, silence about this, brother. We found him; we have limited communication with him. He's asked me to never reach out again."

Hurt flashes in my brother's expression and he briefly looks down to his feet as disappointment swirls around him.

"He's a Corsetti by blood, Raf. That image is evidence. He may have left the family, but does the lifestyle truly ever go away? He has his girl now, which means he'll do anything to protect her."

"You think he'll come home." It's a statement, not a question.

"Not sure," I murmur, leaning back to kick my feet up on top of my desk. "His role here has changed. He couldn't return to a place of power, but I do foresee him making the connection again. For now, the ball is in his court."

Rafael grins, his previous misery quickly wiped away, and taps the side of his head. "And that's why you're the leader, Nico. You have all the good ideas."

"I have all the emotionless ideas," I counter. "Allows me to think rationally."

Rafael stands again and begins walking toward the door. He calls over his shoulder, "Whatever. Just be sure to think rationally this Friday when Mother's throwing potential brides your way."

"Fuck off." The reminder of Father's visit, which now feels like it was forever ago, returns. "It's not happening," I shout at my brother's retreating back.

Before Rafael shuts the door, he turns to wink at me. "You

said so yourself, Hawke found his one. Time for the next in line to do the same."

Never.

The trick to being a rational underboss: don't allow a woman under your skin.

2
DELLA

"Dad wants you," a voice by the doorway suddenly states. I don't have to glance up to see who it is because my body's tense reaction tells me instead.

There are always people with voices that just make you want to snap at them. Unfortunately for me, I live with two of them.

"Hey, did you hear what she said, orphan?" The second chortles.

Continuing to ignore them, I tread around the California King bed to smooth the duvet from the other side, before dragging the lint roller over it, ensuring that Stefano De Falco's bed is perfect, much to my chagrin.

Everything I do must be impeccable or else I risk more than just my life.

Even when his two annoying daughters—my ex-stepsisters —revel in harassing me.

"Orphan!"

"Can you not see I'm busy?" I snap, the anger finally building, bubbling, and exploding over the top. The roller drops from my hand and lands on the duvet, creating a small dent in otherwise perfection. "Your dad can wait the two fucking minutes until I finish making *his* bed."

Rozelyn flicks pin-straight, waist-length blonde hair from her shoulder as she crosses her arms, staring at me, her chin lifted with all the attitude she's perfected. "Careful how you speak to us. One year later, and it seems like you're still forgetting your place."

Beside her, Yasmine, her sister, sneers. "Leave her alone, Roz. Let her do what she's so good at." She pets the black cat in her arms, her strokes slow as she looks down on me.

I fix the wrinkle in the duvet I created before grabbing the lint roller and stomping away from the bed. I approach them, my attention on the cat in Yasmine's arms. Lucifer's dark eyes glint as I come closer, and I swear there's no better name for that devilish cat than the one he has. Fucking animal constantly swipes at me with his overly sharp nails. They really need to trim them.

"Speaking of what one's good at, how's it feel to be the ones sent to fetch me?" I shoulder my way between them, ensuring I shove harder than necessary. "Clearly dear ol' Dad feels you're only good at serving a man. Makes you wonder what else he has planned for your pointless futures." I trudge off, keeping my head high, all while feeling the daggers being shot at my back.

They won't follow me though, because they know I'm right, and now that I've listened to their instructions, they have no further reason to be around me. Especially since I'm headed to their father's office, a place they choose to avoid as much as possible.

Everyone avoids Stefano, if possible.

If only Mom had too.

Rozelyn and Yasmine's dislike for me began nearly two years ago when my mother became the new wife, replacing their own mother, who had died many years prior. According to others around the mansion, their mother and Stefano were a true love match and it was nearly a decade until he allowed another woman in. My mother just so happened to be that woman.

Except, not only did she become their new mom, but she lugged me and my sister in with her, and suddenly, they had two new stepsisters as well. Even though they despised me from the very first meeting, they were at least indifferent and easily ignorable. Once Mom was gone, they were extremely vocal in their hatred of me, and with my new role in the house, they found new ways to terrorize me.

They kicked me out of the room I've had since Mom moved us in here, and up to the dirty, dusty, cold attic. Stefano, of course, couldn't care less about how his daughters treated me.

Outside Stefano's office, I pause, inhaling all the breath I'll need to get me through this coming conversation. The fresh air in my lungs does little to ease the trepidation creeping through my form. Eventually, I muster the strength to lift my hand and knock on the door.

"Come in!" the deep voice immediately hollers.

I open the door and slip into the dim lighting, letting it steal me away from the bright hallway. Stefano has a strange habit of always keeping his blinds shut, ensuring no light can enter. If vampires existed, I swear he'd be one, because the man hates sunlight. Other staff assume it has something to do with his fear of being assassinated.

"What took you so long?"

My eyes adjust slowly to the dusky office, slowly making out shapes, and eventually, finer details of the moderate sized room. Its dark walls are laced with intricate details, hinting toward the mansion's fine age. Shelves line one wall, filled with old books I'm certain this owner has never read before. Directly across from me is a wooden desk, and a figure that stands from his place behind it, coming around to the front, where he props himself on, crossing his arms and staring at me with discerning eyes.

I slowly walk forward, pinning my arms at my sides and lowering my head, even while prickles of distaste course through me. I despise how apprehensive he always makes me feel.

"Sorry." No reason. Only an apology because I've long learned he doesn't actually care about what I say.

"No matter." His voice lowers into a soft murmur and that's when I realize he hasn't summoned me for any good reason. When Stefano speaks like this, it's because he's playing a game he'll inevitably win.

Stefano De Falco was the best and worst thing to ever happen to my family. I can still recall when Mom first allowed him to visit Ariella and me at the house we were living in at the time. It was nearly a year before they wed, only days after Mom mentioned dating someone, but given that Ariella and I weren't kids, she didn't feel the need to hide a relationship from us.

I got home from work one day, when I was waitressing part-time to help bring income into the household, and he was there. Over the next year of them dating, I swear, he was around more often than not, but I didn't mind after a while. Since Dad left when we were young, it was nice to have a father figure in the house again. Someone to join us for dinner and to break up the monotony of only being with Mom and Ariella.

With him, came his own daughters, who were hardly present when we visited their glamorous house. Despite the shared comradeship between me and my sister, and Rozelyn and Yasmine, in having a new parent, they didn't want anything to do with us, but it never bothered me.

Life in Quebec isn't cheap, and even with Ariella and me finally finished with high school and able to work, adding to Mom's own small income, life was challenging. Food wasn't plentiful, not how it was in Stefano's house, and the heat in winter could never be jacked too high, or else our bill would be enormous. So many times, I've wondered if Mom only dated him for his income, aware it would provide us with a better life.

Looking back, I've often wondered if, as they were dating, she was aware of where his income came from—and where it continues to. Stefano De Falco, Boss of the De Falco mafia family: one of two crime families in Quebec. Still, even *I* don't know everything Stefano does to make money, but given the bit I've learned about the mob, I don't ask questions because I suspect I'm not supposed to know.

After they wed and we moved into the De Falco mansion, life got even more comfortable. Stefano insisted I stopped working and learned to enjoy the easy life, exactly as his own daughters did.

Life got good...until it wasn't. Until the veil dropped and Mom died.

An accident. A "tragic car accident" is how the media portrayed it, but those words never seemed adequate. Mom perished, and while Ariella survived, she became a shell of the sister I used to know, so really, it's like I lost them both.

It's been over a year since the accident, and the only person Ariella's spoken to since then is me, and only ever when we're alone. The doctors tossed around words like trauma and psychosomatic symptoms, diagnosing her as having selective mutism.

The doctors gave me everything in basic terminology, but I wanted the truth, so I did a *lot* of research. Officially, she falls under the anxiety disorder category, per the huge book of psychiatric disorders I found online. Her mutism is trauma-induced and the doctors found no sign of neurological damage, which I've learned means there's no physical harm to her mind. Ariella never described the accident though, never explained what exactly happened, but whatever did, her mind believes remaining silent is the way to keep her safe. It's the trauma protecting her from further danger. I'm the one safe person her mental state allows

After the accident, the Stefano who charmed Ariella and me was gone, and he became the unforgiving villain. The moment the funeral ended, he got rid of Ariella, claiming she was no longer useful if she refuses to speak. She's capable, and the doctors recommended she be home with frequent trips to therapy, but Stefano didn't care and ruled her as incapable and wanted nothing to do with her.

Now, she sits silently through therapy, and follows what the doctors tell her to, but there's been no sign of progress. Not that I blame her, being forgotten about in a medical centre, away from everything and everyone she knows.

"I have a task for you."

Servitude. That's the deal. For my life and Ariella's medical care, I serve him. In any way or form, though, thus far, it's only been as a servant in his house.

"You're very pretty, Della. So much like your mother."

I stiffen, the muscles in my neck straining to lift, so I can look up at him, to be prepared should the worst happen. Instead, I allow my eyes to raise, to watch as his shiny leather shoes bring him in front of me.

His hand reaches into my vision and two fingers grip my chin, lifting my head up. Dark eyes, the kind you'd see in nightmares, study me. The dull light from the ceiling bounces off his nearly-shaved head, which sometimes makes him look like a prison convict.

Even though my swallow is rough and I want to look away, I aim to keep my attention on him. I've learned in my time here that my stepfather is like a bear. Watch him, but never run away.

Let him grow bored before trying to bolt because that's when he'll chase.

"Your eyes are identical to your mother's. Blue is such a lovely colour to find on a woman. It's a sign of true beauty." His free hand lifts and he pinches strands of my hair between his fingers, lifting it past my gaze and staring at the hair with a curious expression, the skin between his eyes frazzled, as though struck by the similarities I share with Mom.

Is this why he's called me here? To be my mother's replacement?

Before the inevitable shudder works its way up my spine, he releases me all at once and backs away, even turning around as he returns to his desk. Before he faces me again though, I breathe, taking in deep gulps, preparing me for whatever disaster is next.

"Before I tell you what the task is, should I need to remind you that if you fail, your sister will find herself homeless without the medical attention she needs?"

Dick.

He takes my silence as agreement. "Well, then. You know of the Corsetti family, of course."

I've certainly heard him bitch about them enough. They own all of Montreal and Quebec City, as well as the places in between. They're the largest crime family on this side of Canada, much to the chagrin of Stefano, who's been pushed out of the major cities and claims everything north of Montreal. I often think about the Corsettis and how much control they have over this side of the country, and wonder why they haven't wiped out Stefano De Falco and his line. Then I debate if I'd prefer it or not. It'd free me, but then Ariella wouldn't have medical care because I couldn't afford the level she receives. It goes *way* beyond the country's free basic health care.

"Yes."

"I received intel this morning that they will be hosting a party in two days, on Friday night. It'll be a grand event because most of the country's prominent women will be there, vying for Nico Corsetti's hand in marriage."

Nico Corsetti. Underboss of the Corsetti family, the son of their Don, and Stefano's enemy. He's splashed all over the gossip magazines as being one of Canada's most eligible bachelors, and yet, no matter how many times I pause to study his image, I never grow tired of looking. Sometimes, I allow myself the briefest of moments to stare at his green eyes, captivating me through a picture the paparazzi managed to snap of him. They emit danger—delicious, desirable danger.

"Friday," Stefano continues, folding his hands over his stomach, "you will be outfitted so you can slip into the party alongside the other guests. Get into Corsetti's mansion and find his office. Find me something that will benefit me. I've sent men into his clubs, but they all end up dead."

Ignoring the last part involving my possible death, I ask, "What am I looking for?"

"Anything," he growls. "Documents on trades. Business agreements. Emails. His fucking personal schedule. *Anything* that will help me."

Insanity. Desperation. That's what Stefano exhibits. For years, he's spoken about taking down the Corsettis. One night when he was drunk, I overheard him mumbling to Mom about the day Caterina Vosa wed Lorenzo Corsetti, for he knew the Vosas held true power back then, and now, it's controlled by the Corsettis. Essentially, they're royalty.

I've long assumed there's more to the politics than that. There's no reason De Falco can't move us elsewhere and try to claim another city, I think. Maybe there are reasons he can't do that. But this obsession with the Corsetti family seems a bit...much?

"I'll be picked out instantly."

Maybe. Stefano was very good at keeping Mom, Ariella, and me away from the press. He always ensured any outings were minimal, and looking back, I should have been suspicious why he was so embarrassed to have married a normal woman, rather than someone with connections.

"I'm almost counting on that. Do this or your sister ends up on the street."

There's a huge risk in snooping around the enemy's house, but also, there's as much danger right here in front of me. I must attempt and get in and out of the Corsetti mansion unseen, or I risk death—or worse—by Nico's hand. But all that's a chance; there's no guarantee. Pissing off Stefano and getting kicked out *is* a guarantee, and for Ariella's sake, it's one I won't gamble with, not ever, which means I have to do this.

"Fine."

Stefano smiles, his grin too wide and sickly. "Good, good. Get back to work, Della. We'll get someone in here to make you into a princess."

Charming comparison. I think about that one princess, Cinderella, who went to a ball to meet her prince. She got decked out in the fancy clothing to impress him, before running away to avoid being found out as a commoner.

I'm not Cinderella, since my reason for attending is much different than hers was. I'm not there to make Nico fall in love with me.

I'm there to ruin him.

3

NICO

Rafael's eyes are pinned on the duo of women dancing provocatively on the stage below the VIP balcony. I can practically see the drool falling from my brother's mouth, and the way their own attention is locked on him, it's clear how his night will end.

Too desperate for my tastes. Women here are too blatant in their desires.

A waitress approaches with a tray of three drinks and dips low, her round breasts nearly tumbling from her thin tank top as she removes each shot glass and rests it on the small table between the three leather couches we've stolen in the corner of the VIP balcony. She straightens slowly, glancing at me from beneath full lashes, a promise deep within them. Once she's upright again, she makes a show of tossing her long, dark hair over her shoulder and leisurely striding away, her hips rolling with her steps.

Case in point. Desperate.

Women like her will do anything for cock. It's not me she wants; it's my body. My name. The thrill of being able to claim she's fucked the underboss of the Corsetti family before she's knowingly discarded.

Rather, I prefer a challenge. There's nothing I enjoy more than watching a woman run from me, believing she has a shot at escaping. It's in the way her breath comes out short and harsh; the way her body constantly twists, peeking behind her, measuring how far away she is from me; how long until I catch her. And then when I do catch her, the primal need within me to claim, to remind the woman who dared challenge me in a race, emerges to fuck her into oblivion. To take her wherever I've managed to catch up to her. To remind her who *owns* her, even for that small moment in time.

Somewhere in the midst of my thoughts, Rafael coughs. He jerks his chin toward the retreating woman, his lips pulled in a grin. "Looking to make this a bachelor party?"

"Fuck you."

"Just sayin'." He shrugs, his eyes slowly trailing back to the dancers below.

To my right, a figure comes up, claiming the other free couch. His large frame settles on the leather cushions, his legs spreading wide, his gaze scanning the club, wary and cautious at every turn, despite it being a Corsetti-owned club. Once he's satisfied we're not in immediate danger—which I've already scoped out, but I won't rob him of a valuable habit—he focuses on me.

"Nico," he greets with a jerk of his head.

"Rosen." I gesture to one of the three glasses the waitress laid out as I reach for my own. "Take one."

He does, grasping the glass in his large hand but not swallowing the shot. He continues to watch me, waiting.

"You're too fucking tense, Rosen," I tease.

Rafael spins around, taking the final shot glass as he chuckles. "One day you're gonna relax, Rosen, and it'll be a beautiful day when you do. It's like you forget who we are."

Rosen grunts and lifts the glass to his mouth. As he takes the shot, I spot the hint of a grin, which shows me his exterior is slowly thawing.

Rosen kind of took the place of Hawke, even if it's a hard truth to admit. He's a year older than me—the same age as Hawke—but he's grown up around my house with my siblings and me. As kids, we played together, never caring about the differences between mafia royalty and soldiers. Rosen's father had been a highly trusted soldier for my father before he retired some years ago and was the only one to guard my mother when she left the mansion. Even so, Rosen sometimes struggles to leave his rigid role behind and relax.

For all Rosen's loyalty, Father refuses to allow me to make him a capo of his own regiment. Something about having to appease all the cousins first, who get to rightfully claim those roles. For now, Rosen's beneath Rafael's command, but we all know, he's too skilled and trusted to simply be a soldier. One day, when I'm Don, I'll promote him as I see fit.

"Old habits," Rosen responds to Rafael dryly, lowering his glass again. "I wouldn't dare disrespect my underboss and risk torture." He grins easily.

And that's why I like Rosen. Sometimes even more than Rafael.

Rafael chuckles loudly, downing his shot in one swig. "Right. I've also seen what *you* can do, crazy motherfucker."

If I'm ruthless, Rosen is absolutely insane. I've seen him do shit that's made me downright disturbed. It's also what makes him so ideal for the job I have for him.

"There's something I need to talk with you about," I start, leaning forward, letting my hands dangle between my legs.

"This is in strict confidence. After a recent decision, Aurora will be coming home in a month's time."

Rosen's eyes grow wide and his mouth falls opens. On the verge of speaking, his eyes flick to the other side of the lounge, scanning anyone nearby who could be potentially listening. Even when he finds no one listening in, he lowers his voice to ask, "Your sister?"

Rosen was a kid with Rafael and me, and he knows Aurora, and what happened to her. He and his father are two of the few trusted with the complete truth of her disappearance.

"She's coming home," I continue, "because it's time. My parents should have done it long ago, after realizing that the fear and danger had passed. She needs to take her place in the family...and meet her fiancé."

Rosen still looks shocked, but my attention lands on my brother, who whips back to face me, shaking his head, a smirk curling up the corner of his mouth. I only mentioned planning for a union, not that I had one secured.

I tell them, "Father ruined any chance of a partnership with the New York *Famiglia* when he slaughtered one of theirs. They haven't forgiven, but leadership has changed hands, and the new generation, like me, sees the benefit of a union."

Rafael continues to shake his head. "You're slightly delusional, you know that, right? Smart, yes. I see how you twisted this entire thing to your benefit, but still delusional. She'll hate you. The moment she walks through the door, you'll be shipping her off."

Turning back to Rosen and ignoring my brother's comments, I continue, "She will come back and there will be many questions. I imagine my sister will need to adapt, as well. There will be a lot of pressure while she re-learns her place, and I do fear some could take advantage of that. You, Rosen, will be her personal guard."

He jerks in place, rapidly blinking. "Sir?"

"In a year, she will be wed. It will only be until then."

"Sir?"

I reach over to hit his arm. "Rosen, you know there's no fucker in my employ I trust more than you. You're also one of my youngest, so you're the closest in age to her and won't attract unnecessary attention. You will be excused from your normal duties for this."

Rafael roars with laughter, slapping the couch beside him. "Babysitting duty. Ha! That's great, Rosen. Brother, you're full of the jokes today."

Ignoring my sibling, I pull out my phone to find the most recent image her school had sent me. She's walking through the hallways, her shoulders held high, the breeze blowing her hair from her face. A true Corsetti.

I flip the phone around to show Rosen. "This is what she looks like now. Not the kid you remember."

His jaw falls open a fraction, shock at her growth evident on his face. He shifts, rubbing at his chin as he nods slowly. His eyes peruse my screen, and I know he's committing her to memory. A good soldier—my best, and he'll protect her.

"Only for a year," I finish, putting my phone away and breaking his stare.

Rosen nods, but this time, he seems more distracted.

"Then you'll get the best vacation of your life," my brother tosses in. "I imagine, following a woman around who needs to get used to this life..." He makes a sputtering sound. "Good luck, man. Wouldn't want to be ya."

Neither of us pay him any attention though. Rosen's head bobs into another nod. He swallows roughly, but then lays his hand over his heart, over his tattoo. *"Unisciti a leale. Muori leale."*

25

I accept his oath before my eyes slide to Rafael, who's shaking his head slowly again. "What?" I bark.

He raises his hands up, palms out toward me. "She's gonna hate you for this. First, dragging her home, a place brand new to her, with a family she barely remembers, then adding an engagement onto it, and finally," he jerks his chin toward Rosen, "throwing a bodyguard at her after so many years of freedom."

Aurora's only been "free" because she was placed in a private institution run by nuns. She may not have had anyone shadow her directly, but she's been guarded nonetheless, alongside other children from prominent families.

I shrug, indifferent about my sister's potential feelings. "She will learn her place."

At that moment, the waitress returns with three fresh glasses. She scans Rosen appreciatively, but ultimately her attention reverts to me. She smiles and silently distributes the glasses before taking the empty ones away.

When she leaves again, Rafael nods his head toward her. "Celebrate your final night of freedom."

"Dumbass, I'm not getting married tomorrow." Or even engaged, for that matter. I'm not picking someone tomorrow, no matter how many beautiful women my parents throw my way. I know what I want, and it's not a simpering debutante whose parents are solely trying to 'get in' with my family.

"Makes me so fucking happy for my life, I won't lie," Rosen chimes, leaning forward for his second drink. "To not be part of those games. Women being shown off like they're all cattle." His nose lifts, but I don't disagree with the sentiment. My life dictates it's the shitty game I must go along with. "Makes marriage political."

Rafael's eyes cut toward Rosen. "I hear you, man. It's not so bad when you're the youngest son, though." He grins. "What, no future Mrs. Carrigan yet?"

Rosen shifts, his eyes diving for the drink in his hand. "Nope, no time for that shit. My life doesn't exactly leave room for romance."

Most soldiers eventually settle down with a family, while continuing to work for us, but I understand his preferences. In a life where, at any moment, a stray bullet can go too far and make its mark, ending a life in a blink of an eye, it's difficult to want to add love into it. It's a lot of stress to maintain a family, while dedicating one's life to serving.

"Either way," I start, "tomorrow isn't changing shit. I'll perform as our parents need me to. I'll be there, counting down the seconds until I can be free."

Rosen waggles his brows at me, his mouth finally easing into a smirk. "Doesn't that make you feel like a prize?"

I scoff, but feel compelled to scan the VIP balcony, spotting the waitress by the bar, watching me. Perhaps he's not that far off in his remark.

"Eh. I'm no prince and never will be. They'll understand that really quick." My future mafia queen won't have the happy-ever-after. She'll see me late at night when I'm buried in her cunt, producing an heir, and that's it. If Father insists on a marriage to further the line, that's all he'll get from me.

"Grump," Rafael comments, pulling me from my thoughts. "He was just having fun. Go fuck the waitress and be less grouchy."

As if called over, the waitress appears by my side, smiling down at me. "Is there something you need?"

I study her. The dark hair falling over her shoulders, the desperate smile, all of it makes me sick. How would she react if I told her to run, knowing my goal would be to catch her and fuck her harder than she's ever been before?

The longer I stare, the more her nerves build. Her bright eyes darken with lust and her lip finds its way beneath her teeth.

She presses down on it as her feet shift from side to side. So hopeful. So eager.

But she's here and available and I don't have the energy to search for a woman who'll appease my cravings, simply because there's not many of those women. Most want to be caught, so the chase never lasts long or feels real enough, which makes the entire thing tedious and unsatisfying.

I lift to my feet and pull the tray from her hand, tossing it on the couch I've abandoned. Touching her hip, I place my head in the curve of her neck, my lips trailing the sensitive skin at the back of her neck. My lips nip at her ear, causing her to shudder in the exact way I expect her to.

"There's a car out back. In five minutes, be there, undressed and waiting."

Sending them out back, at one in the morning, to a stranger's car is the exact opposite of safe, and she knows that. Knows who I am and how dangerous I can be, and yet, her cunt's desire for a cock—for *my* cock specifically—is too great for a whore like her to ignore.

Which is why she peeks at me beneath her lashes before slipping away, toward the balcony's exit. Her heels stumble with her speed, eagerness driving her forward. No chase whatsoever, just blind obedience. She'll obey me and I'll find her in the back seat of my car, with her cunt sopping wet and ready to take all of me because I, Nico Corsetti, gave her an ounce of attention.

Pathetic.

4
DELLA

Yasmine and Rozelyn circle me, their sneers permanent fixtures for the past while. They keep it up, they could be risking their face shifting forever into this look of disgust. Neither of them are pleased to do their father's bidding when he instructed them to prepare me for the Corsetti party.

The blue dress he picked out is stunning. It's fitted to my form tighter than anything I'd normally wear, dropping straight to the floor with a long slit up one side. The sweetheart neckline reveals more of my chest than I'd normally be comfortable with.

My hair has been pulled up into a messy but stylish bun, keeping my neck bare. It sours my mind to mentally compliment my ex-stepsisters' hairstyling skills, but I'd be blind not to see how effective they are at crafting me into this beautiful, other persona.

"You're finished," Yasmine states, scanning my reflection in the mirror in front of us. Her lips are puckered, her nose wrinkled.

"Must have killed you both, to wait on me like this."

Rozelyn's nose lifts in a snub. "Charity work is an important part of our lives, if you must know. Besides, you're the one being offered up to the Corsettis. We consider this our final goodbye because once they catch you, you're fucked."

How much do they know of what they're helping me get ready for? To what extent did Stefano keep his daughters in the dark?

I shrug their comments off and move past them and out of the spare room they set up in, going straight for the staircase.

I might look the part, but I certainly don't feel it. Once upon a time, I enjoyed the pretty dresses and doing my hair as such, when Mom was alive and I was one of Stefano's accepted children. Then she was gone and the world turned dark before being made black by Stefano's abandonment and things like shopping and dressing-up became unavailable.

At the bottom of the stairs, I'm stopped again, this time by the raking gaze of a guard. I don't know his name because, honestly, I've never cared to learn them all. There's too many of them to keep track of and Stefano constantly has them going this way and that, completing all the illegal duties he demands of them.

His eyes greedily drink up every inch of me, but I continue past him, trying like hell to resist from covering myself. The guard continues to stare—I feel it—but the unwelcome sensation is soon overtaken by the one Stefano pushes me into instead: dread. His shoes echo down the granite-floored hallway as he strides to a stop in front of me, his eyes also studying me.

"At least my daughters managed to do one thing right," he mutters after a moment.

His hand snakes out and he grasps my chin between two fingers, angling my head up toward him. Instinct demands me to pull away from his unsolicited touch, but I'd rather not anger Stefano tonight. My eyes do lower though, unwilling to meet his intense gaze and create an entire new wave of hate within me.

"Should you ensure your demeanor is up to standard, you will certainly fit into the party. Eyes up," he demands.

I hold back the sigh-slash-groan working its way up in the back of my throat, not wanting him to feel me shudder as I do, and instead, lift my eyes slowly, clashing with his angry, dark ones.

Once he has my attention, he grits, "Keep your head high and your wits about you. My driver will take you to the Corsetti mansion. He will leave and return at midnight." His grip on my chin grows harder, more painful, and he leans in closer, pausing a breath away from my face, our lips uncomfortably close together. "You hear me, Della. *Midnight.* Guests will begin leaving around one, and you need to be out of there before-hand, to slip away when no attention is on you."

"Midnight," I echo softly.

"Do not offer any information about yourself. If you must provide a name, you are Anna Evans, daughter of Edmonton's mayor. She is on the guest list but found herself indisposed tonight," Stefano continues, offering no further information on the case. He releases me roughly and leans away, gesturing to the front entrance on our left. "Get going. Do *not* disappoint me. It'd be such a shame to find your sister on the streets..."

His threat trails off as his slow, paced steps take him backwards. I bite down on a curse and turn away from him, so he can't see the hatred so plainly on my face.

Get this done. Move on. Be his tool for Ariella's benefit.

The Corsetti mansion is fucking *huge*. If I ever believed Stefano's mansion—actually, *house*, compared to this —had any standing against this monstrosity, I was extremely wrong. To think such a place like this even exists in Montreal is fantastical all on its own.

Modern architecture, glass windows everywhere, that are clearly only one-way since I can't see anything through them. The front lawn is easily the size of a few football fields, with a circular driveway cutting right through where Stefano's driver pulls up.

He gets out and opens the back door for me, continuing the act that I'm someone important. I grasp my clutch, which holds my phone, and slide from the vehicle before nerves even have an opportunity to register.

The fact I'm doing this is ridiculous on many levels, but it's also a stark reminder of my life and reality. That mobsters are real. That getting ahead is how one obtains power, and sending an untrained woman into the lion's den is completely normal.

I'm so fucked. My laugh is huffed out silently as I stride up the grand staircase and through the giant, propped-up doors. Two bodyguards line them but neither looks twice.

I enter the mansion and am transported into a new world. A different realm in which everything is flashy colours, fake smiles, and seamless delicacy. The doorman takes my fictitious name, scans the list on his phone, and gestures for me to walk down the long hallway, where music flows. Even the small chunk of time I spent as Stefano De Falco's stepdaughter didn't show me the true style of the mob; not if *this* is what it actually looks like.

I follow the hallway toward the music, trailing after a couple far in front of me, and into a massive wide-open room filled with dozens upon dozens of people mingling around. The most noticeable though are the women. There's a fucking *ton* of them. As if the daughter of every prominent man in the country showed up tonight.

Stefano is kidding himself if he thinks he'll *ever* be able to truly compete with Nico Corsetti. Popularity alone speaks to his power.

Most of the women are talking amongst themselves or with their families, but every single set of eyes is locked onto someone on the opposite side of the room. Somehow, I know who they're looking at, but I allow my gaze to travel there too.

Nico Corsetti is even more gorgeous in person. Like, unnaturally so. The gossip sites and magazines do not do him justice whatsoever.

He looks like a dark prince. Angular jaw covered in a light dusting of facial hair, giving him that sexy shadow just-rolled-out-of-bed look. Mesmerizing emerald eyes scan the room, calculatingly bored, while his dark hair looks like it was brushed through with his hand. He exudes a sense of brooding, while maintaining the deathly haze, like one wrong word and he can have one's life in his firm, unyielding grip. I follow the line of his body, toward his hands, noticing the black ink creeping past his sleeve, and wonder where else he has tattoos.

He's classically handsome in his suit, as he stands in a row with his other family members. The guy beside him, his brother, I assume, given the similarities in their appearance, fades into the background as Nico's own menace is overwhelmingly strong, even from my distance.

My feet move on their own accord, to get a closer look, but then I pause, remembering why I'm here. While I may look like I fit in with these women, I don't. I'm a maid in the enemy's household, here with a task, and it's time to get to it.

5
NICO

Every second passing by adds another tick onto the annoyance level. Every moment has the glass becoming more fragile in my hand. More than once, I've looked to the doorway, wondering if it'd be easy to slip out of here and disappear from the mansion altogether.

"I'm bored already," I mutter into Rafael's ear.

"It's been twenty minutes."

"And? Your exasperation reminds me of our mother." Who I find across the room talking with a group of women. No doubt, handpicking my future wife.

Similarly, Father's off to the side, conversing with men. Mostly fathers or uncles or other fatherly figures who've come with the wanna-be future brides in hopes to secure a marriage deal by the end of tonight. Like we're in the damn eighteen hundreds. These traditional business practices are smart, which is why we do them, but now being the one inside the deal makes me have a different understanding of them.

"Twenty minutes is too long."

One minute was too long. From the moment the first

woman entered my house, I realized what a fucking horrendous idea this is, and the only thing preventing me from shutting the entire spectacle down is the fact that Mother would be crushed if I did so.

"Just pick the hottest one." Rafael leans into me, waving his arm around the room, gesturing to the whole crowd. Those who are watching us pause their conversations and I swear they fucking preen in hopes I'm about to do something, like choose them.

I shove Rafael's arm to his side, burning a glare into him. "Will you fucking stop?"

He chuckles, way too amused about this whole thing. Makes me want to kill him. "Seriously, bro. Pick someone who you can stand looking at for the rest of your life to appease our parents and you'll be done."

It has nothing to do with their appearance though, and everything to do with *who* these women are. The fact they showed up here tells me everything I need to know—they're boring and I'll tire of them after a single night. There's no chase.

Father approaches, his face flushing a light red as he mutters, "Why aren't you mingling? These people are here for you."

"Because this is disgusting," I hiss. "These women are dull."

Father's heavy hand lands on my shoulder and he shoves his face near mine. "Son, *pick* one. Go. You're lucky to have this much choice."

If only to make this night end sooner and get Father off my back, I shrug away from him and stride to the nearest group of women. I barely study any of them, instead holding my hand out to the nearest one. An older couple comes up behind her, their matching hopeful smiles already being directed toward my own parents.

"Dance?"

"Mr. Corsetti," the girl immediately replies, tipping her head in acknowledgment as she lays her hand into mine.

As suspected, she's lacklustre. No chase. No fire.

"My name is Natasha," she says as I lead her into the centre of the room.

"Great. I haven't asked."

She pouts but goes into my arms without a fight. Even being disrespected, she goes along with it. Entirely too submissive for me. My hand goes to her hip, and hers lands on my shoulder. I feel her fingers curl, painted nails sinking into the material of my jacket as though already laying claim.

Like fuck that's happening.

"Can I call you Nico?" she asks.

Brave, aren't we? Needy, certainly. "No."

I spin her, eyes brushing over the dozens upon dozens of women who watch on with envy. A moment later, other couples join the girl and me, filling the centre of the room. We pass Father, who's nodding his approval, his arm around Mother's waist.

"Tell me about yourself."

I sigh. "What do you want to know? How much money you'll have access to if we wed? Or are you wondering what your life would be like knowing, in my role, I could very well never come home one day?"

The girl's—Natasha's—mouth falls open, but no words come out.

I'm nearly ready to signal to the hired DJ to cut the music when a flash of shiny blue catches my attention. Quickly, before it's gone, I spin us again, my eyes locking on the spot I last noticed it.

A woman.

Not any woman though. Even without knowing anything

about her, I just *sense* she's different from the others. Because while every woman is staring at me, this one has her back to the dance floor as she slips between a group of people and heads for one of the room's exits.

Uncaring about the girl in my arms, I release her and lunge toward the side of the room where the unfamiliar woman was, pushing aside the crowd who'd otherwise tackle me for attention.

"Hey!" I call out.

Somehow, sensing I'm speaking to her, the girl stops in the middle of a family, turning around to face me. Red-painted lips form an O and I'm struck by the brightest sapphire eyes I've ever seen, momentarily stunning me still.

My reaction gives her all the time she needs though, as she spins again and pushes past the family. I move in time, catching her wrist at the very last second.

Her muted gasp sounds loud over the crowd of onlookers. She stops, her throat bobbing as those addictive eyes slide toward where my hand is gripping her. She's so small, my fingers wrap her entire wrist. She's so delicate and easily break-able, and it's the differences in our fragility I use to propel her closer to me.

She's fucking beautiful. Her breath catches, her breasts peeking out from her gorgeous dress. Golden hair is wrapped up in a messy bun, and for some reason, I find myself preferring the hairstyle, if only so I can mess it up as I sink into her. Her eyes slide to the side, toward the room's exit, again surprising me. So eager to get away from me.

With her wrist still in mine, I propel her closer, controlling her body. She gasps again, startled by the sudden movement, and I'm able to gain that addictive gaze again. Keeping her eyes on mine, I lift my hand, fascinated as her pulse jumps in response. I stroke a patch of skin on her wrist, noting how soft she is, and wondering where else she's soft.

She never looks away though. Other women won't look me straight in the eyes, thinking that being demure might be the way to my heart, but it's not. It's this. An open challenge. Because even though I hold her, her shoulders continue to slowly angle away from me.

She's like a little mouse trying to scurry away. *Une petite souris.*

"What is your name?"

I *must* know her name. She avoided me, but I've caught her and now she has to reward me.

Her lips part but no words come out. I *want* her voice. I'm so lost in looking at her mouth, in the way her painted lips curl and the way her eyes flash, skirting the room again, I miss when she moves.

I fucking *miss* when she moves, ripping her arm away from me. My stupid hand doesn't clamp down until it's too late and she's gone, a flash of a blue dress disappearing out of the room and around the corner.

I take a step toward her, fully ready to chase her, to hold her down if I must, until she gives me her name—and the rest of her, when I hear the call.

"Corsetti! Aren't you going to say hello?"

My teeth clench in frustration as I stare in the direction my mystery girl disappeared to, while a figure comes up on my right, Mother and Father following on my left.

Run, ma petite souris. Run because I promise to find you.

6

DELLA

F*uck, fuck, fuck!*
Never has there been a better time for crowds to exist. They provide the perfect barrier for me to slip through and get away from Nico Corsetti.

Nico *fucking* Corsetti.

I fucked up. I more than fucked up. I made the fuck-up of all fuck-ups. I have *one* job: to get in and out undetected, and what do I do? Get detected by the last person who should have noticed me.

Our two-minute interaction, which felt like it lasted a lifetime, was enough to ruin this entire thing. If I'm caught, and if he learns who I am, it's Ariella that'll pay the price when Stefano exacts his revenge.

Getting away from Nico as soon as I could is the wisest thing I could have done. Nico can return to dancing with other women in that room. There's enough of them, which means he should have no issue with finding someone and will hopefully write-off our interaction as a one-time, random thing.

Once in the safety of the hallway, I pause, hand to my chest, over my rapidly beating heart. No man has ever looked at me with such attention. Like he was looking *at* me, and not merely through me. My arm is heated from where he gripped me.

I shake my head, clearing all those thoughts because they're silly and a distraction from what I need to be doing.

The hallway to my right has a set of double doors at the end, guarded by two men. Huffing, I turn in the other direction. I won't get past those men, but Stefano did say to find anything that could help him, so perhaps there's something down here.

I wander to the left, past the party again, making it to the end, where another hallway connects. I glance behind me, checking to see if anyone is paying any attention to my less-than-sneaky getaway. Thankfully, the ground is carpeted, and my heels make no noise on the soft padding.

The hallway I'm in has a small series of doors. I head for the first one and open it, finding a few large, leather chairs, a couple small tables, a bar, and a fireplace. A lounge, and based on the lack of storage options in here, I doubt I'll find anything useful, so I back out and head for the next one.

The second room seems to be a game room. On the far wall, a dartboard hangs. Off to the left, an expensive-looking pool table. Another bar, this one smaller, on the opposite side. Definitely a place I imagine Nico entertaining guests, but also, somewhere I doubt will have anything useful. Nico seems too smart to leave anything incriminating around.

The final door is different—glass. A door to outside. I know this one certainly won't be what I need, but I still turn the knob, too compelled at this point to stop.

A greenhouse.

The prettiest little garden is laid out in front of me. I enter the space, shutting the glass door behind me. My skin goes almost instantly sticky with the greenhouse heat, but I'm too in awe of the place to leave just yet. There's a gathering of short trees with bright flowers blooming on them by the back, with other plants I'm unaware of the name of scattered in between. Rose bushes line one side, but it's the centre I'm most drawn to.

A water fountain sits there. Simple and stone, with a small, bubbling brook. The water looks dark, as the only light out here is what comes through the door behind me. I need to return to the house before I run out of time and midnight approaches, but instead, I find myself wandering toward the fountain, my gaze perusing the other side of the greenhouse, out the walls diagonal from me, catching nothing but a black outdoors. On the far side, there's another door, leading outside and to the backyard.

Stopping by the fountain, I lower myself to the stone's edge, mindful of the dress. I rest my clutch down, flexing my hands before dipping one into the small pool of water. The water feels soft somehow, like silk gliding over my skin.

Even Corsetti water is nicer.

Skirting the tips of my fingers over the water, I wonder who comes out here. Nico? His mother? This greenhouse doesn't seem to be growing herbs or anything of the sort, but rather like it was built as an oasis for someone.

Someone who isn't me. I pull my hand from the water, wiping it on my dress, which darkens the material. I stand, readying to wander to the door I noticed on the other side of the greenhouse, curious what's outside.

But as I move, the small light from the house is eclipsed by a figure.

Oh, fuck. I'm caught, but more than that, I'm caught by the very person who shouldn't be noticing me.

I stop breathing and my limbs go limp, caught halfway between feeling overwhelmed and immobilized against the heady weight of his captivating gaze. Green slices through the night and right into me, urging me to take two slow steps backwards.

He takes a single step into the greenhouse, just enough for the door to shut. His electrifying energy fills the small, heated space, making it impossible to breathe. My nerves are seconds away from snapping, while also being ignited with a new vitality. I want to bolt and never look back, while also hoping he'll catch me.

Where did that thought come from?

When he speaks, it's rough but also soft, propelling me toward him. A predator's speech. One I'll imagine for the rest of my days, late at night and in the secrecy of the dark, as I picture it mumbled against my skin.

"Oh, *petite souris*, do you know what we do to people who sneak around?"

Is it possible to die this very second? I want to, but instead, I step to the side, angling myself around the fountain.

He follows, his strides bringing him dangerously close to me, leaving barely any space between us. He moved before I could make it a solid three steps toward the door. Quick as a snake, and something tells me, his bite is just as deadly.

"I-I...um." There's no rational explanation for my presence in his garden, let alone this far away from the party.

Nico lifts a single brow, waiting for me to formulate a complete sentence. "Nothing to say for yourself? You're awfully far away from where you should be. Why aren't you in the ballroom, awaiting my attention like all the other good women are?"

Good women? Is that what he thinks I should be? My chin

lifts a fraction and I fight to rein in my attitude. I'm not like those simpering women in that party; I saw how they all drooled over him. Men are dangerous to allow into your life.

Stupidly, my response comes before I'm able to tell myself not to say it. "Yet, *I* have your attention all to myself. Something they'd surely die for."

When his eyes flash in the moonlight, and there's no sign of irritation at my comment, I realize how severely I fucked up. I answered his challenge instead of scaring him off.

"You are correct about that," he replies smoothly. "I'm sure if I asked any of them to, they'd drop to their knees and suck my cock, audience be damned."

Why does my body heat at the mere mention—the thought —of his cock? A tremble rolls through my form, bringing my thighs closer together, thankful for the dress and the protection it provides me.

"But my attention isn't something *you* want, am I right?" he continues.

Attention can only lead to one thing—the revelation of who I am. So no, I don't.

"What is your name?"

"A-Anna Evans." I provide the name Stefano instructed me to use.

"Hm."

That's all he says though. Nico leans back a fraction, his lips pressing together as he scans me at a torturously slow speed that makes my toes curl.

Get out of here. I've garnered too much of his attention as is, and I need to get away before he asks anymore questions.

I side-step him, angling toward the exit. "Well—"

"Tell me your *real* name."

I pause, my lie clogging my throat. *Fuck.* Of course he

figured it out. In his role, I'm sure he deals with many liars and learned how to pick them out.

Nico's body heat envelops mine as he steals the distance I've managed to gain between us. I freeze, locked in place by his silent command, unable to move even as he touches me.

His fingers lightly trail along the slit in the dress, following it to my hip, and I shudder, my stupid body betraying me. His touch—a stranger's touch—shouldn't feel as nice as it does. It shouldn't make heat expand into the base of my stomach.

"Still no name? Shame."

His fingers trace the edge of my panties, his touch going near where only one man has before. And that guy, the one to take my virginity, did *not* make me shudder and shiver and sigh with the promise of what could be.

Wake up, Della. Get the fuck out of here!

"If you won't talk, then I may be inclined to show you how I treat strangers in my home." His touch lingers, pausing right over my pussy, and he presses his thumb there, enticing a soft gasp from my traitorous lips, which continue to give me away. "How I *torture* them for hours until they're begging me for relief."

"Please," I whimper, but I'm not sure if I'm asking for more or for him to free me.

"Please what?" He lowers his head into the crook of my neck, his lips dancing over my skin as he murmurs, "Please what? What are you asking of me? Do you want me to let you go?"

"No," I respond immediately, followed by a stream of mental curses for not saying what I should have. That, yes, he does need to release me.

His nose skates up and down my neck, and he inhales as a pleased groan comes from the back of his throat. He's sniffing me, but the way my body reacts—the way I jolt in his arms, legs inching apart—has me questioning my own sanity.

"If not to release you, then—" His words cut off as his fingers shift, first to the edge of my panties and then beneath the material, making me jump as his thumb skates over my sensitive clit.

Consequences be damned, I want this. Him.

Fucking the hot mafia guy for a single night rather than completing my stepfather's task is completely acceptable, right?

"You want this then?" He finally finishes his question, his finger sliding through my wet slit. Every pass he takes, I grow more damp, my body giving the truth away with every beat of my heart.

Yes. "No." Logic kicks in when the fog clears the slightest for me to recall why I'm in this predicament. I need to get Corsetti off me and run away before this goes further.

"Hm." He pulls his hand from my dress, taking away his touch, leaving my core clamping on nothing and me silently gasping, tamping down the demand for him to touch me again. "Seems you're uncertain. We might have to play a little game to help you figure it out."

My breath stalls, the endless meanings of that statement rolling through my mind. "A-a game?"

"Oh, yes. You made me hungry, *petite souris,* and for that—"

"Why do you keep calling me a 'little mouse?'" I interrupt. Growing up in Quebec means French is inevitably a part of my life, and I'm fully fluent in it.

"Because," his hand lifts, tucking stray strands of hair behind my ear, "you are one. Scurrying away from me, leaving me to hunt you down. My nameless little sneak, exactly like a mouse."

"I-I told you, my name is Anna."

"I know how to pick out liars, *Anna,* and I know that's not your name. Every letter in it is a lie, and for each of the four letters, that'll be how many times I prevent you from coming. Should I catch you."

There's so much of that sentence that causes alarm bells to chime off in my head, but I focus on the last part. "C-catch me?"

His lips trace the column of my neck, his next words tickling the fine hairs there. "You are going to run, *Anna*, and if I catch you, you will hand over your true name."

Run. Like, flee for my life?

"Um." My tongue licks at my increasingly-dry lips. "And if you don't catch me?"

Nico pulls back, a hint of a grin on his mouth. "Then you get away and I forget all about the liar named Anna, creeping around parts of my house where she shouldn't be."

I'll run fast. So fast because I've inevitably fucked up this entire night and Stefano's plan. I can't sneak around to other places in the mansion now. Leaving is my only option.

I back up a step, eyes darting to the door beyond him. "This is messed up. You do this with all your prisoners?"

Being chased by Nico Corsetti seems thrilling. As though a part of me doesn't want to go all out. I kind of want to see what happens when he catches me.

Snap. Out. Of. It.

"Do you want to be my prisoner? It can be done."

"Um."

"You have a ten-second advantage before I follow, and believe me, *ma petite souris*, you'll need that head start. I wouldn't dally if I were you."

I run.

I don't think. Don't rationalize what it means to be running away from Nico fucking Corsetti, the area's most influential made man. Don't pause at the doorway before flinging it open and sprinting down the hallway, praying I don't break my neck in these heels as they jam into the thick carpet.

My heart hammers in my chest, and no matter how much I want it to be from fear, it's not. Exhilaration, thrill—words that don't nearly explain the feelings coursing through my body.

Nico Corsetti's hands grasp my hips, yanking me to a full stop.

7
NICO

The girl—Anna—*ma petite souris*—pick a fucking name—runs by me and out the small greenhouse garden my father had put together for Mother many years ago.

Ten.

Finding her here was a bit of a surprise, considering no one would dare risk leaving the party and being caught by my guards. Yet, this girl did. Why?

Nine.

She intrigues me. She resisted me at the party, escaping to come here. Being the underboss has its advantages and it's obvious the girl has secrets. She was searching for something or else she would never have made it this far.

Eight.

Little thief. Little mouse. A liar. A girl who avoids a party, creeps through a stranger's home, and provides a fake name. If I was smart, I would drag her down to the basement and hand her over to my enforcer to get her secrets.

Seven.

The thought of anyone touching her, torturing her, gaining her secrets has my blood turning to ice.

Six.

What's amazing is even upon finding her here, she continued her ruse. She defies my every word and doesn't cower.

Five.

Which is why I want her. Unlike so many others, she's worth the chase because she wants it. She denies it, but I can fucking smell how much she actually does.

Four.

She flared to life at the mere mention of being chased. I'm not even entirely sure she was aware of her own reaction, but it was there regardless. The little mouse needs me to show her how stimulating the hunt is—and what it means to be my prey.

Three.

I turn, facing the doorway. It's tempting to go now, but I already know, I don't need to cheat to win. She won't get far.

Two.

Ready or not, here I come.

One.

I run.

Hooking my hand on the doorway, I notice she's managed to make it halfway down the long hallway in the ten seconds I granted her. Her legs wobble with every stride she takes, hindered by her heels.

In no time at all, and with barely any energy, I reach her, my long legs easily chewing up so much of the hall until I'm able to grasp her hips and snatch her, shoving her against the nearest wall, her screech filling the area.

Her hair is a frazzled mess from her run, strands falling from her updo, and I long to mess it up more. To weave my fingers between the strands to get a firm grip, so I'm able to bend her over, control her body, and make it so she can't move as I torture the truth from her.

Her breasts heave against the top of her dress with her gulping breaths. It's humorous really, to see her use so much energy and me so little.

"You weren't fast enough."

"I t-tried."

I tip my head in acknowledgement. "You certainly did, but now, a deal's a deal. I've caught you, which means you owe me your name."

"Wouldn't this be more exciting to remain as complete strangers?"

It's fucking adorable to think I can't see right through that pathetic attempt at keeping her identity concealed. But there's only one thing I'll trade for the truth—a taste of her. With her mouth only an inch from mine, it'd be so easy to steal, but I'll allow her a choice this one time.

"A kiss then. Your name or your lips, *ma petite souris*, you choose."

Somehow, even through all this, she manages to break my stare and look away, down the hall. Her teeth saw on her lip, and again, it's cute catching her uncertainty.

"No one will dare come down here," I tell her, assuming her nerves.

By now, my parents and the rest of the party will have noticed my absence and while I don't doubt they'd search for me, I won't reveal the possibility.

"Nico," she whispers, her gaze coming back to me. It's tortured, shadowed, truly uncertain this time.

I can't focus on the endless possibilities though, when my name on her lips is so fucking addicting, I want to drive her to call it out again. And again. And fucking again, to the point my name wipes away anyone else in her mind, and I become the only one she knows.

Fisting her hair, yanking out the rest of her bun, and pressing my body into hers, so there's no way she'll even consider escaping, I take her mouth, parting her lips beneath mine and tangling with her tongue. Our kiss is angry, animalistic, and unsurprisingly, she's as hungry as I am.

My free hand cups her jaw, maintaining control of her body, so she's reminded of exactly who's in control here. My cock twitches to life in my pants, and with her hips pressed against me, I know she feels it too.

"How's it feel," I start, pulling back to speak, "to know you've succumbed to what you avoided?"

Surprisingly, she responds with, "Intense."

"Deep down, I think you want this. After all, you didn't give a good chase."

She shudders, her eyes shutting briefly, but when she opens them again, there's a fire there I need to stoke. My hand shifts from her jaw to her neck, slowly following the path her bare skin lays out for me. Her skin prickles, and I trace the sensitive marks I leave behind.

"N-no."

Even now, she's *still* fighting, and I fucking love that. She continues to combat her own desires, needing to keep the control she believes she has between us.

"You could have given me your name and this wouldn't have happened."

One way or the other, chase or no chase, I was tasting her tonight, but I won't admit that to her.

"Wouldn't it have?" Her playful smirk makes me want to take her over my knee, or at the very least, to make her run rampant through my land beyond these walls, so I can hunt her. Properly this time.

"You're right," I find myself being honest. "You've awakened a craving, *Anna*. Only one you can satisfy."

Her throat moves with her gulp, but I cup her breast, finger stroking over the material, making her nipple bud. Soon, I'll have this dress yanked down so I can bare her body to me.

"I'm going to devour you, *petite souris*, and you're going to be my good girl and take everything I give. Isn't that right?"

"And if I don't?" she asks, her tone breathless.

So determined. "If it takes putting you on your hands and knees with my cock deep down your throat, so be it, but by the end of the night, I will have claimed your sweet, wet cunt."

Her lips curl, her breath catching, but even so, her response seems natural, as though she isn't trying to figure out how to best respond in a way I'd want, like others do.

"How do you know I'm wet?"

My hand continues down her body, finding the high slit in her dress that provides easy access to her heat. Slipping my fingers in, I return to where I was exploring in the greenhouse. I brush my fingers over the wet spot on her panties.

"So, tell me, what brought this on?" I pause, my finger moving to the side so I can slip beneath the cloth and slide my finger through her folds, her arousal making it so effortless. "The chase, the kiss, or the thought of being on your knees?"

Her eyes shut again, briefly, enough for her to gather herself. "You."

I would accept that if I didn't know it's only partially true. This girl is full of half-truths.

"Another lie," I muse, gliding my finger back and forth. Her nails curl into my biceps, digging into my suit jacket. "You truly won't tell me anything about you?"

"It's better this way." The way her eyes flash informs me that for fucking once, she's speaking the truth.

"What if I want to know every part," the tip of my finger

stops at her entrance, pushing in a half-inch, "of you? How do I explore?"

"By taking."

Permission to take even as she tries to get away. A woman who enjoys being dominated but won't admit how much she wants this. Who continues to run away, even while telling me to chase and trap her.

"Who *are* you?" I voice the question building in my mind. Who is this girl who appeals to me in a way few have before?

"I told you—"

I sink my finger deep inside, cutting off her speech as her words transform into a moan, long and dragged out. I slip in so easily, her core not denying me as her mind continues to do so. Her head falls back against the wall, baring her neck, so I trail my lips there, kissing over her thumping pulse. Her nails dig deeper into my arm as my finger increases its speed.

Nipping at her throat and pumping my fingers inside her, I *take*. Viciously and animalistically, no care for how loud her cries are getting or even how my rock-hard cock demands to feel her heat for himself. I consume her pussy, revelling in the feel of it tightening around me.

"Nico..."

Her cry is unrestrained. Her breath shudders as the orgasm wracks her body and she bites down on her lip, aiming to keep her scream contained.

"Let yourself go. Let everyone at the party hear you whore yourself out for me."

Her teeth release her lip, silently obeying me, and her orgasm immediately ripples into another as I don't slow my onslaught.

"N-Nico." This time, it's panted. Her hands slide from my shoulders and to her side, scraping against the wall at her back.

I pull my fingers from her and push them between her

parted lips, forcing her to taste herself—taste what she's continued to fight.

"Taste that? That's what your desire is. Commit it to memory because maybe the next time, you won't resist me so hard."

She licks, sucking deeply before releasing my digit, obeying the command without a second thought.

"I think you enjoy my resistance." Her hips roll, pressing into my cock, hard with the evidence her words hint at.

"That might be true." My hands drop to my pants and I finally manage to get my cock freed in time for the mansion's clock to chime. Stupid thing, but something Father's uncles insisted on installing way back. Even long after their deaths, we've all gotten used to it, so it'd be odd to have it removed.

The girl freezes, her gaze darting to the side. "What's that?"

"Midnight."

The next thing I know, her hands are pressing against my chest and she shoves me, forcing me to stumble backwards, dropping her to her feet.

"Wh—?"

She rushes by me, taking off. I lunge, hand reaching for her, but she's already too far away.

"Where the fuck are you going?"

She stops a few feet away, peeking over her shoulder. Her skin is flushed a delicious colour, but her eyes have lost all sense of playfulness. There's lust and games, and then there's what's presently in her eyes—fear.

"I'm sorry, I need to go. Don't follow me."

"What are you talking about?" I take a step closer, trying to follow, as I tuck my cock back inside my pants. I want to understand what changed her expression so quickly into something so resolute.

Her hands fly up, palms toward me as her head wildly shakes back and forth. "No, Nico, don't follow me."

There's a gravity in her tone that has me pausing. "A hunter knows the scent of his prey. I will find you."

"I'm serious. Don't follow me. Forget about me. Live your elaborate life and return to your party."

She spins on her heel and runs down the hallway, and this time, I don't give chase.

At the end of the hall, right before moving out of sight, she pauses and peeks over her shoulder. Even with the distance between us, I catch the look of longing.

Then she leaves.

Run, petite souris. I'll find you and I will get your name.

8

DELLA

Like Cinderella, I dash away from the prince at midnight and return to my carriage.

Nico Corsetti isn't a prince though. He's a made man, brutal, and lives his life in total darkness. Disloyalty isn't a language he knows; because should a person act against him, their life wouldn't last past that brief error.

I *know* this too. I should have taken off the moment Nico found me in the greenhouse. What happened afterward had gone entirely too far, even if it's a night that'll live rent free in my head forever.

I barely make it inside the car before it pulls away from Corsetti's driveway. Throwing myself into the back seat, I glare at the driver, who merely shrugs.

"Sorry, girl, I had orders."

I huff, glancing behind me as the vehicle pulls away from the mansion. Somewhere in there, Nico is either wondering why I had to get away so quickly or has already moved onto the countless other women who are more than happy to give him the attention he requires.

Sighing, I fall back against the leather seat and reach for my clutch, feeling around in the dark back seat for it. With every pass of my hand that does not land on it, my heart rate increases. Bending down, I feel around my feet, hoping in my mad dash to get into the car, I tossed it down there.

"Hey," I call up, "could you turn on the light back here for a moment?"

The back of the car is instantly bathed in a blinding light, and my eyes take a moment to adjust before I lift from the seat, getting on my hands and knees to feel around the car's floor.

Fuck.

It isn't here.

Which means, somewhere in that mansion we're leaving behind, is my cell phone.

Fuck! Double fuck. Triple!

"Done?" the driver asks.

"Y-yeah." My voice staggers, but I keep it steady. The driver works for Stefano, and right now, no one can know the truth of what happened. That I'm an idiot and left my purse in the enemy's stronghold.

The greenhouse, I realize.

When sticking my hand in the fountain, I laid the clutch down, and now, looking back, when I ran from there during Nico's game, I don't recall retrieving it.

Blowing out a deep breath, feeling apprehension slithering down my spine, I recline in the seat, lowering myself until I hope to disappear in the leather. If—when—Stefano learns that my cell phone was left in Nico's presence, I am dead. More than dead.

By the time home comes into view, I'm full-on quivering, my nerves visible on the outside of my skin. When the car comes to a stop in front of the house, the driver doesn't get out to open my door. This time, there is no façade. The clock struck midnight and my carriage turned back into a pumpkin, my dress back into rags, and the princess back into the staff.

My feet are heavy as they drag up the steps to the front door, where I push open the door. A guard standing by the door barely looks at me as I continue past him and down the hallway, toward Stefano's office. As tempting as it is to hide away in the attic and evade Stefano altogether, I know he's already been notified of my arrival and it will be minutes before he comes hunting for me.

Knocking once, I wait for his permission before entering. And only after I take an even bigger breath than the one I went into the Corsetti mansion with.

"Hi," I say in a small voice, announcing my arrival. This time, he sits in near-darkness, with only one corner lamp and a desk lamp lit.

"Shut the door," Stefano demands, and when I do, he stands, hands pressing into the papers on his desk. "So?"

He's going to kill me.

But I need to just say it. "I have nothing. I-I looked. I tried."

"Nothing." He states it with a deadly silence that has me wanting to shrink away.

"Nothing," I affirm. "Some of the layout of their main floor, and—"

I don't see him move, but he flies toward me, his hand whipping up in the air.

I flinch, folding myself away instantly to avoid the hit. Stefano's never hit me before, so his action comes as a shock in which I don't know how he'd prefer me to react, so instinct takes over. I hate this. I despise fearing him at every turn, knowing the hold he has on me and Ariella.

The hit never lands, and he slowly, so agonizingly slow, lowers his hand back to his side. The redness in his cheeks gradually fades and his chest rises and falls with deep breaths.

"Why are you so useless, girl?"

"I couldn't," I snap. "One hallway was blocked by guards, and the other had nothing important. Then Nico Corsetti discovered me."

Stefano blinks. "He found you? Good. What happened?"

"*Good?*" I repeat, disbelief emphasizing the word. He thinks me getting caught was *good*? "How is *any* of that good? I could be fucking dead right now, if he realized who I was. That's not *good*, Stefano. You risked a lot."

Stefano leans away, an evil grin slowly growing over his face. His head rocks slightly, shaking away my horror. "No, no. You did exactly as I hoped. I knew Corsetti wouldn't be stupid enough to leave his secrets open for anyone to find and—"

"You sent me in there knowing I would be found then!" Anger radiates up my back and I flex my hands at my sides. There's been a lot of bullshit I've put up with over the past year, all for Ariella's health, but this is horrendous. "You made up a plan for me to follow, all the while knowing I wouldn't be doing that. You set me up!"

In the back of my mind, I know I should stop yelling. The more I shout, the more I risk angering Stefano, but he's reckless in his use of me, and it pisses me off.

"Tell me what happened when Corsetti found you."

I shouldn't. I should stop letting him win, but when Ariella's face flashes through my mind, I bite out, "We talked. He didn't recognize me. I gave him the fake name. I claimed to be a wayward guest and then he redirected me back to the party."

Keeping my expression neutral is a ploy to ensure I don't let on that anything more happened, but the way Stefano's calculating eyes rove over me, has me wondering if I'm doing a good job at all.

His hand comes up beneath his chin and he leisurely strokes the skin there, musing, "There's a reason we dressed you how

59

we did, Della, and it wasn't to ensure you'd fit in. The dress didn't have to be so revealing for that."

That's when it hits. I'm a damned idiot.

"You *hoped* I would catch his attention."

Stefano drops his hand with a pleased smile, as though he was doing me a favour. "Finally, you've caught up. Getting information was a bonus, but yes, your real objective was to catch his attention."

"Why didn't you start with that?"

"Consider it as me testing your boundaries."

My stomach drops. Boundaries. Where is this stupid plan of his heading?

"Boundaries for what?" I ask carefully, linking my hands behind my back, hoping he doesn't notice the nerves creeping up again.

"Does it matter? You've done exactly as I needed. Now that he's met you once, you will integrate into his life again and lead him to a location to be determined by me."

The muscles in my arms go slack, making it a challenge to keep them clasped together because every word Stefano speaks is insanity. He's lost it. I know what leading Nico to a "location" will mean.

His death.

"You want me to, what, get him to follow me to some random place for you to capture him?" I snort. "That's a stupid plan, Stefano. First, he's not going to trust a random girl he's recently met. And second, no. Just no."

Stefano doesn't seem to listen to me and turns, heading for his desk as he continues talking. "That's exactly what you will do, Della. You have one week. Use whatever you need to. Your cunt, your mind—I don't fucking care what. Just make it happen. When you get him away from his family, I will direct you where to take him."

He's insane. I stomp forward, following him to his desk. "Am I hearing you correctly when you say I have to whore myself out for *you*?"

"For us," he counters, hardly batting an eye at my rage. "The moment I have Nico Corsetti in hand, his family will do anything to get their prince back."

Nico's face flashes in my mind along with the expression he had right before kissing me, and I can't do this.

"N-no." The word comes out with hesitation, but I repeat, "No. I won't do that. Stealing is one thing, but you're talking about kidnapping. Maybe even death."

Stefano pays my defiance little attention until he picks up a letter opener, mindlessly scraping beneath his nails. "I see you'll need some persuading, since your sister's care isn't enough for you this time. Therefore, you do this, and I will give you what you want."

What I want? What *do* I even want? To be free from his tyrannical rule, certainly, but there's a reason I haven't run away yet. Where would I go, and how would I care for Ariella?

I stare, waiting for more as my body relaxes, caution overtaking any previous anger. I tilt my head slightly, narrowing my eyes with my question, "Which is?"

"Freedom. Do as I demand and you will be free from my employ forever, with a million dollars gifted to you in cash. You can go anywhere, and take your sister with you."

"Are you serious?" I stupidly find myself asking. For that offer, I can do this. I *can* do what he demands of me, if it means my freedom. Assisting in Nico's capture might twist my gut with guilt and stain my ethics, but this horrible life taught me one thing early on: to be selfish and care for myself and my family above all.

Nico would easily slaughter me if it meant protecting his own siblings. There's no difference in this.

Stefano jerks his head into a nod. "That is how much Corsetti's blood is worth to me. One week, Della. Tick-tock."

For Ariella and me, I won't feel guilt. I won't *allow* myself to be remorseful about sentencing Nico to death.

The first step is to find him, and this time, I will not run away.

9
NICO

Rafael stumbles into the dining room the next morning, bleary-eyed and rubbing at his day-old scruff. Despite that, he's grinning as he falls into the chair across from me, where I'm picking at a breakfast sandwich.

"Where'd you disappear to last night?"

"Where did *you* disappear to?" I counter, gesturing at him with my fork. "You're a fucking mess."

"Well, when the purpose of the party left last night, someone had to console all those broken hearts." He waggles his eyebrows, grinning. "The way you ran out of the room though had some people talking."

"Met a woman."

Rafael reaches across the table and snags a croissant. "Always the case. Whose daughter was she?"

"Wish I knew." I also wish I didn't remain awake half the night, debating if I should scour all of Montreal for her—an impossible feat that I couldn't help but consider. It was around two in the morning when I realized there's a familiarity in her face that I can't quite place.

Hunting a woman is a game of lust. Of chasing her until I can ravage her, but pursuing this girl will take more than speed. It'll involve skill and patience because I *will* find her, and when I do, I'll tie her to my fucking bed until I get all my answers out of her.

"Don't follow me. Forget about me. Live your elaborate life and return to your party."

"What's her name?" Rafael's next question yanks me from my musings.

"Wish I knew," I repeat.

He freezes with the croissant by his mouth. "You're telling me you met someone who didn't immediately hand over her Social Insurance Number as she spread her legs and named all your future children?"

"Brash but funny." I chuckle. "That's exactly what I'm saying, brother. She's...elusive, would be the best word for her. When it hit midnight, she took off."

"Maybe she has a bedtime."

Another humorous comment but, this time, I shake it off, seriousness settling in as I rub at my mouth, thinking back to all the oddities of last night. "No, that's the thing. I mean, she gave me a fake name, I'm sure of it."

Rafael freezes again, this time mid-chew, his brows spiking. "Dude, be careful. She sounds like a danger to you and the family."

"I know, I know. But it's hard to explain." I swipe a hand over my neck, scratching at the itch creeping up as I search for a way to explain.

After a moment of me saying nothing more, he states, "Seems like you have a Cinderella on your hands either way."

"A what?"

"Girl disappears in the middle of the night. No name. Nothing about her."

"Ah."

"Don't follow me. Forget about me. Live your elaborate life and return to your party."

"I guess," I finally agree. "Doesn't matter though because—"

A door slamming from afar echoes throughout the entire bottom floor of the mansion and straight into the dining room. There's only one person who slams a door that hard—Father.

"Oh, right," Rafael ticks a finger toward me, "Father's pissed at you for leaving last night. He sent Rosen after you, eh."

"Guess he didn't look too hard. I was down in the east wing."

"Nico!" Father bellows, his loud steps taking him closer to the dining room. He appears in the doorway, seething, his shoulders rising up and down. Mother steps up behind him and lays her hands on his shoulders, pressing down until he takes a deep breath. For all their faults and Father's callousness, they truly do love one another and understand how the other works: what calms them and what makes them happy.

A strange twist rolls through my stomach. To have a woman know everything about you seems like a horrendous and terrifying concept. To be so exposed, mind, body, and heart, goes against my entire being, but then, my parents always seem to convey the flip side of that belief.

To have a woman know your likes, dislikes, and what makes you tick could be a welcoming thought. To go home, wash off the gore, grime, and death from the day and simply hold someone. The same someone, day in and day out, no matter what shit occurred through the day, who will always open her arms to you. Then to be so attuned to that woman, to know the very thing to bring a smile to her face, is...not a bad thought.

Arranged marriages are too frequent in this life, but it's a sure-fire way to ensure the family's bloodline will be the strongest it can possibly be. There's no room for love. There are unions and making the best of it. Love comes later, if at all.

Father often preached how being weak for a woman is the strongest a man can be. Growing up, his own father hammered in the concept that caring for a woman makes one weak, but when my parents met, he learned the opposite. That being weak for the person you love can bring great levels of strength, and that's what he's drilled into Rafael and me.

But, like everyone else in this life, their romance was a product of blood and death.

Father staggers deeper into the room, his face flushing red as he stabs a finger toward me. "Where the fuck did you disappear to last night, and why was I left with an entire room of eligible women?"

After my little mouse took off, I may have retreated to my suite and never checked back in.

"It was your party." I smack his hand away before returning to my breakfast. "Your party, your problem."

"Well, once again, *you* were a fucking disappointment. You're *this*," he holds up his thumb and index finger with so little space between them, a sheet of paper wouldn't fit, "close to me making an arrangement myself. Last shot, Nico."

Dropping the fork, I push to my feet, rounding on him, fully aware that I'll never hit him, but my sheer size versus his is enough to make him back down. In my peripheral vision, I spot Rafael standing too, hands going out as if preparing to intervene.

I snarl at my brother, warning him to back the fuck up. I don't need my youngest sibling to fight my battles for me.

"You have no right to decide my bride."

"I have every right, boy. Once again, last chance to do it yourself."

"You fed me to the wolves."

The remainder of my argument pauses on my tongue, as I reflect on one particular wolf. Less of a wolf though, and more the girl skipping through the woods.

Lowering slowly back to my seat, I level my gaze with Father's. "There's one woman I met last night who I showed an interest in. That's where I had gone off to."

His eyes squint, skeptical. "Her name then?"

"I'm not entirely sure. Give me time to find her though."

"So the future of my legacy lies on a woman you have no idea who or where she is?"

Precisely.

I lift my fork, ready to resume breakfast as though this conversation isn't happening. "Yes. I'll find her."

Mother and Father share a look of surprise before Mother takes the seat closest to me. She reaches out to pat my hand, her tentative smile one of pride.

I'll find my little mouse. No matter how far away she scurries.

10
DELLA

"Office, Della. Now."

Stefano saunters away, leaving me to trail helplessly after him. My head unwillingly hangs lower than I'd prefer as I walk, each step riddled with a newfound anxiety. Regardless of the possibilities and chances I gain when completing his new task, I still need to somehow *do* it. A feat I fear will be more challenging than Stefano believes it'll be.

He leaves his office door open and doesn't break stride, heading for his desk. By the time I enter and shut the door behind me, he's seated at his laptop, fingers quickly gliding over his keyboard.

Without looking away from the screen, he says, "Tonight at eight, you will be outside The Elixir."

"Corsettis own that club."

"Precisely. You need to weasel your way back into Corsetti's attention. Now that he's met you, he won't be able to resist getting to know you further. My intel says he visits The Elixir, every week on this day at eight."

"Awfully sure he'll fall for it." I resist rolling my eyes. "Besides, when I'm inside, I doubt I'll be allowed where he goes."

Still without looking at me, he mutters, "You won't even make it through the front door. I'm seeing to it. Dismissed."

Gritting my teeth, I leave, mentally counting down the seconds until eight. The sooner Nico notices me again, the sooner I can get this ridiculous, deadly plan underway, and the sooner I can be free from Stefano's clutches.

I slam his office door shut behind me a bit louder than normal, hoping he enjoys the loud sound. Stefano said this task is my priority, which means I'm free from menial house tasks, so I stalk down the hallway and right out the front door without stopping.

The gravel driveway crunches underfoot, the sound signifying every step I take toward peace. A momentary reprieve I take way too infrequently, but one I enjoy nonetheless.

Unlike my stepsisters, I don't have my own vehicle, but I'm not usually bothered by it, since the only place I ever willingly go to now is to visit Ariella, which is a simple, short bus trip away once I make it off the property.

The driveway itself is a small road, and once I make it to the end, I walk down another block, toward the nearest neighbourhood. Mostly affluent people, but I'm lucky a single bus line still cycles through here every hour, providing me the access to get away.

When the bus stops in front of the Douglas Mental Health University Institute, the sun is high in the sky, heat rays beaming down on me as I exit the stuffy bus and stride straight through the glass front doors of the centre.

"Della," Marianna, the friendly receptionist, greets me with a smile as I stop at the desk to sign myself in on the clipboard.

"How are you this week, honey? It's been a while since we've seen you around here."

"Oh, you know," I shrug a shoulder, "busy."

I guess that could be considered an understatement, but I'd rather the centre that cares for my sister not be alarmed to the truth, in fear Stefano might be less charitable one day toward them. Of course, they're aware of him, since it's his credit card on file, but he never visits.

"How's Ariella been?" I ask Marianna, laying down the pen.

"She's been more receptive to treatment this week," she replies, her smile lighting up. "In the sense that she's been attending."

The news makes me a bit breathless for a moment, hitting a deep part of me that was holding its breath. Ariella's been resistant since getting dumped here, not that I blame her. Like me, her life was upended, only she was also shoved elsewhere, out of the De Falco mansion.

"That's great," I respond, throat going thick with emotion. I move past the desk, suddenly eager to get the details of her therapy.

I stride down the white hallway, passing a few other residents as they walk around. I pass the large game room, where a few voices can be heard as they entertain themselves. It's a very clean and relatively high-priced centre, and I should be grateful Stefano paid for somewhere good for Ariella, rather than discarding her in some understaffed, underfunded dump, but I'd still rather we be together.

I take another corner, pass a few more room doors, and stop at one halfway down the hallway before knocking.

The door opens quickly and Ariella instantly smiles at finding me on the other side. She steps aside, allowing me through, before shutting the door and returning to what she clearly was doing earlier—stretched out on her single bed, watching a movie, which is now paused.

Once upon a time, she would have already spoken about two hundred words. She would have regaled her week three times over and animatedly talked about what she'll be doing next. She would have been overly chatty and excited to detail her activities.

And then there's now. Now, where she waits for me to talk. Ariella may only ever speak to me and no one else, but it's at a minimum and nowhere near how she once did.

I shake off the apprehension and slowly pace forward, dropping into a chair situated at a small table. A notebook sits open with a pencil on top, resting right above more evidence of the sister I once had. Music notes line the sheet of paper until abruptly stopping with eraser marks.

While I can't carry a tune, Ariella's always had a special and innate talent for it. She was the kid front and centre at every school Christmas concert. The one found humming in her room as she worked and sang along to every song in a movie. When she was fourteen, she started to write her own music.

Since the day of the accident, I've never heard her sing again. She no longer excitedly tells me about the newest song she's created, and certainly never plays it for me.

When spotting where my attention has gone, red blooms on Ariella's face, a colour that almost matches the deep red of her hair—a trait she got from Dad, according to Mom—and she quickly rushes to the table, grasping at the notebook in such a rush, the pencil rolls to the floor. She bends down for it and tucks the notebook against her chest as she turns her back to me and slips the notebook beneath her pillow.

"You're making music again."

Ariella faces me, the red in her cheeks climbing down her

neck and under her plain tee. She crosses her arms and leans against the edge of the bed, continuing to stare at me wearily.

I sigh. "Will you at least tell me how you are?"

She lifts a single shoulder into a shrug, but murmurs, "Fine."

Fine. Something we tell others when we don't truly want to admit our feelings.

"Do you need anything?"

She shakes her head.

Tracing the edge of the table with my finger, I let my gaze drift away, toward the outside as I muse, "Front desk mentioned you're attending your sessions."

Silence. Still, I don't turn to face her.

"I think it'll do you really good if you open up to the therapists here, Ari. After all, how else do you think this will be fixed?"

The moment the sentence leaves my mouth, I know I've fucked up.

With more emotion than I've heard in a long time, she repeats in a bone-chilling voice, "Fixed."

I turn back to face her, wincing at her narrowed gaze. "You know that's not what I meant. It's just...I want what's best for you. You shouldn't be locked away somewhere like this. You need to be out," I gesture toward the window, "in the world, doing what *you* want."

She looks away, staring down at her hands. Any shred of emotion that was there a moment ago is gone again.

"What if I could get you out of here?"

Ariella snorts but doesn't look up. I don't blame her disbelief though; I'd have it too in her place. But seeing Ariella like *this.* Hopeless. Miserable. If I had any doubts about throwing Nico Corsetti to the De Falco pack in order to provide a better, happier life for my sister, they've vanished now.

For Ariella, I will sentence a man to death.

~

I miss my phone.

That's my only thought as I stand outside of the club, The Elixir, where Stefano ordered me to wait. Wait for what, I wish I knew. Instead, I pace in small circles, bouncing from foot-to-foot as the night's chill ghosts up my arms, making me shiver. I wrap my arms around myself tighter, keeping my head down, despising the short, black dress I'm in.

The street is quite dead, but then, it's probably earlier than usual for people to be at a club. Perhaps that's why Nico chooses this time to come. The club behind me is pitch-black, and I wonder if it's open at all, or if I look like a complete moron waiting outside a closed club at eight in the evening.

I miss my phone because of the useful distraction it brings. Instead, I'm stuck staring at the cement, counting cracks over and over as I literally wait for nothing. For *something*, as per Stefano's vague commands.

Somehow, I get so focused and zoned out on the cracks in the sidewalk that I miss the two large bodies approaching. Their shadows overtake my own on the ground, and I step closer to the building, allowing them the maximum amount of space to walk around me.

Despite two-thirds of the sidewalk being free for them, they continue closer to me, and while I keep my head down, I do peek as that fight-or-flight instinct whirls to life inside me. My heart beats faster, and my feet inch to the side, thinking how best to get away from them.

"Excuse me," I murmur and side-step, continuing to give them the benefit of the doubt that this is all an accident.

The arm of the man closest to me shoots out to the side,

blocking my way, and that's when I know that fight-or-flight instinct needs to be more fight and less flight, if he's refusing to let me pass.

"Nuh uh. You're not going anywhere."

Fuck.

Sadly, I don't actually know *how* to fight, and I certainly can't fight off two fucking humungous guys.

Fuck. Fuck. Fuck.

They crowd me, forcing my back to the wall. I'm calculating on if I can manage to fit between their forms and get out, when one grasps my jaw, turning my face straight and forcing me to look into his terrifyingly unforgiving dark gaze.

I jerk away and my head lightly thumps against the brick behind me, reminding me I'm trapped. That I'm moments away from being assaulted. With my palms flat, I shove into the chest of the one holding onto me, but my attempt does nothing to his towering form.

"Play along, girlie, or we might have to hurt you for real."

By the time his words register, the other one begins pawing me too, his hands landing on my hips as he gets closer.

Wait—what? Play along?

Stefano.

That fucker is getting men to fake-assault me?

"No!" I cry out, shoving them again, not at all playing along to whatever disgusting game was concocted. I shove and kick my legs out, seeking an opening in their wall.

One clasps my arms and pins them at my sides on the brick. His rough stubble scrapes against my skin as he gets closer. Bile rises in my throat when I feel him inhale, fucking *smelling* me.

Now would be a fucking damn good time for *someone* to walk by and help me. In a city like this though, most opt to keep their head down and themselves safe.

"Get the fuck off me!" I yell.

With my arms pinned, I kick my feet out, pushing my body this way and that to get free, but the man's hands clamp down harder. I hear him make this growly sound, like he's some kind of animal.

"I swear, tell him to—"

Bang!

The man in front of me cries out, his eyes bulging and diving straight toward his foot, where a large amount of blood is seeping from, spreading quickly in an arc. I jerk my own away from the blood, not wanting to get dirty, while my mind works to make sense of what just occurred.

In a flurry of movement, both guys are yanked off me and thrown to the ground with a hard *thud*, each crying out. The one not shot immediately rolls onto his knees and begins pushing himself upright, trying to escape presumably, when another *bang* sounds out.

This time, he stills, his eyes finding mine before looking behind him. I follow the man's gaze, catching someone there in the shadows. With the street's dim lighting above us and the shadow, he somehow knows exactly where to hide in, I can't see his face.

But I *know*.

A final gasp and that's all that's left of my attacker's life. He slumps to the cement, lifeless.

The other makes a yelling noise as he cups his foot and begins scrambling away from my shadowy saviour. He crab-walks a few feet until the shadow moves, coming into the spotlight for the briefest second, enough that I can catch his tattooed hand as it reaches down and yanks the man to his feet.

My rescuer lifts his arm and lands a heavy punch to the man's face. A *crack* sounds out, followed up by a spurt of blood that shoots from the man's nose, dripping on the cement.

"This is for daring to lay your hands on her." His whisper is low, gravelly, packed full of dark promise.

In the pitch black, silver flashes and the same gun he used to murder the other man is dug into the second one's chest.

"You shouldn't have touched my property."

His property?

The denial is resting right there on my lips, but then he pulls the trigger and the man slumps, red spreading across his chest. My protector releases him with no care for the dead and he drops to the ground beside his friend.

A heavy silence befalls the street as he tucks away the gun and wipes his hand on his pants, still not looking toward the club or where I'm standing against the wall.

Shit, what do I do? I want to avoid whatever madness I just observed. He *killed* two people in front of me. Stefano is fucking insane to put me on this job.

I need to stay here though. To interact with him and pretend like I'm okay with the fact that he murdered two men without even questioning them first. Yet, my feet inch away. Breaths locked in my chest to limit how much noise I make, I make miniscule steps to the side, hoping he'll be so preoccupied with the bodies in front of him, he won't catch me.

"Where do you fucking think you're going, *ma petite souris?*"

11

NICO

Coincidences do not exist. Nothing "just happens." It's against human nature for people to randomly do things. Everything is premeditated with an endgame goal.

Which is why I find it very interesting that upon pulling up to The Elixir, a club my family has owned for decades, I found my mystery liar nearly getting assaulted. Despite the veil still covering our interactions, I couldn't allow her to be harmed. To be touched by anyone outside of me.

As though I can't notice her attempting to sneak away—a pathetic attempt at that—she still tries, inching away at the most minuscule of speeds.

"Where do you fucking think you're going, *ma petite souris*?" I call out, freezing her in her tracks.

I inch closer as she manages to stutter, "Y-you—I'm—"

"Articulate, I see." Then I add a single word, proving to her, she has no power. She's nothing. *"Della."*

I retrieve the device from my pocket that I've been carrying around since after breakfast this morning. When I was heading back to my room, staff caught up with me, stating they had found a clutch with only a cell phone inside it on the edge of the water fountain in the greenhouse garden.

I knew instantly that my Cinderella left her own version of a glass fucking slipper. The question rolling through my mind all day though, was how purposeful it was of her to leave it behind.

Either way, it's a lucky find, or so I thought. Phones tell a lot about a person, but for some reason, this one is near-blank. Basic apps, one or two games, no social media, no saved contacts. It's way too fucking strange for a person to have a blank phone. The only thing useful it did provide was her first name, listed right there in her settings, but no last name, which means her settings have been tampered with by someone who knows what they're doing.

My private IT guy has been scouring through the phone all day, and only just returned it right before I left to come downtown, stating he found nothing identifiable. Even tracing the ownership of the device has seemingly led to a dead-end. He's running searches on all women named Della. It's a start.

Her eyes bulge in a near-comical way and she lunges out of the shadows and toward me, nearly falling on top of me when I raise my arm higher, angling the phone out of her reach. She leaps, reaching for it again, but her hand only brushes mine.

"My phone!"

"Ah, ah." Shaking my head, I slowly lower my arm, angling my body in a way that she's unable to reach for it. "That's not how this works. Since I saved you *and* I have your phone, I'd say you owe me."

Set the trap. Let people walk into it. One of many lessons from Father.

"O-owe you what exactly?"

Leaning in close, I line my face up with hers, so there's no way in damn hell she'll be unable to miss what I say. "Your secrets."

"You have my name."

"Della," I fill in. "Della with no last name. Your phone certainly doesn't reveal a lot."

Her expression flattens, her lips pressing together once. "You looked through it?"

"Do you forget who I am? A strange woman sneaks around my house, disappears without a trace at midnight, and leaves a phone behind. Of course I had your phone searched."

Her eyes flicker in dismay, confirming what I already suspected—there's more to all this. She quickly blinks away the emotion, pretending to move past it.

"I guess," she finally replies, her tongue swiping along her bottom lip. "What do you want to know then?"

Set the trap. Let people walk into it. She's walked into it, and now, I need to reel her in completely. Make her trust me. Learn what she's hiding.

I pocket the phone again, opting to keep it until I'm satisfied, and turn back toward my waiting vehicle, walking over the two dead men on my way. By the time I'm in front of the driver's side door, I have one of The Elixir staff on the phone.

"There's something you need to deal with out here," is all I bark into the phone before hanging up and focusing on Della, who still stands on the sidewalk, a little dumbfounded. I know she won't run because I have something of hers, and clearly, she's scared at what I'll learn about her, which means safety is now secondary from her perspective.

"Get in."

She looks around, her big eyes scanning the street before glancing toward the dead men. Debate rolls over her expression in the form of a downturned mouth before she side-steps them and walks toward the car, stopping on the passenger side. I watch her, brows lifting slowly as I silently command her to enter the vehicle.

"Don't make me repeat myself. Men have died for less."

"You wouldn't kill a woman."

Some made men won't because they view women as people too gentle to do harm, to be needing protection instead; that if they were to harm them, they have an unfair advantage. I don't think like that because it's sometimes women who are the nastiest of snakes. They use their gender as protection, knowing they can do anything and walk away unscathed. Women and men are equal in their ability to lie, steal, cheat, and betray, and for that, I *will* hurt a woman if the situation calls for it.

"You don't know what I'll do, so if you value your life, get inside the car."

She levels her gaze at the vehicle. "First, my phone."

My teeth grind together, annoyance working at my nerves. It's like she's completely forgotten the part about her being in *my* debt, not the other way around.

Gripping the top of my door, I'm seconds away from going around the car and throwing her ass in the back myself. "You are in no place to bargain, Della. Last time I'm repeating myself. Get in the fucking car or I'll find you a place to sit, and I promise, you won't enjoy it."

The skin between her eyes furrows and her nose does this cute little flaring thing as the spark of fight is still lit inside her, but she finally obeys me and ducks inside the car.

Fucking Christ. I don't know what I'm getting into with this woman, but already, I'm exhausted trying to figure it out. I slip into the driver's seat and immediately start the car, suddenly eager to get back home and be alone with her.

In my peripheral vision, I watch how she squirms, pressing her legs together and moving her body as far away from me as possible, right up against the passenger door. Her head is angled away, watching as we drive down Sainte-Catherine Street.

She remains silent, wisely not asking for her cellphone again. I maneuver us quickly through the other vehicles on the road, managing to make it to the highway in record time, then up toward the Corsetti mansion.

As I pull off toward my house, I wonder how she made it there the first time. Mentally, I list the things I've learned about her, and what I actually know about her. Her name certainly isn't Anna, but if that's what she went with, it means there was an Anna on the guest list. Did Della know and choose a name that would guarantee to get her inside or did the name end up on the list because she managed to get it there? Who was Anna supposed to be? Who brought her to my mansion, and why? Is this some giant ploy to get close to me and she created this whole persona to do just that? The girl I met last night avoided me at the party though, so why would she run off when she gained my attention? Or is that part of the game she's conducting?

And why do I feel like I'm part of some malevolent plan? *I* design the games, no one else, and Della will learn this very soon.

I pull into the driveway, throwing the car into park, and leave it right in front of the house, rather than inside the multi-car garage we have. I'll get someone to put it away later. Before exiting the car, I take her cell from my pocket and toss it onto her lap. The only use it has is gaining her submission, and now that we're at my house, her phone is meaningless.

"Next time, don't leave it around a stranger's house."

She grasps it eagerly, barely glancing at it before sliding it into her small purse. Strange, for someone to be so excited about their technology and not even give it the attention I'd assume she would have.

I get out of the car and by the time I make it to her side, she's also opening the door. Finally learning the rules.

"Come."

Without looking at her, I enter the mansion, walking past the single soldier stationed by the door. She'll follow because she has nowhere else to go. I lead us down the hallways and toward my office.

At the doorway, I stand aside, letting her go first. She stops at the door and glances wearily at me, her brows dipping over her eyes.

"How do I know you won't hurt me once we get in there?"

"That depends. Do you deserve to be hurt?"

Her lips press together and instead of responding, she enters my office. Her silence tells me everything though.

She's stacking up her falsities, but they'll all come crashing down soon. Liars can only maintain deceit for so long before they crack. And I'll be the one to make her crack. To shatter and spread those broken pieces.

She'll reveal everything before long.

12

DELLA

There are things in life that feel like bad ideas, and then there are things that are downright dangerous. Over the course of the drive, I've determined there are things that are even worse than being dangerous, and the term I've titled them is stupid. This is absolutely stupid.

I'm absolutely stupid.

While, yes, I know I'm doing this for Ariella, which makes this the best course of action, I'm literally entering a lion's den with an angry underboss trailing behind me as I enter his elusive office. The very place I was supposed to find last night.

Which makes me stupid. Who the hell in their right mind willingly cons a mafia leader? This has death written all over it, if it goes badly and Stefano doesn't win. And who am I kidding? This is Nico Corsetti I'm dealing with. Stefano isn't winning this no matter how good at deception I end up being.

I'm four steps inside his office. A dark-ish room with floor-to-ceiling shelving. That's all I make out before the door shuts and the room blurs as he throws me against the door. I land with a small *thud* and a sharp pain fires up my back from the impact.

Nico presses himself against me, filling my nose with his dangerous scent. He grasps my wrists and yanks my arms above my head, pinning my hands there and placing me under his complete control. His heavy breaths brush his chest against mine and I feel his rapid heartbeat through his clothing.

"Now," he growls, "you're going to tell me what I fucking want to know."

"Which is?" I drop my weight, hoping to pull from his tight grip, but he holds firm.

"What's your last name?"

"What does it matter?" I shoot back, not missing a beat. My surname isn't De Falco, because Stefano never wanted Ariella and me to take his name, but giving my real last name to Nico is still risky, because who knows what Google has on me. I could lie, to appease him, but something tells me he'd see right through it, exactly like he had with my fake Anna persona.

"I want to know who you are."

"What's it matter?" I repeat. "I'm here. Isn't that enough?"

He growls low, his eyes flicking to my lips and back. Nico Corsetti, firm and controlled as granite, just hesitated in his response. He thinks he needs to know who I am, but it's becoming clearer that it might be enough simply to have me here.

I should feel thrilled by this, since it means Stefano's plan is working. Slowly, bit by bit, I'm slipping beneath his rigid exterior.

"I can always make you," he murmurs, his warm breath brushing over my neck as he leans in closer, his nose tracing all the way to the base of my ear, and I hate the shiver ghosting right down my spine.

"Oh, yeah?"

"Yeah." His tongue flicks out and follows the line his nose just traced.

My next words slip out, consequences be damned. "Prove it."

He pulls his face away from my neck to look at me. His pupils get sucked into the rest of his iris, and the grip he has on me tightens.

After the longest second, he speaks, "*Petite souris,* that was the wrong thing to demand of me. You want me to *prove* it to you, hmm? To use any means necessary to gain the truth from your pretty little mouth? To watch as you crumble beneath my touch and reveal all your secrets."

"Yes," I hiss, and it's not fake—not for show to lure him in. I think about last night and how Nico chased me down the hall, touching me when he caught me. How disappointed I was to have to leave him with everything left unfinished.

"I'll fuck you until you can't sit, Della." His hips roll, pressing his hardening length into my hip. "I'll train your cunt to know I'm its master. I'll own you and your pleasure. You'll regret threatening me by the time I'm done."

"Maybe I won't."

Nothing prepared me for *this*. For Nico Corsetti. For the way he makes my insides clench with desire—with a craving I didn't realize I had. For how different this is than my previous sexual encounter.

I only ever had sex once. It was quick and messy, and overall unenjoyable. It was a long time ago too, shortly after graduating high school. Once Mom got with Stefano, life was taking different turns that kept me too distracted to maintain a social life.

I roll my hips again, flicking my hair away from my face the best I can with the limited control he's allowed me. "I dare you,

Nico. Punish me how you deem fit. *Make* me admit my secrets. Prove to me that—"

His mouth descends on mine, rough, fast, and breathless. In the same lunge, he releases my wrists to regain use of his hands. He grasps the short dress I put on, assuming Stefano would want me to go inside The Elixir and I needed an outfit that would work for the club. From the bottom, the material rips, fragile in Nico's unrelenting hold, until it falls from my form, pooling at our feet.

In the same second, he grips the sides of my panties and yanks them off. I lift my legs to help him, thankful he hasn't ripped these. His lips move from my mouth to my neck, and I drop my head, baring the skin there as he kisses downward, tracing the line of my bra with his tongue.

I arch my back off the door to get my own arms up behind me, removing my bra. He makes an appreciative sound against my skin and continues his exploration, taking a budded nipple between his teeth, scraping the delicate skin there and making me yelp softly with the combination of pleasure and pain.

"I will hurt you, Della, if you don't tell me who you are. Why I haven't been able to get you out of my fucking mind. Why you've interrupted my life."

"Can't you be satisfied with the fact that I'm here?"

"No," he growls into my chest. His fingers trail down my stomach, stopping just short of my hip. "No, I can't because it means you think you're in control, and you're fucking not."

The fire in my stomach is stoking with his touch. Igniting. Building. Growing. Expanding. Until I can't help but say, "Then take charge."

One of his hands drives into my hair, fingers wrapping around the strands until he yanks my head to the side. His free arm wraps around my hip and he turns us away from the door, walking me backwards.

"Nico." I reach for him, resting my hands on his shoulders. When my ass hits the edge of something cold—his desk, I assume—he murmurs, "The only words to come out of your mouth is your last name. Other than that, you will be silent until I tell you to talk. Understand?"

Trick question. He doesn't want me to talk.

Releasing my hair, he grasps my thighs and yanks my legs apart, stepping between them. His hands are large enough that his thumbs stroke over my pussy lips, teasing them. Positioning my hands behind me, I lean back.

"I asked if you understood, Della. You're already disobeying me."

I nod my head in a yes.

"Use your words." With his thumbs, he parts my pussy, baring my clit to the cool air. "Talk, Della."

Anything to ensure he doesn't stop. "Y-yes, I understand, Nico."

"Good girl."

Oh my God. I feel those words ignite every nerve in my body. I'm still trying to rationalize how two simple words can affect me so much, when Nico moves, dropping to his knees, his face in line with my pussy.

Is he...?

He grips my ass, yanking me to the very edge of the desk, to the point it feels like I'd fall off if I wasn't certain he had a hold of me. His thumb circles my opening, dipping inside half an inch.

"Watch me, Della. Sit up and watch me lick you. Watch me *prove* to you that between the two of us, I hold the power here."

He wants me to watch him pleasure me? There's nothing painful about this, so already, his warning of harming me lessens greatly. I follow his instructions, managing to speed my legs farther apart for him.

"You have no fucking idea how sexy you look, *ma petite souris*, looking down on me how you are. Makes me wonder if there will even be a word to describe the sight of you coming."

How can words be so erotic and breathtaking at the same time? "Why don't you find out?" I manage to say, using the last bit of my cockiness before I know he's about to steal it all away with a swipe of his tongue.

Nico moves his thumb out of me, quickly replacing it with his tongue. His mouth covers the entirety of my core as his tongue slips in deeper, pulling a ragged moan from me. My hands curl on the edge of the desk, feet resting on his shoulders. The fact that he's still dressed in his suit, on his knees for my pleasure, while I'm sprawled on his desk is hotter than anything I could have imagined. Being naked while he's not makes this so much more...erotic.

Gripping my thighs, he eats me, his tongue swapping between fucking me and licking at my clit. The stubble on his chin rubs against my inner thighs and I move my hips, as much as his hold allows, trying to chase the feel—the building pressure in the base of my stomach.

The feeling is becoming too much. My unrecognizable noises fill the room; proof of Nico's dominance over my body. The need to wrap my legs around his head is so strong, but his hands hold me in place, helpless to take what he's giving.

"N—" His name is right there on my tongue. A beg for him to quicken his licks, to allow me the relief I need, but I clamp down on the word, remembering his rule for speaking, not wanting to learn what he'll do if I talk.

He drags his tongue from my pussy to my clit, lavishing all his attention there, nipping it with his teeth. I feel like I can come any second now, so long as he stops changing his focus, and again, I almost speak, just to tell him that.

Thankfully, it's like he knows, because he sucks me between

his lips, using both pressure and suction to take me to the edge again.

My moans get louder, telling him what my mouth is not allowed to. I feel it...I'm going to...I'm going to...

Nico pulls his mouth away and releases my thighs, lifting his face altogether until his eyes find mine. A cruel playfulness dances through his expression and he makes a lengthy show of wiping my essence from his mouth with his sleeve.

He's so calm, meanwhile an energized franticness ravages my insides. My chest heaves with viscous breaths and my core clenches, seeking that relief he's stolen.

"Y-you..." I speak, no longer caring about the possible punishment he can dish out because there is no worse punishment than him preventing me from coming.

"Finish what you're attempting to say." He traces the inside of my thigh with his nose, breathing me in, making my mind go blank, unable to bitch at him how I need to.

"You...dick!"

"What's your last name, Della?" he asks into my thigh.

"Not telling."

"Then you don't get to come."

"That's not—Ow!"

Teeth sink into the fleshy part of my thigh, making me yelp loudly, my previous words dissipating into thin air, replaced by the sharp sting of pain.

He bit me! He fucking bit me, like some animal. Right there, on the inside of my thigh. Nico stands, a cocky smirk curling his lips, but I'm too focused on my leg and the clear teeth indent marks left there.

"What the fuck, Nico? You bit me."

He steps between my legs, and with a single finger, crooks my head to meet his eyes. "I have *particular* tastes, and you'll enjoy satisfying them." He brings his face closer, brushing his lips against mine. "Because you already have in so many ways, *ma petite souris*. I felt your wet pussy last night after I chased you down a hallway."

"I liked that," I admit.

He brushes his hand over the bite on my thigh, reminding me of the fading pain. "And this is me marking you. Until you tell me who you are and why you've come into my life, I'm not letting you go."

"Biting me was the only way to manage that?"

Nico's face brushes mine and his teeth nip at my ear, as though to say a silent yes through means of another bite. "I like it rough, Della. I like it animalistic. I like to punish my prey when they don't do what I want."

Other than the pain, I think about him running after me in the hallways last night, and how rousing he is to my senses. How, despite the sting, there's something to him claiming me as such.

Moron, stop. You're falling in too deep already. This is all for show.

Ignoring my inner thoughts, I lean forward and run my palm over his pants and his erection. "I think you were in the middle of proving something to me. What were your words? 'I'll fuck you until you can't sit' sounds right." Flicking my tongue against my bottom lip, I manage to find a sense of bravado. "Make it so I can't sit, Nico."

13
NICO

"Make it so I can't sit, Nico."

How I fucking want to sink right into her wet pussy and feel her clench around my cock the same way she had around my tongue. To feel her come. To *see* her out of her mind with lust as the orgasm takes over her body.

I already know, there will be no sight more beautiful.

But situations like the one Della and I are in require patience and an eased pacing in order for me not to lose control and fall for whatever whims she's brought into my life.

I position my hands on my hips, carefully tipping my head in a way so only my eyes look down on her. "If you want to feel the rest of me, you know what to do."

She immediately goes for the button on my pants, her fingers deftly working and pulling apart my slacks. While that keeps her busy, I unbutton my shirt, sliding it to the floor before kicking off my pants too.

As much as I'd love to fuck her bare, I never risk it. Leaning over, I reach into my desk drawer and snatch a condom. Della watches me straighten, fingers going to the foil to rip it open.

"I'm on birth control. I've been on it for years, to help regulate my cycle."

I freeze, debating. She could be lying, but the woman who continues to evade me, wouldn't suddenly use pregnancy as a trap, right? Studying her eyes, I catch the sense of honesty, rather than the half-truths I've been finding so far. The thought of feeling her bare though is too appealing, so my logic gets tossed aside with the condom when I flick it to the ground.

Pushing against her shoulder, I force her to lay back to my desk and take myself in my hand, angling my cock at her pussy. I rub against her, ensuring she's still wet enough for me to sink in easily.

Without further hesitation, I push all the way inside her, bottoming out. Our groans mingle in my office and her head rolls to the side, her nails sliding against the top of the desk as her body stretches to accommodate me. Her breathing comes heavier and she stills. I do too, allowing her time to adjust.

My mind blanks, my only thought is the feeling of how incredible this feels—so tight, like I shouldn't fit, but so wet that I glide in and out easily.

Hooking my arm beneath one of her legs, I angle it up, resting her ankle on my shoulder. The change in position means I can get a bit deeper, which makes her cry out softly.

"Nico...this..."

I move my hips once, jerking my cock in and out of her, letting her test what's about to happen. I don't do slow. I warned her of my animalistic tendencies, and she's about to experience them firsthand.

"You're taking my cock like a good girl," I croon, sliding my hands up and down her body. I pause at her breasts, taking them both in my palms and twisting her budded nipples with my fingers. "You're so fucking wet, Della. Your pussy knows who owns it."

"Yes."

Keeping my hands on her breasts, I use the leverage to hammer in and out of her at an unforgiving, near-painful pace. I don't let up on her nipples, but she's so far gone in pleasure, she's not complaining about the hold. Her cries grow louder, her pussy constricting, as it works to clamp down and hold me inside her.

"N-Nico, I'm going to—"

I pull my cock from her, leaving us both empty and wanting more.

"What the fuck? Again!"

I release her breasts, placing my hands beside her body so I can lean down. "You've been speaking and I haven't given you permission to. I warned you about this hurting, and believe me when I say, the bite on your thigh isn't all I meant. You dared me to show you all the ways I'll get the truth from you." I pause, but then add, "You can end all this by telling me your full name."

She doesn't speak. Her lips part and her eyes narrow, showing me she's still unwilling to hand over her secrets.

With my eyes locked on hers, and my body bent over her, I re-enter her. She lets out a silent scream and grabs onto my arms, thinking she'll be able to keep me inside her. Her nails scrape my skin. For any other man, it might be considered painful, but I love the feeling of a woman showing how wild and abandoned she is in the moment. How her own primal side begins to expose itself.

She's so sensitive, it takes but a minute until I feel the familiar tightening of her pussy. Her hips rock with mine, chasing the feeling—the build—the release she's about to get.

I slide from her and she cries out a sound that seems like a mix of a groan and a sob.

"So pretty," I murmur. "So beautifully silent as you take your punishment."

No, she mouths, shaking her head. Her hands paw at me, desperate for the release.

I push back inside her.

Two more times, I take her to the brink, only to rob the orgasm from her. No matter how much I also want to come, how tight my balls are, the pleasure I gain from watching her stumble back from the edge she's about to leap from is all worth it. Hearing her cries get louder, her pleas stronger, and watching her eyes water with tears is too satisfying to end.

She looks so fucking lovely in her uncontrolled state taking me. Black streaks roll down her cheeks from her eyes, her makeup smearing from her tears. Her hair fans out around her body, untidy with the amount of times she's rolled her head, helpless as I continue to withhold her orgasms.

With my thumb, I stroke some of the black, further smudging it over her face. Once I've gathered some of her tears onto my skin, I show her.

"You want to come so badly, your body can't control itself. Crying, Della." I lower my hand, lightly stroking over her stomach. "Shaking. It must hurt, doesn't it, to be kept from something you so badly want?"

Yes, she mouths, moving her hips against my cock, rubbing her clit against it as she tries to find her own release.

"Ah, ah, that's cheating."

This time, I'll allow her to come, because I've made my point and she's learned to keep her mouth shut.

With my hand sliding beneath her body, I propel her up, and then continue until I lift her off the desk entirely. Her legs wind around my waist, her pussy in line to take me again.

"Hold on tight," I instruct, my arm shifting around her stomach. My other grasps the back of her neck and as I push inside her again, I take her mouth too, in a sloppy, breathless kiss.

I don't let up, shoving inside her and using my hold on her to push her down onto me. My tongue knocks against hers, fucking her mouth, showing her how much of her body I've claimed in only a short while.

A tightness goes through my whole body: through my abs and down my legs. My own orgasm is right there, but I want us to come together. I want to feel her sweet pussy take my cum.

Her nails scrape helplessly at my shoulders and her head lolls, only remaining up due to my hold on her. She's mindless, helpless—fucking sexier than I ever pictured.

"Come, Della. You're allowed to now."

Her cry is a mix of relief and hedonism. Her pussy constricts at the same time the pressure and heat coursing through my own body is finally released inside her. My hand clamps down on her neck and I bring her closer to me, her neck right beneath my mouth. My teeth scrape the sensitive skin there, the need to bite her here too is tempting with her delectable shiver, but I think I've made my point now.

With a final push, my movements slow. Her body slumps against mine, wrought out, and I feel her heart beat. Rapid. Excited. Content.

Brushing the hair from her damp skin, I press a single kiss there and try to ignore my own satisfaction. I shouldn't feel pleased by this interaction, as I'm no further than when I began, but for some reason, the feel of her in my arms, nearly passed-out from exhaustion, trusting me to care for her now, makes me feel fulfilled by means I never realized I needed.

As much as I don't want to let her go, this isn't the place for us, and I can't—won't—carry her through the hallways and risk anyone seeing her naked body. So, with a groan of dismay from her, I lower her, only releasing her when I feel her feet are stable enough.

She blinks at me with sleepy eyes, and I bend, grabbing my shirt from nearby and slipping it over her. I quickly do up a few of the buttons, enough to shield her body, before slipping on my own pants and taking her hand.

I all but drag her to the door, now eager to get her to my bedroom, but her feet stagger, her energy struggling to keep up with me. She'll never make it up the stairs at this point, so I step around her and sweep her into my arms, carrying her from my office bridal-style.

She blinks, looking at the office we leave, and then the hallway we enter. "Nico, what are—?"

"Carrying you. You don't seem capable of walking right now."

Her responding giggle is breathless and finally, she gives in, dropping her head to my shoulder. "I don't think I could," she agrees. "You've literally fucked me to the point I can't sit. Or stand. Or do anything but die."

"Funny."

I take the stairs two at a time, eager to get her away from any possible prying eyes. While my parents and Rafael both have condos downtown, they also maintain rooms here, and it's too easy for them to wander in at completely random times. Until I know more about Della, I don't want many people knowing about her.

Finally in my room, I shift her to one arm and start flicking on lights. I don't spend a lot of time here, which means I don't keep many personal items either. I've never had to think about such things, as women do not come in here, but with the mysteries surrounding Della, I can't take too many chances.

I head straight for the bathroom, not stopping until we're

in my glass shower. I lower her slowly, catching her gaze and waiting for her to tell me she's unable to stand on her own, but nothing comes. She watches me through those black-streaked eyes as I switch on the shower, keeping out of the water until it warms.

I remove my pants and then do the same to her shirt before moving us both beneath the spray. It's hot against the skin, but my muscles nearly instantly loosen and I stretch, working them out.

Della watches me, waiting. Her lip ends up beneath her teeth again and, with my thumb, I quickly remove it.

"The only person to mark up your lips now will be me."

Reaching by her, I grab my soap and dump a healthy amount on a loofah, rubbing it till it foams, and then I work at every inch of her skin, painting her with the scent of me. At the end, I quickly wash myself before putting the loofah away. I move us both beneath the spray again, washing away the suds and taking extra care between her legs.

"You sore?"

"Not really," she responds. "Just tired. Like you stole all my energy."

I move back up her body, flicking chunks of wet hair off her cheek to reveal her face to me. "Orgasm denial does a lot to the body. Your abs will probably feel it in the morning."

"I feel it *now*." A tentative smile breaks out on her face, and I've never seen anything more lovely. "If I'm sore now, I think I'll be dead in the morning."

"I command you not to be, because you and I are not finished quite yet."

Apprehension flickers on her face in the sign of a partial grimace before quickly removing it.

I should ask her about her anxiety, but I stupidly brush it aside and shut the shower off and then retrieve two towels from a nearby hook. First, I wrap her up, swallowing her form in a large white towel, and then I quickly dry myself.

Once we're both dried, I lead her to the bed, ignoring the red alarms flashing in my mind that Della will be the first woman to ever be in it. My logic shouts she should be nowhere near this bed until I know more about her, but I ignore every rational instinct and lift the bedspread, gesturing for her to get in.

"Your bed," she states. "I'm surprised I wasn't put in a car and shipped off."

"Don't tempt me," I lie, climbing in beside her. "I told you, we're not done yet."

"Yeah, yeah. Threats." Della drops back into the puffy pillows and her heavy eyelids shut right away. Her voice fades, sleep quickly taking over as her body's demand for rest prevails.

But first, before she's completely gone, I again ask, "What's your full name, Della?"

For a beat, she doesn't respond. Her breathing evens out, and I assume I've asked a moment too late. I shut the bedside light off and settle beside her when she finally mumbles an answer.

"I can't tell you. I'm sorry."

Can't. Not won't. Can't.

Which means, something is preventing her from doing so.

I need to figure out what this something is before I pay the price.

14
DELLA

When I open my eyes, a large black comforter blocks my view of the grand room, which I only caught bits and pieces of last night as Nico carried me through it. The silk sheets beneath me feel glorious, way softer than anything that's ever touched my skin. I could happily die in these sheets.

I shift my arms out of the warmth of the bedding, stretching them high above my head, and my spine arches. My body feels like I've had the most gruelling work-out session of my life. Muscles I've never used before ache as I move, slowly sitting up and pushing the blanket off my body to survey the damage.

No bruises, but my abs scream in agony as I sit up. Last night could basically be considered as my first-time having sex. I may have lost my virginity years ago, but it was nothing remotely similar to what I experienced with Nico. I didn't even know it was possible to have so many orgasms, let alone be edged that many times.

My self-survey ends at my thigh, and the bite mark Nico left there. I should be pissed he *marked* me, but the longer I stare at it, the less irate I become and the more...*conflicted*...I am instead, as insane as that brief thought is. I feel like I've only seen the surface of Nico Corsetti. A bite and a quick sprint down a hallway are merely hints of what I could have with him.

He'll be dead soon.

The gloomy thought instantly clouds my satisfaction. Stefano said to lure him in, but I hadn't planned on him and me going as far as it has—for us to have sex.

Nico's my enemy. He's a murderer, as shown last night when he killed those two men in front of me. He's what's between my sister and me being free of Stefano's influence, yet that evil monster called guilt has begun nestling inside my chest, finding a home where he shouldn't exist.

Nico's right to be wary of me, because after last night, I feel like the real game of wits has just begun.

Shaking the thoughts away, I survey the room, spotting a pile of clothes at the end of the bed. Tags, already snipped off, rest on top, telling me they're new. Nico ripped my dress last night, but I assume it's quite simple for a man like him to get new attire.

I slide from the bed, first heading to the bathroom to clean up, and then return to get dressed, slipping on the blue sundress that falls mid-thigh with cap sleeves. It's cute, and I wonder if Nico chose this or if he had one of his many staff members retrieve it.

Nico's bedroom is uncluttered. A massive bed takes up most of it, with a bedside table on each side. Across the room are two doors—the bathroom, and presumably, his closet. I wander toward the bedside tables, opening each drawer and finding them empty.

I have no idea what I'm searching for, if anything. Especially

THE HUNT IN ELUSION

because even if I were to find something useful, I'd have no way of sneaking it out of here.

Besides, nothing you find will be better in Stefano's opinion, than Nico's head.

I leave Nico's room, quite surprised he's left me alone at all.

Unless he's watching you...

My eyes dart to the corners of the hall, seeking evidence of surveillance cameras, but finding none. Still, my steps quicken, my body tingling with discomfort at the possibility that he's left me alone all to see what I'll do with that freedom.

I follow the hallways, recalling the direction Nico took yesterday to get us up here. Once at the bottom of the grand staircase, I'm met with the scent of fresh bread. Taking a left, I let my nose lead me to the source of the smell.

Eventually, the hall opens up to a huge dining room. A long table sits in the centre, fit to play host to at least two dozen people, and I wonder if the Corsettis ever have dinner parties that large. Seems more fitting for their interactions to remain intimate, given the illegal shit mafias participate in.

At one end, Nico sits, an iPad in one hand, an Apple Pencil in the other. He reclines in his seat, his suit fitted perfectly; he's the quintessential image of a man thinking hard over whatever document he's reading. Knowing what's under it—lithe muscles, as well as etchings of dark flowers and symbols I don't recognize, make me wish he was undressed again.

Seconds later, the stylus moves to the screen and makes a *tick, tick, tick* sound as he taps it around. Then he lays the pen down to pick up a coffee mug nearby. Without looking away from the screen, he takes a long chug, seemingly unbothered by the cloud of steam rising from it.

"Morning, Della," he says, still without looking away from the device.

I enter the dining room slowly, approaching the chair nearest him. "How'd you know I was here?"

"Hard to miss your entrance, *petite souris*. After last night, I could find you anywhere."

Heat flashes down my spine and straight to my pussy, but my responding noises come out more as a breathless, tense chuckle that has my hands curling by my side. I certainly hope he can't find me anywhere or else I'll be fucked with a capital F when this is over.

Nico eyes me over the device for a second before he sets it off to the side. "Come here."

As I approach, he scoots his chair back a foot, giving me the space to stand between him and the dining table. My skin feels sensitive as his gaze rakes over me. Without a word, his hands go to my hips and he lifts me easily, placing me on the table in front of him.

Oh. His hands, warm and large, slide up my legs and beneath the dress, not stopping until reaching the edge of the new, black panties I found in the pile of clothes. He traces the edges, and with every pass, my thighs inch farther apart.

"You realize how fucked you are, right?" he asks, his voice smooth. "I'm a hunter, Della, and I'm now imprinted with your scent. Which means all the secrets you keep in here," he quickly removes one hand to tap his index finger against my temple, "are mine."

I don't even know why I talk; why I insist on enticing him more, tempting him with the possibility of learning what he never will. "You still don't know my last name so maybe you're not as good of a hunter as you believe you are."

Nico growls, and in one movement, he has my dress hiked to my waist, my legs spread wide, feet planted on the armrests of his chair. His gaze focuses between my legs, on the dark spot no doubt spreading on my panties.

"I've been waiting for you to wake up. I'm hungry for breakfast."

His fingers hook in the sides of the panties and he slides them from my legs, dropping them onto the table beside me.

"So tasty," he murmurs.

That's all the warning I get before Nico's head dives between my legs and his tongue licks me from my core to clit. My insides immediately jolt with the sensation, the ache in my stomach reminding me how sore I still am, but none of that matters. Not as his tongue lavishes my clit, nipping and sucking, reigniting everything from last night.

No matter how much I shift my legs, I feel like I can't widen them enough, like he can't get deeper inside me. His hands come around to my ass and he slides me to the very edge of the table, urging me to lie back with a subtle push to my stomach.

"Be a good girl and relax for me. Lie back," he mumbles against my thigh, right over top of his bite mark.

His tongue spears me and the noise that bursts up from my throat doesn't even sound like something a person should be able to make. Guttural and pleading, wanton and fearless. He fucks me with his tongue until I explode in a sloppy mess all over his face.

When the orgasm subsides, I'm about to sit up and apologize for what I did, but he doesn't let up. He tongues my sensitive clit and shoves two fingers in my sopping, tight pussy, making another one of those impossible noises climb from my throat.

"You look so fucking beautiful when you come, Della. You're feeding me such a delicious breakfast. I'll never be able to enjoy anything else after this."

My hips rock against his face, the feeling of his stubble on my core making this nearly too much. My lungs feel like they're not getting enough air, like I'm dying.

His fingers hammer in and out of me and when his teeth scrape over his bite mark—his claim on me—I can't hold back any longer. The intensity is nearly blinding, the need to draw this out as long as possible while also wanting to curl up and allow my body time to stop quivering. I feel this orgasm in every part of my body, like he's officially taken every inch of me.

"Well, if I knew that's what was on the breakfast menu, I would have come earlier."

That's not Nico's voice...

I shriek, pushing myself into a sitting position and shoving my messy hair away from my face as I quickly try to cover myself with my hands and right my dress.

Meanwhile, Nico barely looks fazed. He lifts his head, glancing to the side, and I follow his gaze to the doorway.

A guy strides leisurely into the room, his lips pulled into a smirk. He shares so many similarities in appearance to the man seated in front of me. Same hair, same eyes, and same cocky grin. Except, the darkness Nico exhibits isn't shared in this one. Rather, he's more of a grey. Like he's dangerous but opts to only allow that side of him to come out when he needs it.

His brother? I recognize this man as the one who stood beside him at the party when I first spotted Nico.

His forestry eyes flick over my form, pausing on my bare thighs, making me feel more exposed than I already have been. He makes a show of licking his lips, his eyes brightening. "Yum. Is there any left for me?"

Um. How do I respond to that?

While my mind stutters to come up with an intelligible response, Nico rumbles, "Fuck off. This one's mine. You have a club with an abundance of available pussy to choose from."

The newcomer takes the nearest seat and pouts. "But this one looks tastier, brother."

Okay, so that confirms who this man is. My mind goes

through the various news articles I've read on the Corsettis, seeking out Nico's brother's name. While Nico is more prevalent in the news, it's not like his brother is completely kept from it.

As he speaks again, his name appears in my mind, lit up with realization. *Rafael.*

"After all, she's already here and available."

Nico growls, looking from his brother to me. A possessiveness darkens his irises and his fingers sink into the fleshy part of my thigh, nearly making me whimper in discomfort, if I wasn't so turned on by his claim.

"She's mine and I don't share."

"Too bad," his brother muses with a shrug. "She sure looks tasty."

I look back and forth between them, still trying to formulate words in my mind when Nico grabs my chin, focusing my attention solely on him.

"Whatever you're thinking, *don't*. I don't play like that." His thumb brushes over my lip roughly. "This mouth will only know my name. I'll be the one to make you come."

"N-no." He misunderstood why I was looking between them.

But Nico seems to already be moving on, releasing my face and leaning back in his chair, smirking at his brother. "Well, Della, I should formally introduce our intruder. This is my brother, Rafael."

15
NICO

Yesterday, I didn't want Della near any of my family, but thanks to Rafael's inclination to often pop over unannounced, I'm not surprised this happened.

"Hi," Rafael grins, looking at Della through calculating eyes, "it's Della, right?"

"Yeah." On her lap, her hands twist into a knot, and I realize right then how beneficial it is to have had my brother show up. Clearly, being around my family makes her nervous. There's an importance in this fact, I feel, I just can't determine why it is.

His eyes flick toward me and back to her with a speed so quick, I doubt she caught it. But it was enough for me to catch the question, the suspicion, and the wonder in his look.

"And how'd you two meet?"

"The party." She peeks at me, as though thinking she spoke out of turn. I motion for her to continue, hoping perhaps somewhere in this, she'll trip up in recounting the facts. That's when liars *always* fuck up and give themselves away.

I watch her, studying her expression. She's nervous at Raf's arrival, but not for the reasons she should be, I think. Not because she's speaking to another made man, who could slice her neck before she sees him coming, but because he's asking about her.

Red flag.

"Cinderella, I assume?" Rafael glances at me for confirmation.

"What?" she squeaks.

"Ignore him," I command.

Rafael is usually not one to give up until he's made his point, but thankfully, he too gets off the subject, instead asking, "Well, then, *Della*, if you're with Mister Grump over here, you must have quite the story. What is it?"

Della's throat moves with her swallow, but it's more than that. She shifts the tiniest fraction, and her toes curl from where they're still positioned on the armrests. Her tongue peeks out, dampening her lips, and then again, within seconds.

But she reveals nothing.

"Leave it, Rafael," I tell him, feigning to be her hero for now. "Della and I are still working out the details of who exactly she is." I lift a single brow in a dare.

Della shrugs one shoulder, telling us both, "I'm no one special. Right place at the right time."

I doubt that.

Tiring of the conversation I know will simply go in circles, I drop Della's feet from the chair and slide it back, standing and taking her hand to help her hop off the table as I go. Keeping her hand in mine, I pull her by my brother, who watches us with an amused expression.

"You can't fool me, Nico," he calls out as we pass him. "Good luck, Della."

Della doesn't fight when I drag her down the hallway, but she does state, "Nico, I'm hungry. Contrary to you, um, eating, I haven't yet."

I stop, swinging her in front of me. My arm loops around her waist and I propel her to me. She gasps, tipping her head back to look at me. Blonde strands frame her face and I'm brought back to last night, when they were fanned over my desk as she begged for release.

"We'll go out for breakfast," I tell her. "That way, you're not given the third degree by my brother."

"Thanks." The relief on her face, coupled with the fact that she lays her hand on her chest, feeling her breath huff out, has me once again wondering so much about her.

Her bold blue eyes flash at me, her lashes slowly batting. The effect she has on me is so strange, so different than what I've ever felt, I release her before I can think about it a second longer.

"We're going to a restaurant?" she asks as I stalk toward the front door.

"No."

~

"Bagels in the park? Nico Corsetti, you surprise me. This is so simple for a man like you."

Keeping her hand in mine, I sink onto the park bench, bringing her down with me. In one hand, I grip my warm bagel, while my other arm stretches across the bench's back, behind Della's shoulders.

Around us, people enjoy the warm weather by strolling through the peaceful Westmount Park. Mothers with strollers and kids on bikes pass us. Joggers rush by in their quest to exercise, weaving around those who walk slowly.

"It'd be a shame for you to not experience Montreal's finest. We're known for our bagels, you know." Well, the bagels are one of many things, though it seems to be less in recent years, as all the classic shops are closing due to rising rental costs. Luckily, I back one of my favourites, to ensure there will always be at least one place that remains open.

She takes a bite of her sesame bagel, smirking as she chews. "You realize I've lived here my entire life, right, and have eaten many bagels in that time."

"Ah," I roll my head toward her, "I didn't know that, but now I do, so thanks. I'll add it to the few facts I've garnered from you—the very few. So, you're Montreal-born then?" Sarcasm tinges my tone, but I'm also being truthful. For all I know about her, she could have been born in another country.

She chuckles, shaking her head. "Yes, born here and never moved away. You too, I assume, given your family's roots?"

"Oh, yeah." I think about Mother's family, once the adversary to Father's, until they joined together to create a dynasty so strong, no one could rival them. "For decades that I know of, but I'm sure longer."

We're silent as we finish our bagels, observing the scene around us. I finish eating first then shift all my attention to her. Della's legs are crossed, and her free arm—the one not holding her food—is on the bench beside her, propping her up. Anyone passing by would view her position as one of ease, but with my nearness, I can spot the edge she maintains. The way her fingers drum the bench every three minutes, and her legs uncross and recross often. The way her eyes flick over every person passing us, scanning them as though searching for something. I inch closer, and she leans away, putting more weight on her arm bracing her.

"What's in your head, Della?"

She jerks, blinking awake from wherever I lost her to. "N-nothing. I'm fine."

Fine. Such an interesting word. It never means what people believe it does. It's not a word to indicate acceptance, but rather when they're hiding truths. When they'd rather end the conversation and avoid it becoming inquisitive.

Della doesn't want me to probe.

I grunt and look away, feigning acknowledgement of her claim, and slide my phone from my pocket, bringing up the most recent conversation.

ME

Anything yet?

He responds nearly right away:

No, but soon, I think.

ME

Keep searching.

It's a race for her to give me the information I need or for my IT guy to discover it himself. Either way, I *will* get it, and until then, I'm not letting her out of my sight.

"Is there anywhere in this glorious city you haven't seen before that I can take you to?" I ask.

Her teeth scrape her bottom lip as indecision flashes over her face. "You have work to do. Being an underboss has its responsibilities and hanging out with me is probably the last thing you should be doing."

With the hand resting on the back of the bench, I turn her head, locking her into position, so she's unable to look away. "The benefit of being in my position means *I* decide what I do and when, and today, the world can fucking burn for all I care, because I'm too enthralled with you to let you go."

She tilts her head a fraction. "Until you learn my last name, right? Then I'm free?"

No. "Does that entice you to tell me?"

"Hayes."

"A lie," I growl. "All a fucking lie." I feel it. She wouldn't reveal it now, with no further influence or encouragement. The name slipped from her too easily to be the truth.

She shrugs and jerks her head, breaking my hold on her. "Well, that's on you then. I've told you my name. Della Hayes. Not my fault you don't believe me."

I abruptly stand, yanking her with me, garnering curious looks from a family walking by. Her attitude is frustrating me though, and I'm seconds away from throwing her ass in the Lachine Canal. Worse yet, I'm getting pissed at myself for dragging this out. I should hand her over to Flynn, my enforcer, and be done with her bullshit. Then she'll know true pain.

But no. Instead, I take her hand and stalk down the bike path with her, wondering at what point I will lose myself.

16

DELLA

Can my guilt become any heavier?

When I think it can't, it does. When I think I'm managing to play my part well, Nico goes and does something that has my conscience reminding me of the ethics, or lack thereof, in my actions.

After eating freshly baked goddamn bagels in the park, Nico brought me to The Montreal Museum of Fine Arts, a place I haven't visited since a school trip in elementary school, which I can only recall bits and pieces of now.

When you're a Corsetti, visiting a museum becomes the opposite or ordinary.

Private. That's what it is. Private entrance, private tour. With a guide who left us not too long after beginning to lead us around when Nico shooed him off.

Nico was nothing less than a gentleman during the museum visit, even reciting facts of some of the exhibits, surprising me with his knowledge. Seems he's even intelligent in subjects outside of murder, guns, and gang life.

That's when the guilt gets heavier. When we're alone. When

there's no one around to help shoulder the burden. When my speech becomes less because my head's so full of arguments for and against this plan; when I have to remind myself to stop repetitively swallowing and avoid accidentally revealing my culpability to Nico.

After the museum visit, we returned to Mount Royal, this time to become the very people walking the paths we observed this morning during breakfast.

Away from his mansion and clubs, Nico is just an ordinary man.

At every turn, he's tried to probe into my life—childhood, family, hobbies, everything he could possibly think of—and I've been so cautious to avoid mentioning anything that could give me away. At this point, I should just invent a life in order to appease his questioning, but like the first name I gave him, Anna, and my most recent lie about my surname, Hayes, I doubt he'll believe me.

I haven't completely avoided responding though, managing to divulge *some* things that have no connection to my real life. I told him about my childhood, and that I grew up without a father. I talked about old school friends—nameless to him— that I haven't spoken to in many years, but it gives him something to latch onto. What music I like. What movie I last watched. Where in the city I enjoy the most. Which restaurants are my favourite.

On one hand, the facts Nico has learned about me are details that people who just met wouldn't be aware of. They're the deeper, little things in a person's past that only gets revealed with a lengthy relationship, when both parties have time to discover it.

I've also learned about his past. I know when he was ten, he broke his arm by jumping from a swing when Rafael dared him to. He talked about his childhood pet, when he begged his mother for a dog, and that dog lived a long life, dying only a few years ago. He told me that for a while, he wanted to attend public school and not the private ones his family instead made him go to. He claims to have hated them, because they didn't have a floor hockey team, which he wanted to be a part of.

It's strange to know these things about him. Like what I've revealed about myself, he's only given the innermost facts about his past. Both of us skirting the truth of our reality and revealing the smallest fragments of what we can.

We share another outdoor meal for supper, this time, poutine—something I never thought I'd see a man like Nico eat. The combination of curd cheese, fries, and gravy might be a common food item here, but it's not exactly a delicacy. Nico merely shrugged when I pointed this out and mentioned something about it being a Canadian classic that he too appreciates.

Back at the mansion, he takes me outside to one of the many balconies I hadn't noticed during my first visit. I walk to the edge of it, scanning the side of the house. I catch sight of the greenhouse below us, which means we're facing the backside of his property. In the far distance, on the edge of a large land, there's a treeline outlined in black.

"I think you're trying to woo me, Mr. Corsetti."

Nico comes up behind me, the heat of his body stifling. He places one hand on the balcony on either side of my body, caging me in. His words are mumbled against my cheek, his face buried in my neck. "Do you need to be wooed, Della? Last night took very little effort before I had you on your back."

Dick. Whipping my head around, I hit him with my hair, making my point. "Are you calling me a whore?"

With force, he twists my head to face forward again. "Yes. But you're *my* whore, Della, so it's okay." His hand travels the length of my body, his hand pausing on the base of my neck as his thumb pushes against my rapid pulse. "I don't hear much of an argument from you."

"Well, when you put it like that." In truth, I have no fucking clue how to feel about this conversation. Given the future, I don't have time to allow myself to *feel* anything. "What's over there?" I gesture to the darkness at the edge of the property, changing the topic.

"A small forest. It's the best at this time of night. Dark. So easy to get lost in." He pauses, leaving the bait there, and I fucking take it.

"Lost?"

"Mhm. So easy to be scared, running through it, your heartbeat hammering in your chest with the knowledge that I'm right *there*. So close. And when I catch you..." His threat trails off, and by now, I don't only hear his words, I *feel* them.

So I, again, answer his taunts. "What would happen when you catch me?"

The hand he has on my throat slides down my body, his fingers disappearing beneath the edge of the dress and dancing along the skin there. "You want to know what will happen, *ma douce petite souris*? Your pussy will be soaking wet, all primed and ready to take me." His hand trails up my thigh, and he presses a finger over my core, making my breath catch. "Right here, Della. When I chase you through that dark forest, and inevitably catch you, because I'll be able to scent this dripping cunt, I'll take you on your hands and knees, shoving your face into the forest floor, reminding you of exactly where you are. You'll scratch, scream, try to get away. Will try to fight being my whore, but you won't win because, in the end, your pussy knows its master."

Holy. Fuck. Am I still breathing? Are any thoughts working in my head? Am I shaking or imagining my own reaction? What. The. Fuck. Is. Happening. To. Me?

His finger pushes the material of my panties inside me and his teeth scrape my shoulder, enticing a delectable shiver. "It'd be the ultimate chase. Now I won't be able to go a day without imagining that fantasy playing out."

Speak for yourself. Before two minutes ago, that wasn't even a fantasy I had. Something I would have never entertained. I was right in thinking that last night only brushed the surface of Nico's preferences.

Stop considering being chased. That'll never happen.

But it could. Right now. Before Stefano's plan continues...

With his hand beneath my chest, he uses the leverage to push my hips back into him, letting me feel his hard length.

"Nico, we're outside."

"And?" he murmurs into my skin. "When has being public ever stopped you before? Should I remind you about the hallway I chased you in? Anybody could have found us."

"Still..." I roll my hips into him, lifting my hand to place it on the backside of his neck, locking our bodies together, even as I continue to point out, "Don't you have cameras out here?"

Nico chuckles dangerously, his warm breath painting my skin. "Trying to learn the best way to break out?"

"I mean, your staff could be watching. You're not one to share. You said that yourself. You want them to see us?"

He growls, and his teeth scrape the delicate skin at the back of my neck, doing more to me than my words did to him —*clearly*. Always one step ahead.

"You're right, I wouldn't. So it's a good thing I know where the cameras are, where they're not, and where there are blind spots."

In a blur, Nico grasps my upper arms and he spins me away from the balcony edge and into the darkness—into the shadows. He pins me against the wall, the chilly brick wreaking havoc on my body through the thin material of the sundress.

THE HUNT IN ELUSION

"This," he murmurs low in my ear, "is a blind spot. Lucky you."

"Oh, yeah," I breathe. "Why am I lucky?"

Instead of responding, he hikes my dress to my waist and pushes my panties down my legs. His fingers brush over my damp core, and the cool air follows right behind them.

"You're lucky," he finally answers, "because this location isn't on camera, which means I can fuck this wet pussy and no one will be seeing you."

My response is quick, instant, driven by extreme lust. "Then what are you waiting for?"

In a swift moment, he has the front of his pants undone. Then he's lifting my leg to the side, opening me to him. "This is going to be quick, Della. I'm not holding back. We've spent all day together, with the memory of your hot cunt constantly on my mind."

"Please."

Please don't.

Please take me.

Please claim me.

Please go slow.

Please go quick.

So many possibilities for my single word. Which one did I mean? Maybe all of them.

Nico lines his hard cock up to my core and in a single thrust, he sinks the entire way inside me. Our cries mingle in the nighttime air as he grasps one of my hands, linking his fingers with mine. It gives me something to look at, something that has my thoughts going blank for a second. A simple action, a simple touch, and yet something so powerful and impacting. Genteel and romantic even, if it can be taken that far.

"Take me like the good girl you are." His hips slam against

me and I curl my spine, arching my back to take him deeper.

"Tell me how much you're enjoying this, Della."

He wants me to speak? He wants me to actually formulate words? "So—much."

"Tell me what you want."

"To...come," I manage in between dense breaths.

His hand comes around to my front and he roughly slaps my swollen clit, the impact nearly painful yet fully pleasurable. "Come with the pain. Give me your orgasm. Della, *come*."

Perhaps it's the command, or it's simply the timing of his strokes and his slaps on my pussy, but I obey him, squeezing his cock, feeling my insides pulse as I take him deeper. He follows my orgasm with his own, his groan making me shiver.

His cum floods me, and after long minutes, when both our breathing returns to almost normal, he slides out of me. His cum drips down my leg, but neither of us move to wipe it away.

"Your pussy is magic." Nico rights my dress and turns me back around. As he drags me toward the balcony door, he continues, "You're way too compelling to release."

And that'll be your downfall, is what I want to tell him.

"So don't," is what I actually say.

"I won't," he promises, his tone dark, with a seriousness that has me believing him.

17
NICO

The next morning begins much like yesterday, in which I leave Della in bed. This time, instead of going down for breakfast, I dress and head straight to my office because as much as I claimed yesterday to have been able to put aside work in order to spend time with her, it was a lie. My phone constantly vibrated with notifications, but none were the ones I was hoping for—information about her.

Last night after Della went to sleep, I responded to one particular email because its importance was too great to ignore. An email from Diego Rossi, Boss of the New York *Famiglia* and father to Erico Rossi, Aurota's future fiancé, requesting a meeting to go over the details of the agreement.

Aggravating, but leader to leader, I can respect his request. Father really fucked things up years ago when stealing Mother away from the union between his family and ours, so I can understand Diego's hesitation to go all-in on this deal.

Once I'm seated at my desk, I text Rosen to come to my office. While waiting, I pull up my email, as well as another contract I need to read at some point today, and then the video chat program, preparing for the upcoming meeting.

Meetings. Contracts. Family. It's all so easy to forget when I'm buried in Della's pussy. A woman I still know nothing about because, while I may have learned plenty yesterday, it was nothing of substance; nothing actually valuable or indicative of her identity. It's all surface-level shit.

A knock on the door pulls me from my thoughts. Seconds later, the door is opened to reveal Rosen, who enters and shuts it behind him.

"Boss," he greets. "I feel like we haven't seen you around since the party."

I suppose I haven't been. I haven't looked in on any of the clubs, taken any calls, or even visited our fucking gym since Della entered my life.

"The men miss sparring with you," he adds as he treads across the floor. "They've been asking about you."

I grunt, waving my hand to dismiss his concerns. "Tell them I've been busy." If the men have noticed my absence, even after only a day, I wonder who else has too. "Sit," I order.

Rosen drops into one of the chairs across from me.

"Diego Rossi wants to discuss details of the arrangement between Aurora and his son. Since you'll be around Aurora most, I want you to listen in, in case you pick up anything of value I don't."

"Understood."

When the time on my computer's clock matches the meeting time, I click the link, opening the meeting room, spotting Diego already there. His greasy hair shines through the camera, catching on the sunlight past his shoulder. His expression remains flat and ready for business.

"Corsetti," he greets.

"Rossi," I return the sentiment. "You wanted to discuss something."

"I want to ensure the safety of your sister until she's wed to my son."

Not words I expected. Blinking twice to ensure he said what I believed he had, I steel the agitation bristling my nerves by taking time to adjust my jacket.

"Define safety, Rossi." My jaw tics. "If you're insinuating I would dare place my own sister in harm's way…" I trail off, allowing the threat to go unfinished and up for interpretation.

He waves his hand, feigning innocence. "Not at all. I simply mean to say the girl has been raised away from your family, which means her upbringing is…questionable."

"You better be fucking careful how you speak about my sister," I snap, uncaring that the name Rossi holds more influence than Corsetti. "And of what you're demanding. Her 'questionable' upbringing, as you've referred to it, has still been controlled. Are you claiming she's unworthy of your son? Because I can promise Aurora Corsetti has been raised no differently than if she was home."

Lie. Aurora's been raised in an elite and extremely private institution, funded by the families of privileged children. Raised by three nuns, she's been more closed-off than if she was home, but taught about our life and what her role will be upon returning. In truth, though, none of us really know what we'll be getting when she arrives.

Over my monitor, I spot the skin between Rosen's eyes crinkling as he too reacts to Diego's suggestion.

Diego shifts in his seat, crushed by the weight of my stare. "No, I mean to say, without the guidance of your family, Aurora could find herself tempted by outside influences upon her return. No fault of your own, or even hers, but rather, a fact we may need to deal with. She simply hasn't had the same upbringing as you and your brother, no matter how much you claim she has. Therefore, I'm concerned about possible *complications* that can arise in the time between her re-entry into society and the union of our families."

Ah. Over the screen, I catch Rosen's gaze, and he too shares the same realization. Diego thinks Aurora will fuck the first man she happens across because she hasn't been raised in the Corsetti household. The rules we gave her school were strict: her freedom limited, so there would be no opportunity to lose her virginity.

"What are you proposing exactly?" I curl my hand around the edge of my desk, gripping it as I imagine it being his neck instead.

"A bodyguard. Not only for her protection, but also my son's."

Someone to watch her and make sure she doesn't fuck anyone.

I meet Rosen's eyes again, shrugging as I respond, "I already have my best man set aside for her. Aurora will have complete protection upon her return."

But Diego is already shaking his head. "No, Corsetti. I would feel much safer if it was a man of my own choosing. I'm sure you understand."

It's laughable at best and I hold onto the edge of my chair, steadying myself before I ruin all possibilities of this union. "I don't, in fact," I answer slowly, thinking about every word before I speak. "I respect your desire to ensure your purchase, but in case you have forgotten, she's *my* sister. *My* family. She's a Corsetti, and until she bears the name of Rossi, she's *my* responsibility. This agreement only works with trust, and right now, I will not be having one of your men staying in my home. I'm sure you understand." I toss his own ending statement back at him.

He scoffs, throwing his head back dramatically. "You speak of trust when it was *your* father who murdered my uncle."

"That was the past. My father made his choices, but mine are different. As are yours, which is how we've come to an agreement at all. Was it not you who said that since your family is under your leadership, we can appreciate the changes and begin anew?" I pause, allowing him to swallow that before finishing off with, "Do not confuse me with my father, Rossi. As I've said, Aurora *will* have a bodyguard, but it'll be one of my men. I wouldn't dare repeat the mistakes of the past and insult you by sending Aurora to your son without her virginity." I cross my arms, signalling that we're done.

Indecision flashes over his face and his jaw tics. A man who's not used to having to follow the orders of another. The situation is a tough one. Tricky, because he holds more power between the two of us, but he wants the Corsetti connection, and Aurora—the long-lost mafia princess—is the way to obtain it.

"Fine, Corsetti. I agree."

He shuts off the stream without another word. With him gone, I huff out a long breath and look at Rosen. "What do you take from that?"

"That he's going to be a pain in our ass."

"I agree. Which means, to save us all the headache, don't let my sister out of your sight." I rub at my forehead, at the headache beginning to bloom there from all this. I could be balls deep in heaven right now, but instead, I'm playing this stupid political game.

Rosen signals his agreement with a two-fingered salute. I dismiss him with the customary wave of my hand and he leaves.

The moment the door shuts, it's reopened. This time, blonde hair peeks through followed by the face I continue to see in my mind.

"Knock, knock. Someone mentioned you being in here." Della steps through the door entirely. "But if I'm interrupting, I can leave."

"No, you've come at the perfect time. I was in a meeting, but it's over now."

"Who with?" she asks, her expression completely innocent and clear.

Does she think me stupid to fall for that? I push away from the desk, creating a small amount of space between it and me, and gesture to the spot. "Come here."

She does without question but narrows her eyes. "So bossy. I should walk away, to make you chase me."

Please do. "You'd like that. For once, listen to me."

She steps into the space I indicated, rolling her eyes playfully. "As if I ever *don't* listen to you."

Cocking my brow, I lift a hand, ready to raise fingers as I list every time she hasn't obeyed me. "Regardless of my ongoing questions about you and your life, you haven't told me anything of substance." One finger. "You disobeyed me when I instructed you not to talk when I took you right here on this desk." Two fingers. "You continuously evade all my questions regarding your emotions, because, Della, I know you're not *fine*, which is what you claim to be. I see it in your eyes."

"Fine." Della leans back against my desk and crosses her arms, looking down on me in the sexiest way possible. "I guess there were a couple of times I didn't listen. But just to make a point, demand anything of me, and I'll do it."

I chuckle darkly, instantly overwhelmed with the numerous possibilities I can ask of her. "Della, careful making offers like that because that's way too open-ended." Taking her arm, I break her hold and make her fall into my lap, wrapping an arm around her waist. "I could fuck you relentlessly and deny you all your orgasms. I could have you kneel in the corner over there," I tip my head to the right, "unmoving for hours as I work. Or have you beneath my desk, my cock buried deep in your throat. I could tie you to my bed with a vibrator strapped to your pussy and watch you lose your mind with countless orgasms." When she grins, I wag a finger in front of her face. "Ah, ah, it'd be nearly as painful as being denied. Either way, *petite souris*, what you offer has endless possibilities, so you might need to be careful what you propose."

She presses her lips together, a smirk curling the edges, hiding how much my words have turned her on. I know they have; it's in how her eyes have darkened with lust and her body bends toward mine.

"You're insatiable," she mumbles. "Point made though."

I laugh. A lightness courses through my chest that I try to ignore. A feeling I've never felt with anyone—

The door opens again and an uninvited visitor strides in, crossing his arms as he stays in the doorway. "Well, well," my brother drawls, "look at how busy you are. And here Rosen warned me you'd actually be working."

Unwillingly, I drag my gaze from Della to Rafael, a tenseness tightening the tendons in my neck as I rumble, "Fuck off."

"On the contrary, you should be happy I got here first. Because Mother and Father are on their way up. Figured I'd give you a warning."

Fuck.

Della meeting Rafael was manageable because Rafael won't say shit, but my parents will demand to know everything about Della. They'll expect *me* to know these things, and when I admit I don't, Father will send her straight to our enforcer.

Della looks over at me, her own eyes bulging. Good. So she doesn't want to meet them either. This could be a prime excuse for escaping.

"No warning needed," I tell my brother smoothly, feigning relaxation. I don't want him noticing my tension.

My brother grunts and walks farther in the room, leaving my office door open. He smirks though, knowing me all too well and recognizing the anxiety I've learned to hide. He takes up residence by leaning against a far wall, crossing his arms and ankles.

"Well, then, by all means, let me stay here and watch the shitshow about to go down."

As though they were waiting on my brother's permission, my parents instantly appear in in my doorway. Mother enters first, her eyes sweeping the room, landing on Rafael and then me, before spotting Della. It's subtle, but her steps falter. Behind her, my father enters, but instead of scanning the room, he immediately looks to me, and like Mother, he stiffens at the sight of Della on my lap.

"Well, hello there," Mother says to Della. She slowly treads into the room, her high heels barely wobbling on the thick carpeting. I've often believed my mother looked like a true queen, and I see it again now, as she approaches us, looking down on us.

Della scrambles to her feet and pats her blouse flat, more clothing I had the staff purchase for her. Red blooms across her cheeks, and I'm lost somewhere in wanting to flee with her and leave her to my parents' inquisitive gazes. Perhaps this is finally what'll break her. All the Corsettis together in one room.

"H-hi," she rushes to say, and then takes Mother's outstretched hand in a shake.

I stand too as Father approaches behind Mother. To Della, he might look impassive, but the way his jaw is locked and his gaze firm on me, I know he's hiding a curious rage. "Who's this lovely lady?"

"Della," she answers, even though he was speaking to me.

"Della...?" Father ends in a question, seeking a surname.

"Hayes," she answers with the previous lie she fed me.

"Della Hayes," he repeats her full name. "Hm. You look familiar. Would we know you from somewhere?"

A wave of protectiveness overcomes me; a need to get her away from them. But I don't. I don't because of Della's reaction. Her chest stops moving, and I assume she's stopped breathing altogether. Her shoulders curl inward, like she's trying to hide. She licks her lips three times and rubs her hands together.

She's nervous.

Interesting.

Which means, my parents do know her from somewhere.

When Della finally manages to speak, it's with a nervous, light chuckle. "N-no, no I don't think you would. I'm new to the city."

New to the city. She's either lying to me about having been born and raised here, or them. And I know it's my parents she's lying too, given her behaviours.

Her gaze darts to mine and the plea there is so loud, it'd be challenging to ignore. *Don't say anything.*

"Hm." Father grunts, his attention sliding to me.

I'm stuck between both of them. One demanding I learn about this girl and the other begging me to hide truths from my family.

Why though?

Father doesn't let up, rubbing at his face as he muses, "It's your features. I've definitely seen them before." He glances at my mother. "Caterina, would you agree?"

"Maybe you saw me in passing?" Della offers, shrugging. Her look of panic is back, and if I can see it, I know they can too.

Enough of this. Snatching Della's hand, I begin dragging her around the desk and past my parents. Rafael watches us, looking seconds away from bursting out in laughter.

"Excuse us," I call back. "Father, I'll be back later if you have something you wish to discuss."

Then we're out of the office and I don't stop dragging her along with me until we're out of the mansion completely, standing in the middle of the gravel driveway.

Della breathes out a sigh—probably one of relief—but I'm too far gone to care. To really notice. Not releasing her, I roughly swing her to a stop in front of me, towering over her.

"No more fucking games, Della. Tell me who you are. Tell me why I've just lied to my parents for you." All the previous flirting, the jokes, the lightness, it's gone. Zapped away by hardened demands.

"Y-you—" She shuts her eyes, tilting her face away. Her lips fold together, defiant to the core.

I jerk her arm roughly, garnering her attention again. "No, Della. First, tell me which is it: did you lie to me or my parents regarding your life here in Montreal?"

"Them," she whispers, her voice breaking.

"Why? They were correct, weren't they? They know you from somewhere."

"Probably."

"That's not a yes."

She shrugs. "They shouldn't know me, but it's a possibility. I can't say for certain."

"You're scared as though they do."

She swallows. "Nico...don't."

"Don't *what*? Don't what, Della? *Tell me* what I shouldn't be doing." Clamping down on both arms, I shake her, releasing a modicum of pent-up anger. I've shoved shrewdness aside for her magical pussy, when there's clearly more to this. Instincts I've ignored that I now wonder if I'm about to pay the price for.

"The game's up, Della. Before I find it in me to lock you in my basement and throw away the key, tell me who you are and why my family *possibly*," I go with her specific term, "knows you."

Her eyes shut again. She breathes once, twice, and when she opens them again, there's a new hardness. A new Della. A Della I haven't seen before.

A girl who's turning back into a pumpkin before my very eyes.

She nods once, more of a jerk of her head. "Okay, Nico. You win. I'll tell you everything, but not here."

"Where then?"

"My house."

18

DELLA

Some-fucking-how, Stefano's plan might actually work. When I awoke this morning, there was a text from an unknown number. Unknown, because it's how my phone lists it, but the digits are very familiar to me. Stefano. Only, he's always ensured I never had his contact programmed into my phone, or anyone else's for that matter.

The text listed out an address. No instructions, only an address, which I then Googled. It leads to a house.

The message was clear though. This is where Stefano wants me to lead Nico.

That's when the guilt resurfaced.

All-consuming.

Empowering.

Immobilizing.

An emotion chaining me to Nico's bedroom, long after I woke up. I paced the floor countless times, hoping to eventually tire myself out to the point that I wouldn't feel that useless emotion, but as much and as fast as I walked, I could never seem to outrun it.

I've known Nico for a matter of two days, but I've spent more time with him than I ever imagined I would. It's a ploy though, I continue to remind myself. Not real. For him, he's keeping me around all to see if he can uncover who I am, and I'm merely getting close to him for my freedom.

Lie. Or at least a partial one.

I found Nico in his office and I was going to suggest a drive when he was available. A drive in which I would somehow lead him to Stefano's address. Stefano had given me a week, but if I could end this sooner and resolve this sickening feeling in the base of my stomach, it would be better. At least, I can go away and pretend these short days never happened, even though I already know they'll stick with me forever.

I can't sentence a man to death and simply forget about it.

But then his parents showed up and his father started giving me the third-degree about possibly knowing me and I froze. I'm one thousand percent certain they've seen me before, even if Stefano attempted to keep Mom, Ariella, and me away from the media.

When Nico dragged me outside, I knew the game was up. There was no way he'd allow me to continue my made-up realities. The look of utter betrayal is only a hint of what I'm expecting to soon see when he realizes how deep my deception actually goes.

Then he gave me the perfect opportunity. Nico won't return to fucking around, like he's been doing so far, knowing there's more to me, rather than only suspecting. If I want this over soon, there's no reason to drag this on.

Nico leaves me in front of his house to go get a car, rather than having me follow. I wait for the second he disappears into the large, multi-bay garage to take my phone out and reply to the address.

ME

We're coming.

Within seconds, the reply comes through.

UNKNOWN

We'll be ready.

Nico drives his black sports car—I can't even begin to guess the make and model of what I'm sure is a very pricey European vehicle —to the front of the mansion and stops beside me. I get in, barely glancing at him as I take the passenger seat. Shame has my shoulders curling away, angling my body, so I stare out the window instead.

"Address?"

I recite what I've memorized, and I assume Nico inputs it into his GPS, but I don't check.

As we drive, my remorse worsens, becoming so thick, I can't focus on anything else. Can't breathe.

This time, not regarding robbing a man's freedom and life, but for the outcome this will have on his family. I don't completely know Stefano's plans for him, so perhaps Nico will make it out alive, but I have a strange inkling he won't.

The Corsettis will lose a family member soon. For all the death and destruction surrounding their name, it's not the same when they're losing their son and brother.

I'm aware of what it's like to lose someone close to you.

Mom's death wrecked me. A piece of me will forever be gone. Nico's parents will soon be experiencing the same, and it's a pain I'd never wish on another person.

But I must do this. For Ariella. For me.

The car maneuvers through streets and toward Westmount, an upscale neighbourhood. I've walked through there once in high school, curious to see its offerings, but given the nice housing and high price tags attached to the life there, it's only ever been for a brief look-around.

Nico will wonder how I can afford a house in such a rich neighbourhood, and when I shrug and make up an answer, it'll be my only truthful lie: a deceit in which I don't need to pre-plan for.

What if I told Nico the truth? What if I didn't do this? Would he spare me? Understand why I agreed to this?

I glance over, studying his tight grip on the steering wheel. His knuckles are nearly white. There's a hard set to the planes of his face, a crinkle around his eyes that tell me, no. No, he won't understand, nor will he forgive me. It's not in the nature of his role.

So I remain silent, for my life and for Ariella. At this point, I'm so close to having accomplished my task. Maybe an hour more of the falsities and it's over.

When Nico turns into Westmount, I peek at the GPS, reading the remaining length of time on this trip.

Two minutes. Two minutes and we'll arrive at "my house," and Nico will get the truths he believes he's getting—but not in the delivery method he assumes.

ME

Two minutes.

My warning is to guarantee Stefano is ready because, if this goes wrong, I don't think I'll live past today. I have no clue what kind of house we're walking into, which means there's no lie I can feed him that will appease him.

The two minutes pass way too quickly, and Nico slows in front of a pretty, two-story house. The brick is a dark red, rather than the plastic siding most modern houses now have. The roof is angled, drawing my attention to the large front window.

Short bushes line the stone walkway, leading to a white door that has a small, half-moon window in it.

"Cute house."

Somehow, I think it's an insult. *Cute* to rich people means *small*.

Nico parks the car in front of it and immediately scans the area. There are no number of breaths I can take that can ease the mix of troubled emotions inside me, so I don't bother and just quickly follow him out of the car.

Nico's scanning up and down the street, his eyes passing over all of the similarly, old-style homes.

"This is your house?" he checks, doubt heavy in his tone.

"Yes," I manage to say, without choking over my words. "I've lived here since I was a kid."

That's a plausible lie.

I walk away from him and up the path, eyes studying the neighbourhood, searching for any sign of Stefano, but finding none.

You better fucking be inside.

My feet feel like stone. My steps slow as I drag myself to the front door. Nico trails behind, and I realize, I have no way to get inside. Panic rises due to yet another fuck-up in Stefano's planning.

At this point, I have nothing to lose, so I touch the knob, angling my body in a way to block Nico's view as I test it, already mentally dying with the knowledge it won't be opening.

Maybe there's a spare key around somewhere... There's a doormat at my feet, and I've heard that people often keep keys beneath them.

Instead, all my worries evaporate as the door falls open.

Nico comes up behind me. "You leave your door unlocked?"

How do I explain this one? I shrug, playing my response down. "My sister often leaves it unlocked."

"Your sister," he repeats, brows lifting. "So you live with your sister then?"

I did. "Yes."

"You never mentioned her."

"I haven't mentioned a lot."

I enter the house, hand scraping against the nearest wall for a light switch, hoping I find one quickly, in order to continue the ruse that this is my house. My fingers catch on one almost instantly, giving me a flash of victory as I bathe the small foyer in light.

"You live here?"

"Yes," I say with conviction. "I said I do."

"This place looks quite bare."

I agree. There's a single table nearby with a small bowl on it, as though meant for holding keys. Beside it, a shoe bench with no shoes, and a coat rack, also empty.

Where did Stefano find this house?

I force an eyeroll and a giggle, aiming for the lighthearted jokes we shared earlier. "Yeah, well, I've seen your bedroom, Nico. You're not one to talk."

He doesn't laugh. Instead, he moves by me and into the attached living room.

"Give me a tour, Della. I want to see every inch of this place."

19
NICO

The living room is simple. A light blue couch with a single blanket and two pillows for décor. A sizable TV sits on a stand across from it, and a small coffee table in the centre that's completely empty of all items.

The room looks staged. Unlived in. Certainly nothing of the vibe I would match with Della.

I continue toward the kitchen. No matter how orderly a person is, the kitchen will *always* show signs of life. Food in the fridge, that single cup used before bed. I find a spotless kitchen instead. Also almost staged. A small round table with four chairs is in one corner, and the counter stretches across the parallel wall. The other has the stove and fridge, which I wander over to, to open.

"I'll show you upstairs." Della's voice cuts in, pausing my hand on the fridge handle.

Something is off. Something about her behaviour, about this place, about everything I've learned about her so far.

I release the handle, albeit semi-reluctantly, and turn to face her again. "You said you live here with your sister?"

"Mhm."

"What's her name?" I don't believe there's a sister at all, so the name she'll provide will be made-up, I presume.

"Ariella. She's out though. Often is."

I make a sound of agreement and step by her, heading back toward the living room, as I head for the foyer, where I saw a staircase leading up, and a door, likely to the basement.

"We can talk now, if you'd like." Della gestures to the couch. "You have questions, I know."

By the door, I pause, gaze skimming everything I've so far seen. The mysteries with this girl are great, and a large part of me wants to follow her suggestion and sit and hear her story. I want to learn everything about the woman who's snagged my attention. But my instincts are screaming at me to check this entire house, from top to bottom. Father always said to leave no room unturned when entering someplace new because you never know what's there.

And right now, there's a lot I don't know.

"My first question is what do you do for hobbies? Because people have movies, game consoles—*stuff* in their living rooms, Della, and you don't."

She shrugs one shoulder, her gaze dropping to her feet. "I don't know. Not a movie person. I spend a lot of time at work."

"Which is?"

Her lips press together as she slowly raises her head again and replies, "House cleaner."

That's not what I would have expected from Della. She seems like a person who'd enjoy a bit more excitement in her life. If she's a house cleaner by trade, it could explain why this house is so tidy.

I glance at the stairs, leading up to where her bedroom should be. A bedroom reveals a lot about a person, and suddenly I'm eager to see what it'll reveal—if anything—but the door to the side of the stairs calls to me.

"Basement?" I guess.

"Yeah."

A basement is where people hide everything they don't want others to find, so I grasp the knob and turn it, opening the door and feeling a chill rising from the bottom. I feel around for a light switch first.

Then I place my foot on the first step, hand going to my waist where my Glock is stored.

"Nico," Della calls out, her voice spiking.

I pause, glancing toward her. "Yeah?"

"Never mind."

Before I turn away, I catch her looking behind her, toward the front door.

At the bottom of the steps is a very empty basement. No boxes of holiday décor, no shelving, no nothing, besides a washer and dryer tucked in the corner.

I move to the centre of the room, a new wave of frustration making me curse. I run my hands through my hair, tugging on the strands as my hand moves through, trying to use the pain to lessen the other emotions coursing through me.

There's *nothing* in this place indicative of who Della is. This house is a lie.

Exactly like she is.

Della's steps are slow as they trail behind me. "There's nothing down here, Nico. We can go upstairs."

"No," I growl. Lunging toward her, I grasp her upper arms, just like I did outside my house. I shake her once, twice, hoping that, at the end, I feel more controlled. "Della, you do not live here, so stop spewing bullshit. What the fuck is going on?"

Her lips part, an answer right fucking *there*, only to be interrupted by a sound that chills me to my core.

The door at the top of the steps slams shut.

Della gasps, her gaze darting toward it.

I release her, taking out my Glock, cocking it immediately. Careful steps bring me to the front of Della, inching toward the staircase.

When heavy footsteps echo above us, I glance at her, asking a question I already know the answer to, but needing her to give the answer regardless. "Would that be your sister?"

"No."

"Stay behind me then. I might have to fight our way out."

There could be numerous reasons for why people are in this house. I have many enemies in the country, and if the wrong person saw us entering this small, unguarded house, they could be taking their chance. This could also just be a common break-in, though it's certainly coincidental.

And I don't believe in coincidences.

When the door flies open again, I throw myself backwards, becoming a human shield in front of Della. Until I know how many people I'm dealing with, running upstairs and trying to fight my way out could prove more dangerous. Instead, down here, with my vantage point, I'm able to take them out one-by-one.

I pull the trigger on the first person to make it into partial view, and my bullet shatters his shin, causing him to cry out and stumble the rest of the way down. I don't look twice before shifting my aim straight for his head.

The second follows quickly, and I shoot but miss, and then, more legs that appear. And more, and soon, there's a gathering at the base of the stairs. Men in black armour with large rifles circle the room, caging Della and me in.

Fuck. My weapon is nothing compared to theirs, and with Della here, I won't win this fight. Our best opportunity is to run, to get out of this house.

Della's fingers curl into my shirt and I feel her press into my back. The heat from her body warms me, reminding me why we need to get out of here. I still don't know who this woman is, but her life doesn't need to end in this house.

"Nico," she murmurs, fear lowering her tone so only I can hear.

My free arm bends behind me, shielding her body the best I can as I slowly spin, scanning the small, amassed army, searching for anyone who looks familiar. They all stare us down through unrecognizable faces, presumably waiting for someone else.

Someone who gives the orders.

Fuck.

"I got you, *petite souris*," I reassure her.

More steps come down the stairs, these ones slower. I shift the trajectory of my gun toward them, ready to shoot on sight.

Then he appears.

I should have fucking known.

Stefano De Falco, in a suit much too large for him, smiles his fucking rat smirk. His two front buck teeth stick out from his toothy grin and the dim light passes over his balding head, as he crosses his arms over his chest and walks to the middle of the room.

Shoot. One bullet to the forehead and this is over.

But then his men will attack.

I can fire and throw Della up the stairs. Fight our way to the top. Once I kill the head of the snake, the rest will be easier to get rid of.

My finger tightens on the trigger at the same time, feet scuff behind me. I don't turn to look, though Stefano's eyes slowly drag toward the noise.

"You shoot me. She dies. You choose, Corsetti."

Following his gaze, I spot the three men who have re-angled their rifles so the barrels are now pointed at Della.

My teeth smash together, mind working to determine every possible way I can get us both out of here. "De Falco," I greet in the meantime. "Quite the charade."

"You have no idea." His chin jerks toward the gun in my hand. "Drop that and then we'll talk."

"Fuck off."

"So be it." His fingers flick toward a soldier closest to us. "Shoot her."

"Fine," I shout without a second thought. "Fucking fine." Bending, I lower the gun until it drops to the floor, still keeping my body around Della as much as possible. Being weaponless leaves my gut in knots, but it's best to play this slowly until I can get us out.

"Kick it over here," he demands.

Huffing, I flick my ankle until my main form of protection exits my perimeter. The soldier nearest bends and slips it into his holster, making my jaw clench as I watch it become completely unavailable.

"Let her go, Stefano, and then we'll talk. You don't want an innocent's death on your conscience."

He *tsks* and steps forward. "*Innocent* is such an interesting word, Corsetti. I suppose to you, she is though."

My stomach drops. My entire form—my fucking *soul*—goes cold as the realization I think I fucking knew, deep down—so far down, I resisted even considering it—rises to the surface.

Then the bastard continues, his voice dropping into a croon. "You did so good."

His eyes aren't on me. They're staring over my shoulder, landing on the woman who releases my shirt and takes a few steps around me.

Della's eyes are pinned to the ground, her hair falling forward to cover her face, but it can't hide the duplicity. She stops by Stefano, and when she finally lifts her head, those beautiful ocean blue eyes I've come to love are cold, lost, and apologetic.

Stefano claps softly and wraps a single arm around her shoulders. A visible shudder courses through her, but she doesn't move away, and still, despite what I already know—that she's involved in this, that she's the reason for this moment—I want to rip his arm from her body.

"Good job," his eyes slide toward me, his lips curling, as he smashes the last bit of faith I held for Della, "daughter."

Daughter. His fucking *daughter?* Della...De Falco.

Della De Falco.

That's why she resisted admitting her surname to me.

Ma petite souris est un rat.

My little mouse is a rat.

20

DELLA

If I thought the guilt earlier was horrible, it's nothing to the storm ravaging my body as Nico puts the final piece together. Despair makes my throat tight with the sob I want to release. Nausea rolls through my stomach at the self-disgust. My heart beats slower with the horror of this moment.

This moment. The one I've orchestrated in the past couple days. The one where I shatter a man's trust. A man who's been nothing but good to me. A man who I've wanted to steal me away from this reality and make it all disappear.

Stefano's arm presses into my shoulder, heavier with the disgust I feel toward him, making me want to shrink away.

I've done it. Let me go, bastard.

In the middle of the room, Nico stands poised, his body shifted into a partial crouch, readying to fight his way out, if it wasn't for the betrayal locking his feet to the ground. The normal liveliness of the green in his irises is flat and dead with his stare.

I want to cower, to shield away from the look that's calculatingly planning my death. I want to go to my knees and beg him for forgiveness and explain why I agreed to this. That, at the time, Nico Corsetti was simply the name of my stepfather's enemy, and not a man I found myself enjoying being with.

Stefano's disgusting breath blows over my cheek as he speaks, and I flinch, mentally praying this torture will soon be over and that I haven't made the biggest mistake of my life.

"That's right," Stefano fills in. "Della here has gotten close to you, to lure you here to this very spot. She works for *me*, Corsetti, and you fell straight into my trap."

Just hearing him say those words—the claim he has on me—makes bile rise to the top of my throat. I *hate* this, but this was for Ariella. I betrayed a man, but now, I'm free from Stefano's horrible household.

Is the price worth it, though?

"Della." It's a half-growl, half-plea, rumbled through a tone that nearly has me going back to his side. "Della?" he repeats, this time, an unspoken question tacked onto it.

Is this true?

I swallow three times and it does nothing to the burn in my throat. Nothing makes my response more comfortable. "It's true."

Nico looks like he's about to respond, but then Stefano removes his arm from my body, letting me breathe a bit more normally, and he mumbles something to one of his men nearby. A moment later, a black duffel bag appears in Stefano's hand, given by the soldier behind us. He lowers the duffel bag to my hand, and my arm drops a few inches with its weight, before readjusting.

I don't unzip the bag to peek at what's inside, because I already know.

Money. The money as part of this deal.

"You're free to go, daughter. Enjoy your life." Stefano steps aside and gestures for his men by the staircase to do the same.

Every set of eyes stab into my spine as I walk past them all, over the corpses Nico created, reaching the bottom step.

Don't look. Don't turn around. Don't—

I turn to face Nico. I *have* to. This could be the final time I ever see him. I'm selfish enough to take one final peek.

His dark brows blend together as he once again pieces the final part of this together: that money was involved. That I did this for a payday. That his life is equivalent to the million in the bag.

I've never felt more ashamed than I do right now. Beneath the weight of his glare, my shoulders curl in even tighter. My throat gets thicker, my breathing becoming impossible. I need to move, to get away, but I also want to say goodbye. I need him to *see* in my expression how fucking sorry I am. How I wish I hated him from the first meeting, rather than feel in my heart what I do, making it nearly impossible to leave him now. How I wish I could rewind and admit everything to him yesterday and later beg for his forgiveness and his protection. How he doesn't need to detest me because the amount of self-hate I feel is enough for both of us.

When I manage to turn away, when my hair falls to the side of my face and blocks his penetrating hate, he speaks, locking my feet into place.

"Della, you better run fast and run far because I promise you, there will be nowhere you go, I won't be able to find you. No games this time. *That* is my promise to you, so you better enjoy your sliver of freedom while you have it. Once I find you, you're fucking done." He pauses, his grin entirely too devious, too welcoming for the situation. "And *petite souris,* this time, I *will* stick to my word."

You won't find me.

You won't make it out of here alive.

Hate me.

Don't hate me.

I hate myself.

My lips part, dry and cracking. There are so many other things I could respond to him with, but I manage, "I-I had to. I'm sor—"

Stefano spins, his hand swinging out and making contact with the nearby wooden post, inches from where I stand. "Leave. Now. Before I lose my patience."

Just the threat makes my feet move again, lifting to position itself on the stair one up from where I stand. But I can't look away. Not yet. Not until I spot some understanding in Nico's deep, hateful gaze.

But it's empty.

So before Stefano makes good on his threat, I turn away from the person who was quickly weaving his way into my heart and ascend the steps, not stopping until I'm outside of the house. I rush past Nico's car and the row of black vehicles, lining the residential street.

I walk faster than I ever imagined my feet could manage until I'm blocks away and then hail the next cab, beginning my trip to put as much distance between Nico Corsetti, Montreal, and myself.

21

NICO

There is not one word in the motherfucking English, French, or Italian dictionaries that accurately describe the level of betrayal I feel toward Della. The level of *hate* I feel for the lying bitch.

There's no statement to describe how fucking idiotic I feel either. I should have seen it. The damn signs were *there* and I ignored every single one as they were flashed in front of me. Gaining my attention at the party, conveniently outside of The Elixir the very next night, the inexplicable draw I had to her, her resistance in answering any questions, Father's insistence on recognizing her, even her behaviour in the last twenty-four hours as she claimed to be "fine." No. The pressure to pull this off was getting to her.

Coincidences do not exist. I've always believed people will plan with an endgame in mind. Nothing "just happens," and today is a prime example of that very idea.

Everything with Della was pre-planned, right down to her willingness to admit everything to me and come here. She was agreeable because she never planned on our conversation reaching that point.

The lying cunt will pay for this. I will revel in stripping the skin from her body, inch-by-inch. By making her feel an ounce of the pain she's shot right into my heart. Everything about Della De Falco was a lie. *She* was a lie. A woman designed to tease me in all the right ways, to get me to this very point.

Retribution will occur, but at this second, my lying little mouse can't be my top priority. Getting out of this basement alive is.

"My daughter played her part well, I see," Stefano comments, forcing my attention away from the stairs I've been having a stare-down with, reliving the moment she stopped on them and looked at me with the fakest sorrow I've ever seen a person muster. "Look at you. Totally smitten with the little liar."

"She's dead."

Stefano purses his lips. "She was merely a tool for my actions. I needed someone who you wouldn't recognize to lure you in. But it's not her who will be dying this week. That's a future reserved for you."

He snaps his fingers and immediately three guys are on me, their hands snatching my arms, yanking them behind me back, trying to immobilize me.

I allow them to believe they have a firm hold on me before throwing my body weight backwards, shoulders jamming into their chests, breaking their hold. The slightest loosening is all I need to free my arms and I throw them out to the side, punching the other two in the face, hearing the *crack* as I hit their noses.

I whirl, leg kicking out to take down anybody near me, while I reach for a gun on the nearest soldier. He's still disoriented from my initial shove and his grip on his rifle is feeble at best. I manage to get it in hand, immediately positioning it as I spin back around.

I don't think, don't aim, don't plan, just clench the trigger of the gun, feeling victorious when the familiar *oof* of a man's death reaches my ears. I shift to the side and hit another in the leg, dropping him, as blood seeps from the wound.

From the side, a body slams into mine, throwing me to the cold cement ground. I land on my arm, pain immediately shooting up, but I shove it aside, rolling to my knees to stand.

By the time I'm righted, a room full of rifles is pointed in my face, a group of soldiers circling me. Through their legs, I spot the one I've injured dragging himself into a sitting position, his face white and bloodless. Beside him, a body lies, ideally dead.

My chest heaves with deep breaths, staring into death. I won't make it a single inch before they pull their triggers. The rifle in my own hand gets heavy as my adrenaline begins fading.

Two men part and Stefano's there, staring down at me with that same winning grin he first came down the stairs with. He claps twice, nodding appreciatively.

"That was some show, Corsetti."

I ball up a wad of spit and throw it straight up, pleased when it lands on his oversized shirt. "I won't go easily."

Lazily, he glances down at the wet spot I've left on his shirt and wipes it with his sleeve, his expression rippling in annoyance, his eyes narrowing as his jaw gets tight. His tongue runs across the front of his teeth.

"Oh, but you will." He backs up, his hand gesturing in the air.

Thud.

Black instantly overwhelms my vision and my muscles go lax, the gun slipping from my grip as easily as this entire day has.

Fuckers knocked me out...

The moment fuzziness lifts from my senses, I start completing a mental scan of myself.

My head is slumped forward, and I begin to lift it slowly, eyes still closed. My arms are wrenched tightly behind my back, tied to the hard chair I'm seated on. I try to move, noting my ankles are also secured. But not impossible to escape from.

The chill of the air implies we're somewhere where little heat is, so I suspect a basement or a warehouse. I doubt it's the same house Della trapped me inside because Stefano would have had no need to knock me out if he was going to keep me there. The air rolls over my arms—my bare arms. Which means at some point, they've removed my jacket.

Slowly, I pry open my lids and my eyes adjust to the dim lighting of whatever room I'm in. I blink a few times, trying to activate awareness to study the stone walls, with wooden beams every few feet, and a windowless room. A basement, as I've suspected.

Right in front of me is De Falco, seated in a chair, one leg crossed over the other. His arms rest on his lap and he watches on with a serene expression, as one would observing a show they're bored with.

When he catches me awake, his leg drops from his other one and his toothy grin returns. "Oh, good, we can get started."

Pretending to ignore him, I turn my head, seeking the exit and finding the staircase behind me. At the bottom, a soldier stands, a Beretta angled toward the back of my head.

Rolling my head back around, I look at Stefano with a lazy, bored expression. "If you're going to kill me, you better start now because I'm not an easy kill."

He shrugs a single shoulder and stands, pacing in a slow

circle around my chair, like he's some villain in a movie. I don't bother stalking him, instead letting my ears determine his exact positioning.

"I've heard you're not. After all, how many others have targeted you and your family, all to perish."

"I suggest you take a fucking lesson from them all and save us both the time."

"Nice try."

"Then, like I said, start now. Kill me and show my body to my family and demand whatever you want because that's your plan, right? Use me to get power." I scoff, shaking my head. "You're predictable, De Falco. Always have been."

He stops in front of me, his brows lifted. "That so, Corsetti? So you saw Della coming? That was a predictable move?"

No. But I won't give him the satisfaction. "That was a wrong move on your part. We'll leave it at that."

Stefano's hands slide into his pockets and he continues his slow gait around my chair. "You have no idea how good it feels to have you in my grasp. Nico Corsetti, Underboss and heir to the Corsetti family. They will hand over anything to get you back."

Father will do what he must, so long as he continues to have children to rule the family. He hesitated saving Hawke; he'd do the same with me, because that's who he is.

"You think so, do you? So you're not planning on murdering me then? You want to keep me alive and use me."

"They won't pay to get a dead man back."

"You're a fucking moron."

I don't see the fist before it lands on my face, straight into my jaw. A swell of pain flashes over my face and I rotate feeling back into my jaw as I look up at him, grinning.

"That's better. You're learning how to treat a prisoner."

This blow, I see coming. He hits the same spot and the force fills the back of my mouth with the metallic taste of blood.

"You're mighty cocky for a man who was played by pussy," he snarls, pulling back for a moment to roll up his sleeves.

I spit the wad of blood, angling it toward his shoes. "Who is she really, De Falco? It's a known fact you have twin daughters. Neither of them are Della. She's not your biological daughter."

"She is. From a relationship long before my first marriage. I kept her hidden from your family for many years."

Della looks *nothing* like Stefano De Falco, which means if he's telling the truth, she's bound to take after her unnamed mother.

I think about the house though, and Della's mention of a sister. Ariella, her name was. Either Stefano is lying and has another daughter buried somewhere, or Della is, and right now, the possibility of either of them deceiving me is too probable. The puzzle I've begun piecing together expands into a larger one filled with so many pieces similar in size—so many falsities to trip me up.

"If you've kept her hidden, it means you've had this planned for some time now."

Stefano doesn't reply, continuing to keep silent on the subject, but he's revealed just enough for me to know how big this game truly is.

"She did her job well," I compliment, causing his eyes to widen in surprise with my agreement. "So well, I've found myself in your hands. So what is it exactly you want, De Falco?"

"This city. Hand over all your control, your deals, your clubs—everything. Take your family and leave here alive."

"No."

He throws another punch, this one into my stomach. I curl forward to lessen the impact, but the ropes around my arms and legs make it challenging, so I take most of the brunt with a grunt and a deep inhale through clenched teeth.

"Fuck you, De Falco," I push out, when I'm breathing almost normal again.

Another hit. This one to the jaw.

I gather more blood and spit it at him. It lands on his cheek.

He wipes it away, flicking his fingers, and the blood spray lands on my pants. "Big fucking mistake, Corsetti. You could have agreed and this would be over and done with."

"You'll have to kill me, fucker."

Punch.

Punch.

Punch.

Impact over my eye, my nose, and my jaw. His blows are getting harder, more desperate, as if this isn't going how he thinks it should. I'll bruise tomorrow, and no doubt, there will be swelling as well.

Punch.

This time, when my head rolls back from the impact, my muscles don't have the strength to lift it again and another wave of darkness takes me under.

22

DELLA

The airplane seat under me is firm, but comfort is the least of my worries. By now, Nico is either dead or coming after me. I won't relax until we're thirty-two thousand feet in the air.

Pulling up the hood of the sweatshirt, I press my body into the small window and watch through the evening darkness as airline staff load the plane. With every bag they stack, I pray it'll be the final one and we can get in the air. Glancing at the time shown on the screen in front of me though, we're not scheduled to take-off for another twenty minutes.

Which means another twenty minutes of listening to people get settled all around me, while every little noise, every person who talks, has my heart in my throat, as any one of them could be Nico.

Does he know where I am? Is he on his way?

At my feet, I kick my backpack beneath the seat in front of me. After getting away from Nico and Stefano, I rushed back to the De Falco mansion and hastily ravaged through my

154

bedroom, grabbing as many articles of clothing, my ID and passport, and toiletries I could jam into a single bag.

That's it. Life on the run means limited items.

I left my cell phone in my bedroom too. The technology could be tracked and I'm not taking any chances.

Then I grabbed a cab to the nearest bank and deposited the million, minus keeping a few thousand dollars cash on me, so I can survive these next few days or weeks. I added Ariella's name to the account, so she has access to it should anything happen to me.

From there, I went to her medical centre and changed the card on file to mine. Of course, I won't be using my credit card, in fear Nico can track me through that, but for now, I'll take over her medical expenses. I left reception with very clear instructions that if they don't hear from me in six months to have Ariella retrieve the money I've left for her. She'll be cared for, no matter what happens to me.

Then I left, without saying goodbye to her, even though there's the risk this could be the final time she sees me alive. I couldn't jeopardize her safety by warning her in any way.

Until I have confirmation of Nico's death, I'm not going anywhere near Quebec again. I can only hope Nico has forgotten her name and won't go searching. Handing that truth over was a moment of weakness I despise myself for.

Every hour passing since I left that basement, every step farther I've taken in my getaway, his threat rings in my head.

"Della, you better run fast and run far because I promise you, there will be nowhere you go, I won't be able to find you."

A guy shuffles into the seat beside mine. He places his bag between his feet and glances at me as he settles. His smile is small, blond hair hanging over his bright eyes. He's cute. Seems like the kind of guy you'd take home to meet your parents and who would promise you the white-picket-fence-style life. Not at all like Nico, who is the epitome of darkness.

I angle away from him, indicating there will be no casual conversation between us, and shut my eyes. I'll only open them when we arrive in Toronto.

≈

Toronto isn't my final stop, but I've seen enough movies to know what not to do. If Nico survives and comes searching, no doubt the airport will be the first place he'll look, and if I were to purchase direct or connecting flights, then he could find me quicker. When inquiring, Toronto will be listed as my final destination. Instead, I booked a direct flight to Toronto, and then a separate one that'll leave hours later, as the sun climbs into the sky, to Edmonton.

Toronto is larger than Edmonton and extremely tempting to hide out in, since it'd be so easy to become one of the six million people, but it's too close to Montreal for my comfort.

With my backpack in hand, I find my next gate and wait out the hours in the corner, curled up on the ground, lightly napping while I'm able to. With my hood, I'm able to shield myself from prying eyes.

By the time morning comes, I feel as though I'm more exhausted than I've ever been. Constantly peeking over my shoulder, ensuring no one looks at me twice, has been a complete energy drain. When it's finally time to board, a weight lifts from my shoulders as more distance is placed between Nico and me.

Once again, I've booked a window seat, allowing me a place to rest my head and continue stacking up much-needed sleep. I stare at the time listed on the screen in the back of the seat in front of me, waiting for it to match the take-off time reported on the ticket.

Once the plane's in the air and I leave the Eastern Time zone altogether, I think, once again, about Nico. By now, Stefano's had him for over twelve hours. Is he still alive, or is he already freed and coming for me? Is he injured? Bleeding? Near-death and thinking about the woman who's at fault?

I can't *not* think about him, to the point my head's so rattled and can't focus on anything else. My thoughts seem to follow two main paths. One being that I may have destroyed a family. They'll lose a leader, a son, and a brother. I think about Rafael, Nico's brother, who'll most likely become Underboss in Nico's stead. Humorous and easy-going, he'll have a lot to do while he's mourning his brother, taking over Nico's role, and planning his revenge against the De Falcos.

The other thought is how I felt being *with* Nico. The emotions he dragged out of me. How, in such a short time, I found myself getting addicted, even though I knew we wouldn't have a happily ever after, and feeling anything other than dislike would only lead to heartbreak.

Still though. I felt wanted, safe...desired.

Happy.

I smiled more with him than I have in a long time.

He saw me as Della, and not as a tool for his own gain. Even when he had no idea who I was, though he certainly tried to figure it out, he still turned his back on his duties to spend the day *with* me. He could have locked me up somewhere and only let me out when I admitted the truths he knew I was holding back, but he didn't. He seemed to care. To want to be with me.

In the short time with him, I've gotten to experience first-hand how different he is from Stefano. Stefano, who I curse Mom all the time for ever bringing into our lives. What kind of asshole dangles an injured sibling over someone? A villain, clearly, which is what Stefano is.

By the time the pilot announces our descent, my anger is a living beast inside me. I *hope* Nico breakouts, not only for his own life, but to destroy Stefano's. I will happily hand myself over to Nico in exchange for the evidence of Stefano's death.

I laugh out loud, garnering odd looks from the passenger beside me, but I ignore the elderly man.

I want him to live. I fucking shouldn't, as I continue to run across a country to escape him. I don't want him to come for me, but I don't want him to lose his life, even if those two desires can't survive in the same world.

Once deboarding the plane, I maneuver through the Edmonton International Airport quickly, making it outside, where I slip into the first cab in the line of many, and provide the name of a hotel downtown.

For the drive, I rest my head against the seat and just breathe. Many, many deep inhales as I reach the conclusion of my trip. I'll hide out in Edmonton for a while.

I'll live.

At least for another day.

23

NICO

My head lolls to the side, but I still grin through my cracked lips, split with the number of times I've been hit. Blood drips into my eyes from the cuts on my forehead, blurring my vision.

But De Falco is one hit too late because I haven't stopped seeing red since learning who Della really is.

My cheek feels swollen. My mouth has been hit so many times, the pain barely registers. At some point, they took my shirt off me, to make the cuts they sliced into my chest more painful. They certainly revelled in cutting over my Corsetti tattoo, but didn't go deep enough to leave lasting scars.

"Tell me who your weapons' dealer is."

"Fuck off."

Stefano's enforcer lifts the blade in his hand, angling it toward my chest again. "Give up the city or your life."

"Take my life then."

The guy growls and sinks his blade into my pec, creating a fresh line of blood. The cool basement air brushes the cut, making it sting.

I take it though, because there will be a time to fight, and I won't waste my energy now. Even as the enforcer destroys my strength hit-by-hit, cut-by-cut, I conserve what I can for when it matters.

Nearly a day has passed since De Falco's had me in his hold, but the fact I'm still alive speaks to his weakness. If he truly wanted to make a point, I'd be dead by now. Or, if he wanted to use me to bribe my family, that conversation would have happened already. Instead, he seems to revel in keeping me injured.

He's on a power trip, but it's this high he's riding that'll make him crash.

Part of the family's training involves being tied up in a room for days with minimal food and water. So the single day I've been down here isn't remotely close to what I've lived through before.

Stefano kicks off the wall he's been leaning on and emerges from the shadows. "Stop," he tells his enforcer. "We'll give Corsetti a break."

Never give your enemy a break. It only gives them an opportunity to strengthen up and plan an escape.

I grin through split lips, rolling my head until my gaze focuses on Stefano. "You're sweet. Need to give your stomach a rest from the sight of all this blood?"

"Fuck you. It's time for you to become a movie star."

Ah. He'll film me looking broken as bait to my parents, believing they'll care for me more than our legacy. The issue with De Falco's plan, though, is that they'd never give up control of the city because they know, I'll get out of here myself regardless.

De Falco snaps his fingers toward his enforcer. "I'm going to find Thomas. He has the filming equipment. Don't hurt him while I'm gone."

Not sure who Thomas is, but I'm grateful for the fact that he's not down here. When De Falco goes, it'll leave me with only one other person.

Stefano walks away and the moment the basement door is shut, his enforcer turns his back on me, heading for the table across the way, stacked with the bloody knives he's been using on me.

Just like you shouldn't give your enemy a break, you also shouldn't turn your back on them.

Breathing through the aches, finding strength in my body, which is exhausted from injury and blood loss, I uncover the adrenaline I need. Ripping my arms out of the pre-loosened rope, I get to work on my ankles before I'm noticed.

Being locked in a room and tied to a chair was a training session I've done more than once. Lesson one: survive for a predetermined length of time. Lesson two: escape.

The knots that were around my wrists were basic at best. I've had them undone a while now, but I knew taking on two of them would be challenging in my state. I have one chance because, if I fuck this up, De Falco will make it impossible for me to get away a second time.

Once my ankles are freed, I stand, keeping light on my feet as I lunge, catching the guy off guard and taking us both to the ground. He grunts with surprise and, as expected, fights back immediately, grasping my body and trying to roll us around.

Bringing my legs up between us, I kick, hurling my foot into his stomach and tossing him off of me. I manage to get over him again and throw fist after fist into his face, not slowing, not pausing, because the moment I do, my adrenaline will break and my body will recall how exhausted it is. He's not injured, giving him the edge, but I have determination on my side.

He manages to block one of my final hits, grasping my fist and twisting it until my teeth slam together in a silent cry of pain. I push away from the ground, yanking my arm with me, and reach for the table. For the multitude of weapons there.

He sees where I'm headed and kicks out a leg, trying to trip me, but I notice at the right time and leap over him, nearly crash-landing onto the table instead. I grab the first thing my hand lands on, which ends up being a large blade.

Once I have a firm grip, I whirl, not giving him another opportunity to fight as I stab it down into his heart with a sickening squelch.

His eyes bulge wide, and with the final spark of his life, he reaches for the knife—for the source of his pain—but it's too late; his muscles, nerves, and life give up, his arms slumping to the side, the light fading from his eyes.

Hand to my chest, I feel the rapid beats of my heart. Pain ricochets throughout my body, my injuries more sore than I let onto. They cause me to sway, my arm reaching out toward the table to keep me upright and steady. I could very easily pass out this second, but De Falco will return within moments, and I need to get the fuck out of here.

I grab a second weapon and then pat down the enforcer, finding keys in his pocket. Not sure what they're for, but I'd rather have them and learn I don't need them than not have them when I do.

With the remainder of my energy, I throw myself up the wooden steps, pausing at the top. Beyond this door, I don't know what I'll find or how I'll get to the nearest exit. They likely have guns while I only have two knives.

This is it.

A flash of blonde hair fanned out on my desk invades my mind. Her heels digging into the desk as she attempts to push herself onto my dick further. Her nails endlessly scraping against the top of my desk as she reaches her orgasm. And those fucking addicting sapphire eyes, filled with tears as her body convulses, being brought to the edge time and time again, only to not receive the release she requires.

It's with Della on my mind, I open the door and peer out into what looks like a hallway of a mansion. The De Falco mansion, presumably. Slowly, I step into it, scanning up and down the hallway and finding no one.

Interesting. Has a Corsetti prisoner in his basement, and he doesn't have an army guarding the door? He clearly had a lot of faith in himself.

I make it partially down the hallway, hoping I'm heading in the right direction when I hear footsteps. I throw my back against the nearest wall, waiting for whoever it is to come around the corner and hoping it's Stefano.

The moment the steps cross the threshold, I dive, throwing my knife into flesh. The guy hollers out, but before others can hear him, I drag the other blade across his throat, gleefully watching the line of red cross his neck. Gasping, he drops to the floor, and I jump over him, continuing at a faster pace down the hallway.

I pause at the end, pressing against the wall, once more, as I peer around the corner. I'm approximately ten steps away from the front door, and so far, there doesn't seem to be many people around here. Scanning up and down the connecting hallways and the staircase leading to the upper floor, I find no one.

One. Two. Three—

I bolt, grabbing onto the door handle and yanking the large, ornate door open. It takes more energy than expected, but doesn't slow me.

On the step, a single soldier stands, spinning at the sound of the door opening. His eyes widen and he's stunned for a moment before yelling out, "Prisoner esc—"

His warning shifts into a gurgle as blood pours from his neck. I slide the gore-stained blade against my pants, wiping the freshest blood off it, and don't stick around to watch his body fall to the ground.

The De Falco mansion is on the edge of the city, but I just need to make it into civilization again. Pumping my legs, using the last fragments of adrenaline my body clings to, I push myself forward and toward safety.

Toward revenge.

~

"*F*inally, you're home." Rafael's voice rings out the moment I fall through my front door.

The second the door opens, that's it. I've made it this far beaten, bruised, and bloody, but no more. I slump to my knees first, instinct managing to shift my arms forward to catch my fall before I break more of my face.

"I mean, walking out on our parents like that with Della in tow was colourful. But you've been gone all night, man. They're getting pissed and...Nico?"

My brother's steps pause before quickening again. I can't turn my head to see him approach. To see him fall to his knees, his hands pressing onto the multitude of gashes decorating my body, trying to slow the bleeding.

"Nico! What the fu—Help! Anyone!"

Darkness creeps into my vision, the moment I know my brother has me. That I can die right here on this step, but I've returned. I made it away from De Falco and back home.

In the last seconds I retain consciousness, I push out, "De Falco...Raf...De Falco. Della De Falco is fucking *dead*."

24
DELLA

Two days pass and I'm not entirely sure I've managed a complete night's sleep, or even had a rational thought since leaving Quebec. My days are spent pacing the hotel room until I stealthily leave to retrieve food. I could order room service or delivery, but it's a small reprieve of freedom before I go absolutely insane locked in a room all day. Although, once I return, and my senses have gone haywire and my heart is in my throat, I question how smart of an idea leaving was at all.

I observe Edmonton in small pieces when I get outside or from my window. High-rises stand nearby, blocking a lot of the faraway views, but I've gotten the gist that this is a much smaller city than what I'm used to. Downtown seems to be limited to a few square blocks, while the rest of the city is fairly flat.

Presently, I'm lying in bed and staring at the ceiling as a news channel plays in the background. It's been my constant companion, filling the silence in my life, as I go back and forth on fearing to hear any mention of Nico and hoping he's made it out alive.

He *must* be dead by now, right?

The other thoughts rolling around in my head consist of where the future will take Ariella and me. Montreal has been home for both of us our entire lives, but once all this is over with and Nico either gives up searching for me or is dead, I can return for her. We can go somewhere—anywhere. Here in Edmonton? I suppose it's not a bad city. Farther West? Maybe out East? Ontario, so there's a semblance of home nearby?

"Just in: this video, which appeared on the popular app, TikTok, late last night, has already gone viral with three million views. It seems Montreal's own It Boy, Nico Corsetti—"

I shoot up in bed and scramble to the edge, peering intently at the TV, blinking to ensure there's no way I can't *not* distinguish what the news is telling me. The screen flashes with a blown-up TikTok reel scanning over an unidentifiable street. The owner zooms in, focusing on a particular spot across the street—on a person climbing inside a taxi. The video's too blurry with the distance it was shot at to catch details of the person's face, but who it is, is undeniably recognizable.

Nico.

He's alive.

Breath catches in my throat. Air won't get through, not even as the news flashes to its next topic. The need to bolt, to hide becomes prevalent, but my muscles lock and are unable to move. With numb hands, I manage to click the power button on the controller, shutting the TV off.

He's alive.

He's alive.

He's alive.

No matter how many times I repeat it to myself, it doesn't seem real. Like it's impossible for him to be. He *can't* be alive. He can't be...

He is. Between Nico and Stefano, Nico's stronger. More

resilient. It always seemed unlikely that the impenetrable force that Nico Corsetti is would ever be defeated by someone like Stefano.

How long will it be before he comes for me?

Ariella. Will she be safe?

Yet, through the fear, a small sense of victory plants itself in my mind. My own life aside, Nico is alive. Breathing. Safe. I rub my chest over my heart, which feels like it's clenching tight, trying to tell me something I can't understand.

What do I do now, though?

Nothing, my logic slips in. *You do nothing because he has no idea where you are.*

Yet.

Stupid intrusive thought. But it's not totally incorrect. Nico's expression in that basement said it all.

"I promise you, there will be nowhere you go, I won't be able to find you."

He won't let my treachery go unpunished. He'll track me. That's who he is—a hunter.

And I've just become his prey.

My gaze slides from the spot on the bed I've been staring at but not seeing, toward the window, to the city beyond the hotel, and farther. To a whole other province, wondering what happened over there that allowed Nico to getaway. How many of Stefano's men are dead? Is Stefano still alive? What happened to Yasmine and Rozelyn? Are they safe? As much as I despise my ex-stepsisters, they're innocent where Stefano's ploys are concerned.

They can't be my concern, though. Because I have my own, and it's too pressing to focus on anything else.

Nico's revenge.

25
NICO

The moment light breaks through my consciousness, I push myself into a sitting position. I sway, my eyes struggling to pry open. A wave of dizziness attacks my head, trying to push me back to the pillow, but I merely shake my head, trying to rid myself of the response.

"Nico!" Mother's voice.

My eyes rapidly blink, clearing sleep from them before sliding my legs to the side and onto the floor.

Mother's right there, her hand pushing against my bare chest. "Nico, no, you can't get up yet." Her attention darts to the side. "Enzo, call the doctor."

I follow her gaze, spotting my father near the door. He straightens from his slouch and throws open my door, disappearing.

"N-no." I push Mother's hand away from my body and manage a shaky step forward before my body lets me down and another surge of faintness clouds my mind, stopping me where I stand. I waver, hand reaching out for my bed—for anything, really—to catch a potential fall.

"Nico, what are you doing?" Mother stands in front of me, her height bringing her only to my chest, but her arms go out to the side, fierce as ever, and trying to block my path. "You are not well enough to be on your feet."

"Doesn't matter. I have to go."

While my lungs work to catch their breath from the effort it took to straighten, I survey my body. My chest is a mess of red marks, but they're no longer bleeding. My body's clearly been washed, as there's no smudges of blood either. I touch my face, my hands darting away from my cheek as fast as initially brushing it, a pained hiss slithering from my teeth. Still swollen and sensitive. With my tongue, I check my teeth, noting none seem to be missing. Rolling my jaw, it's less sore now than when it was freshly punched.

"Nico, your body is exhausted. You're injured."

Father reappears then with Dr. Shappo, the doctor the family keeps on retainer. Mother steps aside for the doctor to approach, who gestures for me to sit.

"Mr. Corsetti, you need to rest for longer. You should not be standing."

"See!" Mother screeches, coming up beside the doctor, her hands on her hips, reminding me of the woman who'd scold Rafael and me all the time as children, when we got into things we shouldn't have.

Father appears on my other side, his eyes narrowed and scanning my injured body. "Son, what the fuck happened? Two days ago, you fell through the front door. Rafael claimed you mentioned something about De Falco. Did *he* do this to you?" His voice becomes harder, a war battling in his gaze.

Two days. Two fucking days have passed in which I've asleep?

I side-step the three of them, pushing by the doctor and heading for my closet to dress. Even the sound of De Falco's name reinvigorates me; it makes the injuries feel like they've healed on their own with the pressing necessity to finish what's already started.

Della De Falco. Every ache, every cut, every wounded muscle is secondary to the retribution I'll slice from her perfectly smooth, deceiving skin. Every punishment I deliver will be another one of my wounds healed.

"Has he been here?" I demand, even knowing the answer. Stefano wouldn't dare try, knowing what kind of army we have. No doubt, he's licking his wounds, trying to determine how fucked he exactly is.

"No," Father replies. "I insist on you telling us what's happened."

Meanwhile, Mother returns to fussing. "Enzo, stop. Put that aside for now. Our son is injured. Dr. Shappo, please do something."

The doctor shoots me an apologetic look. "I have to agree with your mother, Sir. I insist on at least one more day of rest and then we can evaluate how you feel."

I slice the air with my hand, brushing aside all worries as I continue to my closet. "I'm fine. I wouldn't be awake if I wasn't." Focusing on the only person in this room who seems to understand the severity of what's happening and the importance of action, I say to my father, "Office. Get Rafael. No one else though. We're keeping this under wraps for now. And find Rosen. Tell him to get me a new fucking phone."

∾

To Rafael, I bark, "You're in charge."

I move past my brother to Rosen, who stands by the door, a new iPhone held up between two fingers toward me.

I snatch it with a mumbled, "Thanks," and pocket it. At some point, I lost mine when getting captured by De Falco.

"When will you be back?" Rafael asks, his eyes widening. Rafael hates when I go away for extended periods of time and he's forced to pick up my duties.

"Not sure." Depends how long it takes me to track down a rat.

I open my laptop and immediately start writing an email to the contacts I have at the airport. Della would be an idiot to remain in the city, which means she took off. If she's extremely smart, she's still running because, now that I'm free, I'll have her location within the hour.

With the email sent, I focus on my father, who stands a few feet away, his arms crossed, waiting for me to speak. Normally, I'd avoid admitting my fuck-ups, but this is bigger than me. If De Falco's morality dropped so low, he's using his daughter to do his dirty work, then the family's safety is a priority. Father has his role of Boss, and I have mine, and we both need to protect our name.

Allowing Della into my life was a mistake I'll freely admit to having made.

"Della is Stefano De Falco's secret daughter."

Three expressions drop into mixed emotions of shock. Rosen shifts on his feet, and I know him well enough to know he's mentally readying for battle. Rafael jerks, blinking as he looks off to the side, as though trying to piece things together. Father though turns absolutely deadly.

"That girl you had in here yesterday? Son, that doesn't make any sense. De Falco didn't have another child."

"That you know about. He's hidden her well from us. He sent her undercover, to lure me to their fucking hideout and succeeded."

Father's eyes bounce over my face, cataloguing my injuries.

171

"The girl was a trap then. We need to handle it."

"Yes," I growl, my nerves tightening. I glare at my laptop screen, willing the email response I need to pop up. My hands curl into fists, agitation making it difficult to remain still. They have two more minutes before I'm calling and demanding an answer. "She will pay for her crimes." I stare him in the eyes, lifting my chin until he understands I will handle this how I see fit. Della is *my* issue; I'm the executioner of her sentence.

Rafael approaches, breaking through the tenseness between Father and me. "Where did she go?"

"And De Falco?" Rosen also moves forward, glancing at my family. "Della aside, there's still the issue of him."

"Find him," I snap. "Put all our men on it. I don't care what has to blow up for us to find the cunt, but do it. Bring him back alive." *I* want to be the one to make him pay. To put the barrel of my gun between his eyes and pull the trigger, for him to see who's reaping his life, but only after many delicious hours of torture. Of screaming.

Pausing my ire for a second, an email pops up. My eyes eagerly devour the information.

"Edmonton. That's where she is." *Mon petit rat* scurried to the other side of the country. A stop in Toronto, with a secondary booking to Edmonton. At least she has some wits in that brain of hers; she certainly tried to throw me off her trail.

I push to my feet, scanning the three of them for a final time. "The truth about Della's identity stays between us." Specifically to Father, I add, "No uncles. No cousins. Not Mother. We don't need them concerned right now. *Unisciti a leale. Muori leale.* We protect them."

Hatred ices over my nerves as the seconds pass. Energy expands in the room with the fact that there will be one champion, one winner, in this entire fucking thing.

Me.

26

DELLA

After learning the news of Nico's survival, another two days pass, and I'm stupid enough to believe I may be all right. Maybe it's the morning air, or the scent of hope and a future threaded with the fact he hasn't found me yet.

A month, I decide. One month of hiding and if Nico hasn't located me by then, I'll assume he's let this thing pass and I'll return for Ariella and get us the fuck out.

I leave the hotel for the first time since learning the news and wander half a block away to a coffee shop I discovered the other day. It's close enough to the hotel that I feel semi-okay with the distance.

As I stand in a short line of three people, I readjust the bag on my back when the straps begin digging into my arms. I never leave the room without all my items, just to be certain.

"Whoa, look at that fancy car!" A man's voice rises over the dull conversation in the coffee shop. "Some big wig must have left his ivory business tower to come mingle with the poor folks."

I doubt that's what it is. Still, compelled, I twist around, finding the speaker—an elderly man seated with a friend—and look past them and out the window, spotting the car he shouted about.

It's not the same car...but I know who's driving. I know even before he fully steps out of the driver's seat and the sun catches on the dark strands of his hair. I know even as his head remains tipped down and sunglasses prevent me from being certain of his identity.

I know because I can *feel* it. When my body goes numb, but my instincts go erratic. When the air cools to a temperature impossible to survive in.

Nico.

"Miss?"

I think the barista is calling me, but I can't turn. I can't look away as death scans the street around him while he adjusts his leather jacket, looking entirely too calm for the fury rolling off his shoulders. It's nearly visible; a thick cloud of red that seeps beneath the shop's glass door.

He found me.

Go! I snap awake to respond, and my feet move before I can even debate the most rational way of escape.

There's one door in this shop, and while he's a mere twenty feet away, I have to take it. I shove out the front door and bolt around the corner, hoping he didn't notice me.

I take off, probably looking insane as I sprint through the streets. My legs push me as fast and as far as they possibly can. The urge to peek behind me is so pressing, to see if he's noticed me, if he's pursuing me, but I don't in fear of freezing up.

At the first corner, I turn, pushing through a small group of people, before rushing down that block. Across the street, heads turn, but I pay them no attention. When there's a gap in traffic, I lunge into the road, not caring that I'm technically jaywalking. If I can take an unpredictable path, I may get away.

At the next corner, I go left this time, exhaustion quickly creeping up on me. I'm no marathon runner; I shouldn't be able to do this, but I suppose when one's life is literally on the line, you find the energy to keep going.

For a second though, I slow to a walk, hand to my chest to feel my heaving breaths. I can't keep this up, but I must have gotten far enough away to have lost him. And that's only if he knew I was in that coffee shop.

Why else would he have parked right there, if he didn't know I was inside?

I can't begin to consider all the possible ways he's tracked me. I continue walking, managing a near-jog, searching for something to provide the ultimate escape, even if I don't quite know what that is yet.

My silent prayer is answered when a taxi slowly drives by. I rush to the edge of the sidewalk and wave for the car's attention. It rolls to a stop and the driver, an older gentleman, peeks out the window, waiting for me to get in.

He doesn't need to wait too long; I immediately throw myself inside, demanding through heavy breaths, "Airport. Please."

The driver meets my eyes in the rearview mirror. He might spot my insanity, but shrugs regardless and pulls the car away from the curb. As we drive through downtown, I study every single person we pass, hoping that none of them look like the vengeful mafia prince who haunts my dreams.

I'm safe.

For now.

～

I settle into the only available seat on the soonest international flight I managed to snag, right at the back of the plane by a window. Around me, flight attendants are helping other passengers settle in for the lengthy, overseas flight to Germany.

Upon arriving at the airport, I made a swift decision about my destination. The U.S. would be plausible, but it's too close to where we are now. Travelling overseas means that it'll take Nico a while to catch up, and by the time he figures out where I've gone, I can be lost in one of the many European countries that surround Germany.

I tip my head back, tuning out anything nearby. Minutes pass, and while my other row companions have yet to join me, based on the number of people standing in the aisle, waiting for their seat, I suspect that I'll be boxed in soon.

My contented sigh is long and drawn-out, rattling my lungs, and eases me the slightest fraction. Very slight.

In the corner of my eye, a passenger claims the seat beside me. He's large and his spread legs tread in my area, but given how close I lean to the plane's wall, I can't really complain.

Then my senses pick up on what's happening.

My neck prickles in utter terror; my hands grow clammy and icy, and my breath seems to catch in my throat. Even before I glance over, I know *he's* found me.

Nico's eyes blaze and his lips curl upon capturing my attention. I almost gasp in surprise but not because of his presence. His right cheek is slightly swollen and there's multiple cuts around his eyes. I have a feeling though, there's more injuries covered by his clothing.

A hand lands heavy on my thigh and he leans in close. His delicious scent momentarily clouds my flustered brain, making me forget the risks he brings.

"You truly believed you could run from me, *petite souris*? You certainly figured out how to play the game well."

Somehow—some-fucking-*how* I manage to reply through numb, frozen lips, through a panic-stricken mind. "Survival isn't a game, Nico." Saying his name aloud reminds me that this is, indeed, happening.

"Oh, but it is, Della." He leans in even closer, his fingers curling strands of my hair around my ear, so his lips can brush along the skin there, making me shiver—unfortunately, not in fear. "It became so the moment you chose the wrong side."

I chose my side.

"So," he pulls back a fraction, releasing a bit of air for my lungs to capture, "do I drag you from this airplane myself or do we sit back and enjoy the ride you've so nicely booked us?"

I don't know how to respond to that because if he's here, there's nowhere else I can go. I've lost. He's won. He kept his promise.

"I promise you, there will be nowhere you go, I won't be able to find you. Once I find you, you're fucking done."

"H-how did you find me?"

He chuckles, but it's not at all a sound of amusement. Rather, it's cold, slithering darkness. "It's intriguing to hear you believed you could get away. You truly give me no credit, if you think I don't have contacts inside the airlines. It was all too easy to discover where your flight took you."

"You found me at the coffee shop."

"I watched you leave your hotel room."

How long has he known where I was? "Did you chase me?" *Was my running for nothing?*

He snorts lightly, his sparkling jade eyes raking me in disgust. "And waste energy? No. I knew you'd try to get on a plane. The moment you entered the airport, I was notified. The second your booking was complete, I knew."

"You managed to get a seat beside me on a plane that was fully booked."

With his hand on my leg, his weight presses my thigh into the seat, making me whimper in discomfort. He whispers in my ear, "I have capabilities, Della, and if you haven't learned that by now, I anticipate showing you. Keep that in mind the next time you decide to stab me in the back."

"I didn't..." The denial is immediate, though I can't finish the lie.

His fingers curl into my leg, making me flinch and look around toward the other passengers. How has no one noticed the obvious distress emitting from me, the animosity from him? Nico lets out a low growl, his other hand coming up to grasp my neck, angling my head toward him.

"You deceived me, Della. You whored yourself out all to lure me in for your father. Be proud of that because you're the first and last person who can have such a claim. For that, you *will* pay."

His fingers flex around my neck, stealing my air supply, making me gasp. Again, I peek around, wondering how no one has caught onto the abuse happening here, but everyone is so focused on stowing their bags and getting comfortable in their seats. My tongue feels thick, being pushed into my airway. His thumb caresses the column of my throat, taunting me with his authority. Then he crowds me, getting closer than ever before. His lips brush over mine, painting a promise onto them.

A promise that it'll be the final bit of pleasure I receive from him.

He releases me altogether and I gulp in large breaths, replacing what he stole and hiding away more, should he strangle me again.

"Will you kill me?"

Nico's cold gaze stays locked on me. "If I'm being honest,

which is more than you deserve, I haven't decided yet. Right now, there are no words to describe the level of hate I have for you—or for myself. Because as much as I'd relish slicing into your neck and watching the blood drain slowly from your body, I still want to be inside your cunt."

Oh my God. My insides clench, utterly betraying my rational fear. How could I still lust after a man who wants me dead? Or worse, react in such a way to words that should completely terrify me.

Nico brushes a thumb over my wrist, right over my pulse. "Hm."

I assume he'd say more, except our final row mate joins us. An elderly lady settles beside Nico and barely spares us a glance.

Nico rests his hand over my lap again in a possessive manner as he shifts, pressing as close to me as he can. While I nudge myself right up against the plane, I know I can only stay like this for so long, considering it's a twelve-hour flight, and eventually, my limbs will need to stretch.

He shifts again, trying to expand his reach as far as possible. Either way, he looks entirely too large for the economy seat.

"If you're uncomfortable, I'm sure you can pay your way to the first-class section."

Nico smirks and tips his head back against the headrest, feigning relaxation. "Nice try."

"You know, just because you've found me, it doesn't mean you've caught me. I'm not done running."

"Oh, *petite souris*," he grins maliciously, "I'm fucking counting on it."

27
NICO

There's one thing I desire more than chasing a woman. And that's a woman's submission.

The moment she realizes, even after her long, harrowing battle, she's lost. When she has nowhere else to flee to and I hold the metaphorical chain around her neck: the ability to make her submit to my every whim.

The terror radiating from Della is so overwhelmingly potent, it makes me shift in the uncomfortable seat of economy class, as I aim to hide my thickening erection from the little old lady beside me. My legs try to stretch the best they can, and I realize with absolute certainty, I despise commercial planes. The benefit of the Corsettis owning a private jet means I never deal with this bullshit.

The same plane that's on its way to Germany, to meet us upon arrival and begin the trip back to Montreal.

I debated taking the jet there and grabbing her when she arrived. Precisely when Della believes she's safe on international lands, I'd be there to remind her of her new reality. Instead, I chose to pay my way into this seat, to force her into twelve hours of torture and anxiety with me beside her because knowing the torture my presence has on her is enough.

Della moves, her arm brushing mine, but she quickly jerks away. A moment later, her leg kicks out at mine. I open my eyes, watching her squirm and readjust in three different positions.

Keeping my tone flat, I bark, "Are you done?"

After a long moment, in which she sighs and readjusts again, she turns to me with hunched shoulders and mumbles, "I need to pee."

"Too bad."

Beside me, the old woman glares, her red-painted lips parting in an O, causing me to sigh in annoyance. I suppose while we're still around people, I can't make her life too unbearable. The elderly woman stands and slowly shifts herself into the aisle, opening a path for Della and me, making my decision for me.

Della catches the woman's response and her gaze slides to me. Her lips curl up in the corners as though to say, *See?* She stares expectantly at me, and then the clear aisle beyond us.

Clamping my jaw from snapping with all the curses rolling through my mind, I push to my feet and shuffle into the tiny aisle. To imagine people travel like this every day. Thankfully, the bathrooms are right behind us, so she won't be gone for long.

Della quickly moves past me, her chin lowered, her gaze at her feet.

Before she steps too far away, I grasp her upper arm, yanking her body against mine. I tower over her, and she feels so fucking soft against me, I despise my thoughts for going there.

Through a low voice only she'll hear, I whisper into her hair, by her right ear, "You breathe a fucking word to anyone and I will slaughter them all."

Her throat moves with her swallow, her eyes flashing in a

subtle fear. She gives me a subtle nod and then strides away to the small bathroom mere feet away, not glancing back. Her spine is rigid though, and I catch the tremble in her hands as she slides the bathroom door handle open.

In her absence, I don't sit, but the woman does. She looks up toward me, her expression oddly fierce for a little thing. "Is there something wrong between you and that nice girl?"

"Nothing, ma'am. Simply a game we enjoy playing."

Her eyes narrow, the wrinkles around her eyes making them disappear for a second. She grunts, seemingly accepting my lie.

Another moment passes before I hear the loud airplane toilet flush. *Classy.* And something I've unfortunately heard one too many times on this trip so far.

Della returns, this time with her head down, her gaze locked on her feet. Once we complete the awkward seat shuffle again and Della's by the window, she mumbles, "Thanks," before shutting her eyes and leaning her head against the window.

I stare at her a beat longer than I should, observing her chest rising and falling with her soft breaths. I remember her sleeping like that in my bed after being thoroughly fucked. Back when she was this strange, unknown woman creeping into my life, my bed, and my damn heart. Before she was a traitor to me and all the people I love and protect.

I turn away, glancing at the live in-flight map, noting the hours we still have remaining. Six. Blowing out a long breath, I shut my eyes for my own nap, the long journey starting to catch up with me. A few more hours though, and then the fun begins.

Her life ends.

～

Deboarding the plane is a torturous event that takes entirely too long. Since we're in the very back, we're literally two of the last people off the plane. It's some ungodly time in the middle of the night for our bodies, but the morning sun in Germany shines brightly through the plane, reminding me of the annoyances of time zones.

The moment we're in the tunnel, her steps quicken, pushing past a family. Chuckling at her pathetic attempt, two large strides take me to her side and I grasp her hand, pinning her against my body.

"Give up."

Of course, she tries to yank her hand away, but I tighten my hold to the point of pain, making her gasp.

"Don't bother trying, Della. You won't be getting free." Once out of the tunnel, I drag her toward the right, following the path I was instructed earlier to take. "We have another flight to catch," I tell her, "and this one will be much less comfortable." Because we'll be alone, and I won't be restricted by the innocents around.

"Because sitting beside you for the first one was *so* pleasant."

She sinks her heels into the floor, but the epoxy on the flooring gives her no traction, so I easily pull her along with me.

"If you put up too much of a fight, people will question." I pause, waiting for her to understand the importance of what I'm saying. "And then I'll have to go on a murder spree."

Through the thick of the crowds, over the noise, over everything, I hear her whisper, "No, you wouldn't. Because that's not you."

She obviously didn't want me to hear and I pretend I didn't, so I don't have to respond. Using the signs hanging from the ceiling, I quickly get us to the private entrance I was instructed to find, where a single airport security guard stands, looking bored.

Flashing my ID, he stares extra-long at it before nodding and stepping aside for us to pass. My pilot takes care of a lot of the airline shit, so I don't have to when we're unable to use a private airfield, like now. Which means, if he did his job correctly, none of the staff will even blink an eye at Della. The influence of a lot of cash.

Beyond him, we enter a small waiting room, filled with large, cushioned chairs. A single desk in front of another entrance sits at one end, and that's where I stop.

The attendant, a middle-aged woman, smiles up at me, her eyes briefly flicking to Della and back. "Welcome. Your name?"

Silently, I flash my ID. She reads it and types something into the computer in front of her.

A moment later, she says, "Ah, yes, Mr. Corsetti. Your plane arrived an hour ago. If you'd like to go right outside," she gestures to the door behind her, "it's on the airfield."

She's barely finished speaking before I haul Della past her and down the short hall, to the door at the end. I'm eager to get Della on the jet and into the air because it means the fighting is over.

I throw open the door and the force of the airfield's air is nearly strong enough to throw us backwards. Keeping a tight grip on her, I drag her down the three metal steps and over the smooth cement, toward the familiar white jet on the other side. A single black stripe is painted on the wing, keeping our transportation's identity as discreet as possible.

As we approach, my pilot, James, appears inside the doorway. He quickly comes down the plane's steps to acknowledge us. "Sir!" he yells his greeting over the bustling, loud winds. "Good trip here, I hope? We're all ready for take-off whenever you are."

"Thank you, James. Let's just say, I've missed you. Commercial planes are horrible."

He chuckles and gestures for the stairs. "If you and your guest will get settled then, I'll be sure to get you home as quickly as possible."

Despite the numerous people we've passed inside the airport—the guard, the woman at the desk—Della only now stupidly decides to awaken and beg for assistance.

"Help! He's trying to kidnap me."

Pushing into her back, I force her onto the staircase as I glance at my pilot. "We'll be seated in a moment."

Her steps falter on the second step and she leans back, throwing her weight into me, trying to knock me away from the plane. Her legs kick out, her arms whacking me in the face, but her attempts are pathetic and easily controllable.

James discreetly looks away while I allow her to fall on me, because as I catch her, I swing her into my arms, over my shoulder, and stomp up the stairs.

"You asshole!" Fists pound into my back as I walk. Her legs wiggle, kicking out into the air. "Put me down!"

With my free hand, I send a firm smack to her ass, warning her to keep still. "The next one will hurt more."

"I can walk."

"Could, but you didn't. Therefore, I will help you."

I stalk down the short aisle lined with large, leather couches on either side. At the back, there's a bar on the right and a table on the left. I breathe in the familiarity of rich comforts, thankful we're here and not on another commercial flight back home.

Unceremoniously, I drop Della onto one of the couches. She scrambles to sit upright and in a flurry of movement, gets to her feet in front of me. In a storm of fists, she hits me, doing little damage to the wounds already there.

"You're a fucking asshole, Nico Corsetti! This is kidnapping. Let me go!"

I allow her a moment to release her pent-up anger. A brief second to relive the sliver of freedom she's had for the past couple days. And by her tenth punch, I block her fists with a single swipe of my arm, knocking her to the side and back onto the couch.

Towering over her, I position an arm on either side of her head, leaning into her. She shrinks back into the black leather, her eyes flicking to the side toward the exit, but this is it. There is no more escape for her.

"Give. Up."

"No." Her eyes narrow into slits and she straightens. The new position puts her lips a fraction away from mine, and I spot the moment she realizes this because her eyes darken to a midnight blue and her tongue peeks out to dampen her lips.

I stare at the spot she's licked, clamping down on the desire to chase her tongue with my own.

She quickly breaks through my hunger with her next words. "Mighty big of you. Catching the woman who was only trying to save her own skin. That's why I did what I did, Nico."

Leaning away an inch, I bark out a humourless laugh. "Is that so? You really can't come up with a better excuse than that?"

"No, because it's the truth."

Bullshit.

"Truth or not, *rat*, you betrayed me, which means you pay the price for that choice."

28

DELLA

at. He's calling me a rat now.

Pressing my lips together, I force a deep inhale until I can preserve some semblance of self-control as I maintain my stance of being frightened and fighting for survival, so the ongoing lust coursing through me can't rule my senses.

For days, I've imagined the possibility of this moment, but the one thing I hadn't counted on was my feelings toward him. How him being so close to me, his face inches from my own, throws my mind to days ago, before all this went down.

"Listen to me. I did what I had to for my own life."

Nico's nose scrunches into a sneer and he backs away, granting me the reprieve to breathe again, and moves to the couch across from me, settling into the puffy leather. Despite being alone with him and not having the protection commercial planes allow, I'll admit, this plane is much more comfortable—if it didn't feel like I was sitting on pins, anxious regarding my immediate future.

I expect him to reply, but instead, he reaches into his pocket and pulls out his phone, unlocking it and scrolling over the screen. The plane jerks into movement, backing up and turning to begin its taxi down the runway.

That's it? *Now* he chooses to be silent, when we're alone and he can say anything he wants?

Doesn't matter. Stay silent. Silence equals remaining alive, which means Ariella won't lose her sister.

That's what the slightly logical part of my brain says anyway. The rest of me opts for a different path, one where I can recognize it's a bad idea, and yet, I continue doing it, unable to stop.

"That's it? You said your piece, so our conversation is over?"

Nico slowly drags his eyes away from his phone. So slowly, you'd think I was interrupting him from the most important business ever. His bored expression annoys me to no end.

With a flat expression, he states, "There's nothing else to say. Whether I believe you or not is irrelevant because it doesn't change the way I now feel about you."

Now. That single word weighs so much.

Unfolding my body, I slide to the edge of the couch. Fear prickles in my neck, but my curiosity is worse. "Have you decided to kill me or not?"

"Do you deserve anything less?" he shoots back.

The plane quickens, and the jets whirl louder. It tilts and I clench the edges of the couch to remain steady. Nico doesn't budge as he watches me struggling through the takeoff.

Once the plane's higher in the sky and begins to level out, I reply, "I already told you why I did it."

"And I don't believe you." His hand tightens around his phone; his only physical reaction to indicate that my words affect him. "Della, for the remainder of this ride, you will shut your mouth and sit pretty and fucking *enjoy* it, because once we land, there will be no more luxuries in your life. If I were you, I'd nap."

His attention lowers back to his phone and I see the moment he chooses to shut everything else out. When his expression flattens and a metaphorical brick wall erects around him.

Fine. Whatever.

I slept on the plane ride to Germany, but not well. The seat was cramped and uncomfortable, and with Nico right beside me, I couldn't completely doze off. Between the change in time zones and losing track of the days, my sleep schedule has been wrecked.

His suggestion of a nap is something I won't ignore because I suspect once we arrive back in Montreal, I won't be getting much sleep. The couch I'm sitting on is large enough for me to stretch out on, so I kick my feet to the side, reclining back and turning until my back is to Nico. Curling my arm beneath my head for a pillow, I close my eyes. The mystery surrounding my future is my final thought before sleep overtakes me.

W hen I awake, the plane is still in the air. I stretch my arms and legs at the same time a large yawn emits from me. The movement makes it obvious that something is over me, and I lift my head to see what it is.

His leather jacket.

Huh.

Rolling over, cognisant to not fall off the couch, I'm unsure of which version of Nico I'll be getting.

Across from me, Nico has his head reclined against the back of the couch, his eyes shut, fast asleep. His chest rises in small, eased breaths through parted, full lips. He looks so content, and nothing like the monster who stalked me onto a flight.

Careful not to make noise, I sit up, keeping his jacket over my lap. How could a man who claims to want me dead care enough about my comforts to cover me? I bring it to my nose, breathing in his scent, letting it drag me back to a better time, to only days ago.

I glance down the length of the plane to the back, assuming there's a bathroom down there. Sliding his jacket from me, I lift to my feet carefully, gaze locked on the sleeping monster. I wouldn't put it past him to prevent me from using the bathroom, like he tried on the trip here.

At the back, I find the bathroom. It's easily triple the size of the ones found on commercial planes. When I return to my seat, Nico is still asleep, leaving me to sit and stare out at the clouds, my busy mind focusing on everything I don't want it to.

Ariella. Her safety is the only thing that matters. If Nico kills me, what happens to her? She'll be cared for with the funds I've left, but what about her mental state?

"Stop chewing on your lip. You'll harm yourself."

Jerking, my teeth release my lip, which I was unconsciously chewing on. "You're awake."

"Been awake since you first opened your eyes," he says, his voice lined thick with sleep, giving his lie away.

Either way, I play into it and mutter, "Pretending to sleep then. Childish."

Nico shrugs a shoulder and leans forward, wiping sleep from his face. "More like I was curious what you'd do while I was asleep. I'm quite disappointed actually. You didn't even search for a weapon."

"Would it have made a difference?"

"Not in the slightest. In fact, it would have made me more

pissed and given me more leave to punish you. But you've never been one to roll over and take it."

"And you're not the villain you continue to claim to be," I shoot back, lifting the leather jacket beside me. "Covering the girl you hate to keep her warm is a kind act."

"Your chattering teeth annoyed me. Made it hard to fall asleep."

"So you *were* asleep."

Even from here, I hear when his teeth snap together. His jaw tics, and while to other people, he could look the picture of ease, I see how close he is to cracking.

Yet, my rambles continue. "I mean, I'm still alive. You could have killed me the moment you found me. You haven't tied me up. I must say, this whole kidnapping thing isn't as bad as movies make it out to be. That, or you're not as wicked as you claim to be."

I learn then, how quickly a man of his size can move, even in the small body of a private plane. Nico's by me in an instant and his arm shoots out, snatching me by my throat. He lifts me, slamming my back to the side of the small plane. My feet dangle inches from the ground and my hands fly to his, nails scratching at the impenetrable grip he has on me.

With his thumb over my pulse, he puts pressure there, making me gag instantly, gulping excessively for air.

"S-stop."

He doesn't. He leans in close, his bared teeth a fraction from my face. If I were able to breathe, I'd be able to taste his breath.

"The only reason you're still alive is because shooting you is too quick and painless of a death. Fucking enjoy surviving while you can. *Take it* because after we land, your life will be in my hands; your sanity in my control; your soul mine for the reaping." His lips curl in a downright terrifying grin. The kind of grin only a psychopath could make. "Do not mistake my charity as being anything more than that."

"N-Nico..." My feet kick out, seeking reprieve—searching for breath. Life. Anything.

But he's not listening. Doesn't even seem like he pays my movements any attention. His rampage goes on, his grip tightening to the point that black covers my gaze. "You are *mine* now, to do with as I see fit. If I want to keep you as my own personal fuck-toy and tie you up for my convenience, I will. If I want to sell your ass on the black market and earn back every dollar you and your father tried to take from me, then I will. If I want to slit your throat so you bleed to death slowly, I will."

I open my mouth, ready to beg again, to tell him I'm minutes from dying, and he won't have any of those choices, when a voice over the speakers interrupts me. "Mr. Corsetti, we will be landing in a few moments."

Nico releases me with a rough shove, dropping me back onto the couch. I gulp in large breaths of air, my lungs working overtime to catch up, to bring me back to life. He retakes his seat, spreading both arms wide over the couch's backing.

"Y-you're...an ass—hole," I gasp out, glaring at him with all the hate I can muster in my condition.

"And you're trapped, *petit rat*. Enjoy your final moments of freedom because they're soon to be a memory."

29
NICO

The most discerning part of all this has been my hesitation to *want* to kill her. I should have already, so I don't have to look upon her betraying ass any longer, but when I think about it, something in me pushes back against the idea.

Maybe because in the back of my mind, I reflect on her insistence that she was protecting herself. Against her own father though? It doesn't make sense.

You want there to be more.

No, I don't.

I do. Maybe if there was a reason for her treachery, then I could have a reason for keeping her alive. To allow her to live though means she can return to De Falco at any moment, and to do so is a threat to my family, which I will not risk.

If there's no good reason, then she dies. She must, to end this. If I was wise, I'd march her straight to Flynn and have my enforcer deal with her. I could be done with her ass and move on with my life. Follow Father's advice regarding my future, marry a woman who'll bring good relations to the family, and forget this week ever existed.

But the thought of Flynn handling her has me feeling deadly. *He* who would cut into her smooth skin, leaving *his* marks on her. *He* who would hear her beg, see her tear-streaked face as she becomes terrorized in her drive to live. No. Those considerations make me want to kill him instead. If there's anyone who will get the pleasure of vengeance, it'll be me. One cry at a time; one drop of blood at a time.

Will you though?

I gaze upon the soon-to-be-broken girl as she sits across from me. When the plane begins its descent, she turns, watching our approach to the Corsetti private airfield. Her pulse rapidly jumps in her neck the nearer our approach. Her hands tighten their hold on the cushioned seat, anxiety rolling over her in pungent waves. Her neck is red from where my hands gripped her and I feel a strange sense of welcoming possessiveness. *My* marks are on her. I wonder if there's still evidence of my bite on her thigh.

Minutes pass as the plane completes its descent. The plane lands on the tarmac with a loud *thud*. We taxi for a short minute—the benefit of a small plane—and then it stops with a jerk. The moment I hear the door being opened, I lurch to my feet and reach for her, propelling her to her feet.

"You will walk or I'll carry you again. You pick."

I push her in front of me, deciding for her, but remaining available to toss her over my shoulder if she attempts anything.

At the bottom of the stairs, warm familiar Montreal air greets us, leading us straight to the black car waiting only feet away. Wisely, she doesn't try to run, not that she'd get far if she had. She stalks toward the car, her head down and shoulders hunched.

"Say goodbye," I tell her.

"To what?" she asks, without peeking at me behind her.

"Freedom."

At the vehicle, she pauses. In the reflection of the window, I watch her teeth scrape along her bottom lip. She looks away altogether, up and over the car, into the tarmac. I rock back on my heels, waiting for it. The run as she attempts to escape again.

Please, petite souris, do it. Give me that pleasure.

"If you had a really good reason, you would have made the same choices I had."

Speaking to her reflection, I reply, "I wouldn't have made the decision to betray someone who could easily become my enemy."

Her lip curls. "You talk of betrayal like we were aligned at all, Nico. Up until just days ago, we were strangers."

"Strangers, yes, but you were certain to get close to me. Fucking user." Refusing to look at her any longer, I flick a finger toward the car and demand, "Get in."

"It wasn't like that," she mumbles in a small voice, but shockingly, she listens and gets into the vehicle, sliding straight across the bench to press herself against the opposite door, the same way she sat on the flight to Germany.

I follow her into the car and shut the door, instantly banging my fist against the roof to signal to my driver to go. The sooner we get home and I put Della in her new rightful place, the better.

"Don't get comfortable. It's not a long ride."

"I wouldn't dare to ever be comfortable in your presence again."

Other than her snarky comment, she remains silent for the entirety of the drive. I watch her more than I should be, strangely fascinated in the sweet scent of disgust that rolls from her as she tries her fucking darndest to not show her emotions.

She's not scared though. Not in the ways she should be.

I've taken enough people captive to see the trends in how they respond to me compared to how Della is now. With Della, there's no sniveling, no crying, no begging. Just a fierce quietness, as though she's lying low and waiting for her opportunity to fight back.

We finally arrive, and the car barely stops before I open the door and step out, gesturing for her to follow. She doesn't move from her rigid spot, continuing to stare out at the opposite window.

"Thirty seconds. You won't enjoy it if I have to come around and get you."

Her spine goes rigid and her shoulders drop once with a huff. She can be annoyed all she fucking wants, though.

"Della," I warn. "Final time."

She slides across the leather seat and out the door. She glares for a long beat before breaking it and glancing up at the mansion. A sense of longing passes over her expression, her hate breaking for the briefest second before her walls rebuild. It's enough though. Enough to easily spot the memories pass through her mind.

"Walk. You try to run, I shoot you in the back."

She steps in front of me and her shoulders lift and drop slightly. I can nearly see them knotting beneath the material of her shirt. She strides up the stairs, her feet dragging over each one. I'm not sure if she's doing it unknowingly or to piss me off, but it's beginning to work.

"I remember when I first walked up these stairs," she mutters. "I was dressed like a princess."

"You're a boss's daughter." I grunt. "I'm sure it's something you're used to."

She doesn't comment on that, instead saying, "I was so scared when I arrived. Figured you'd see right through me."

"I should have." Perhaps that's the maddening part in all

this. Not what she did, but who she is and how no one knew of Stefano's secret daughter.

The mansion's heavy front doors are opened for us, and Della enters without a secondary command. The moment she's passed the entranceway, I clamp onto her arm and drag her to the right, toward the hallway that'll eventually lead us to the basement. It's where Della will be finding a new home amongst the age-old blood stains and walls that have heard many tortured screams as they pled for survival.

Our arrival doesn't go unnoticed though, because feet quickly pound down the hall behind us.

"Nico, you're back," Rafael calls.

"Not now." I don't bother to look behind me.

He catches up to us, his gaze flitting between Della and me. She glances at him quickly before her eyes dive to the floor.

Interesting.

My brother doesn't have the same reaction to her though. His voice is hard—a tone I don't hear frequently from him. "You found her."

"Don't follow us."

Rafael's steps pause as he actually listens to me and we continue on without him. At the end of the hallway, I pull open the wooden door, gesturing for her to enter first. Unlike the rest of the ornate mansion, this room has been likened to hell by previous guests who've stayed down here.

"Walk."

There's nowhere she can go. Not at the bottom of the stairs and certainly not inside this mansion, where someone will always be able to stop her.

She grabs a hold of the railing and walks down without a fight. Like on the plane when she hadn't searched me for a weapon, her compliance is unsettling and even disappointing, but I shove the soft emotions aside. I need to be hard for the next part. I need to be an underboss and protect my family.

At the bottom, I switch on the single light that hangs over a wooden chair, stained with many different blood types from over the years. At this point, it's more red than brown.

"Welcome to your final resting place."

Her head whips around, her eyes narrowing. The fight in her is right there, right on the tip of her tongue, but then she backs down, looking away, toward the chair.

"So you've decided what to do with me then?"

I don't know.

I've never wanted to kill a person so much.

I've never wanted to keep a person alive so much.

Feet pound down the steps behind us, and I move my body in front of Della, uncertain who the intruder is. Once he pierces the basement's dim lighting, I catch the familiar face of my enforcer. He flicks dark bangs off his face as his crazed eyes look past my shoulder and lock on Della. His menacing growl echoes through the room; a sound that I've witnessed makes grown men piss themselves. Muscles bulge from his tight shirt, built from his time spent carrying bodies around.

Della lets out a screech, oddly similar to a squeak, and her hands land on my shoulders, using me as a shield. The aroma of her fear is so strong, it overtakes the rancid scent of blood, piss, and death that's long tainted this basement.

Curious of her reaction, I side-step her, dropping my arms, and the unnecessary need to protect her. Her eyes flick back and forth between Flynn and me, and with every pass, her breasts rise faster with her quickening breaths.

Then Flynn takes an intimidating step forward.

She skitters back, falling against my chest. Wild eyes meet mine, inflamed with panic. Her head shakes back and forth, the speed causing her hair to tangle against my chest.

"N-Nico." It's the only word she manages, but it's heavy, strained with horror and a plea.

I've already decided to handle her myself. Flynn's arrival is simply to show her what she could have instead.

"You're dismissed."

Flynn tips his head in acknowledgement and turns to return upstairs, leaving us in what's usually his domain. The second the door shuts, Della rushes to the right, now recognizing I'm the worst thing in the room again.

"How easy your loyalty shifts."

"It's called self-preservation."

"Hm." I grunt, folding my arms over my chest. "I get the sense you do this often."

Della stops by the chair, her attention inspecting the evidence of previous deaths. After a long look—more curious than scared—she glances toward me again. Her arms spread wide and open.

"It's how I've stayed alive this long. You win, Nico. You want the story? The truth? I'll tell you anything."

"Careful. You might not like it when you have to keep that promise."

30
DELLA

Loyalty.

An odd concept.

Allegiance. It's the basic definition of loyalty. Who am I aligned closest to? Who do I support above all? Who do I believe in the most?

I'm loyal to my own happiness and to my family. To Mom and Ariella.

Until it became only Ariella and me. I was devoted to our safety, our sibling bond, her happiness. Unfortunately, that meant shifting allegiances to our stepfather. For my loyalty, Stefano gave me a house to live in and safety for Ariella, even if I was transferred from stepdaughter to staff. The outcome of that change made it worth it.

Loyalty meant going undercover into an enemy's house and trapping him.

Loyalty never meant enjoying my short-lived experiences with that very man.

Then when the task was complete, I was able to alter my commitments again, focusing solely on Ariella and me.

THE HUNT IN ELUSION

But when one's back is up, when there's nowhere else to go, you have to give in. To remain alive, I might need to be faithful to Nico instead.

The basement Nico has brought me to is disgusting, but perhaps it's the kick I needed. I will *not* die in this piss-reeking, blood-stained room. I will *not* die tied to this chair, where so many others have obviously perished.

I turn to Nico, who's lit by the single bulb above our heads. The angle he stands at casts his face in the shadows, while his body remains in the light. The muscles in his arms flex with every breath, while his expression remains passive, simply observing me. He's never looked more like a mobster than he does in this moment, and I'm foolish enough for it to turn me on.

To respond to his previous statement about shifting loyalties, I say, "It's how I've stayed alive this long. You win, Nico. You want the story? The truth? I'll tell you anything."

"Careful. You might not like it when you have to keep that promise."

"Try me," I challenge, lifting my chin a fraction and pretending like my insides aren't shaking in trepidation.

I expect Nico to come for me. To demand I speak. To do *anything*.

Instead, he gives me his back, stalking to the staircase.

"Wait!" I call. "That's it? You're not..." I trail off, my tongue in my cheek to shut myself up before I give him any accidental ideas.

"Consider yourself lucky I'm fucking exhausted." Then he turns and continues his ascent. Every heavy stomp of his polished shoes nails the annoyance in further. Every stair he climbs, my teeth mash together harder until I'm on the verge of a headache, and when the door slams shut, my insides are a jumble of feelings: all of which I'm unsure how to sort through.

For all his threats, he didn't chain me to the chair, which is its clear purpose. I'm free to pace the room and—My gaze darts to the staircase. Nico isn't stupid. The door would be locked behind him, and probably even guarded.

Still...

As fast as a possible plan forms in my mind, I hear the door open again and booted feet appear in view. Not Nico.

A man appears. His large strides take him to my side quickly. I've barely studied his features: his beard, hard eyes, and arms the size of my head, when he grabs hold of my wrist. In a blink, a metal cuff is snapped on my wrist and tightened.

"Hey—"

He doesn't listen. The other cuff he straps to the chair, the metal clang echoing through the basement. Then he releases me altogether and turns for the stairs.

"Hey, wait!" I call. Unlike Nico, this man pays me zero heed as he climbs the stairs and exits the basement.

So, I'm not free, it seems.

Tugging lightly on my wrist as a test, I find the cuff is fitted in a way I won't be getting free of it. Yanking harder, to see if I can move the chair, all it does is dig the cuffs into my skin. Eyes skimming down toward the base, I spot the giant bolts holding the chair to the stone ground.

At least I can walk around, even if it's not comfortable and only a few inches of space. I can stretch my legs and sit on the ground too.

Clearly, I'm not escaping this. Which means I need to hold on until Nico decides to return. I won't hold anything back, but I'm not offering it up completely free. Not when it's my insurance.

He wants my loyalty, then he needs to do something for me too.

At some point, I finally give up standing, and sink to the disgusting ground. Exhaustion is making my head light and my eyes blurry, and if there's any chance of me making it through what Nico's bound to send my way soon, I need to be rested. He suggested I sleep on the plane ride, and I'm thankful for that, but at some point, those few hours need recharging.

The cold seeps through my jeans, likely soon to be making my ass numb. It's good enough that I'm able to awkwardly lay my arm on the seat, giving my head a pillow.

Where did my life go wrong? *How* did this become it? I could die down here, and Ariella won't even know. Maybe she'll read about my death in the *Montreal Gazette*, when they report my body found in the Lachine Canal with all the other bodies criminals hide in there.

Just the idea of such an outcome should drive energy and life through me, but instead, my spine compresses and my body gets heavy with sleepiness. I won't get a good sleep, but anything will count at this point.

Being loyal to Stefano might be the biggest mistake I've made in a while.

31
NICO

At the top of the stairs, Rafael waits, his pacing only stopping when I shut the door behind me. I walk by him, continuing toward my wing, fingers moving over my phone's screen as I shoot out a message to a few soldiers, requesting someone go handcuff her to that chair, giving specific instructions how to.

Handcuffing how I've instructed them to is a mercy she should appreciate. No one gets that good of treatment. I don't know why I'm even bothering.

Liar.

"I'll get your report tomorrow," I tell my brother. "Time zones have fucked me up."

Rafael waves his hand as he keeps pace with me. "Nothing happened while you were gone. You found her."

"Insightful," I comment, hooking my hand on the banister and climbing the stairs two at a time to gain distance between him and me.

He gets the hint and stops following, remaining on the bottom step. "Funny," he calls up. "What's your plan?"

Halfway up the staircase, I stop, twisting around. "Make sure everyone knows not to go downstairs. No one is to interact with her except," I glance at my phone, toward the name of the soldier who responded to my call out, "Dario. He's to feed her twice a day and she's permitted moderate bathroom breaks."

Rafael blanches, his mouth falling open, his brows rising. He quickly shakes it off though, and his shock is replaced by a chuckle. "Food. Bathroom breaks."

It's not a question but I know what he's asking. It's very rare we ever feed a prisoner, depending if we need them alive or not. We torture them. Rip skin from their bones because that's what their behaviour warrants. They piss and shit themselves because that's what they deserve. They are never permitted bathroom privileges.

Deserve. Such an interesting term.

Della deserves all that and more for her actions, but not yet. For now, she'll receive some kindness until I get the complete story from her. She might be to blame for holding the executioner's knife, but something inside me says there's more to what she did.

"Yes," I reply, turning away from Rafael.

"Then what?" he asks, his voice travelling up to me.

"Torture comes in many forms, brother, and driving her mad is nothing less than she deserves."

I give it two days. Two days in which Father harasses me constantly about ending this and getting the answers we need. He doesn't understand why she's still alive. He never gives a direct order though, which I could be forced to follow, and that I find interesting. Almost like he's testing me.

Della is where my mind has been most nights. During the

day, she's easy to forget about as I've thrown myself into the field with my men, searching for evidence of where Stefano may have disappeared to. Like fucking smoke, he's gone, his house cleared out.

If I'm not out searching for him, I'm working. Avoiding any and all meetings, but popping into the clubs to check on progress.

I only think about Della when getting the reports from Dario. She eats both meals he brings down each day, but consumes minimal water, which has resulted in few bathroom breaks. It makes me wonder how much work Stefano put into training her because these are actions of a trained soldier.

It gets really bad at night though. When I'm lying in bed, inches from where she once was, or in my office, as I sit at my desk and recount every moment with her. Not only fucking her in here though, but *every* moment. Every conversation, every action. Anything that would hint to any hidden truths, any signs I've missed.

That's also not to say I haven't watched her through the camera feed. The night-vision cameras down there have tracked her every move. Every time she paces around the chair. Every reposition her entrapment allows for.

Dario tips his head as I pass him to finally visit her. "She ate a few hours ago."

At the bottom of the stairs, I find her standing poised, looking almost regal. As regal as someone can be in a place like this. She watches me approach, no fear in her expression.

When I reach her side, I use my finger to crook her chin up, aligning our faces. She maintains her farce of bravery by looking past my shoulder. Her neck is blemished red, almost blistered from where I gripped her the other day. She's wearing another one of my marks and I shouldn't enjoy the prospect as much as I do.

Her beauty truly pains me. Makes me wish our outcome could be different. That I could have her in my bed right now. She thinks De Falco was her path though, and now I'm here to learn why.

"What was Stefano's exact plan when he sent you to the party?"

She jerks her head away and I let her. She paces back as many steps as her cuffs allow for—two. If she feels she's in control, she'll more likely reveal everything, so I tolerate that much.

"Originally, I was supposed to enter the party, sneak into your office, and search for anything that would help him get ahead of you."

Unoriginal. "Look for what exactly?"

She shrugs a shoulder. "Weapons deals, upcoming trades, your schedule. Anything like that."

That's a pathetic attempt. Does he think we're stupid enough to have every document in my office and not spread amongst the businesses, for this very purpose?

"You said 'originally' you were supposed to sneak into the party. That obviously changed."

Della snorts lightly, glancing at her hands as her lips roll together. With a slight shake of her head, she reports in a bitter tone, "Stefano played us both that night. When I returned home, he told me there was more to my attendance. If I found anything, it was merely a bonus. Getting close to you seemed to be the focus. You know this though. He told you as much."

"Sorry if I want to be certain of all the facts first," I reply dryly. Not that I didn't believe De Falco's claim, but I want the complete story direct from Della.

I approach her. My moves are sudden and unable to be tracked. Her eyes bulge and she tries to step back again, but the cuffs limit her. My arm wraps around her waist and I propel her to my chest, feeling her rapidly beating heart against mine, her breaths huffing over my neck.

The scent she imprinted on me has faded and is now masked with the gore of this basement. It makes me want to sweep her away from here and scrub her skin until the scent of violence is replaced with only mine.

"Is Stefano your real father?"

"No," she answers right away.

"So you're not his child from a previous relationship he hid away?"

She jolts, scoffing, and finally looks at me, her brows dipped with incredulous shock. "Is *that* what he told you?" Her chest thunders with what sounds like genuine laughter, to the point she wipes her eyes with her free hand. "That's fucking funny."

"So who are you really?"

Her laughter almost immediately dies and her gaze drops. She returns to this shell of a person, almost limp in my arms. Shut down.

"Della," I growl my warning.

She rests her hand on my chest, right over my heart. The heat of her palm sears through my shirt, my heart beating quicker, almost like it's responding to her touch. She peeks up at me through full lashes, scraping her teeth over her lip again.

I move before I realize what I'm doing and caress that lip with my thumb, pulling it from her teeth before she injures herself.

"Della," I repeat, a bit gentler than before, "if you're not his daughter, why did he say you were? Why didn't you deny it?"

"I'll tell you but I need something in return."

"You are in no place to demand anything."

"I can't tell you then."

I shift the hand I had on her face up to her neck, right overtop the marks there from the flight. She flinches. I don't put pressure though; only the silent threat of what can happen. She could fight with her unchained hand, if she chooses to, but she remains still.

"You would have done it by now," she whispers, meeting my gaze. "If you were going to kill me, I wouldn't still be here, two days later. You're keeping me alive because you *can't* murder me, no matter how much you want to."

Surprise flits through my mind that she's come to that conclusion, but I lock my expression, unwilling to allow her to see she's correct. Any other traitor would be dead by now, but Della...I'm hesitating.

"Who are you, Della? Right now, you haven't earned a request. Maybe I'll reconsider when you start handing over valuable responses."

Her lips fold together and her eyes narrow, but she quickly rids herself of the frustration and finally replies, "I'm his step-daughter. My last name is Lambert. Della Lambert."

Stepdaughter.

I release her, almost stumbling back. It makes so much sense. She's his hidden weapon. If she's his stepdaughter, it means—

"Your mother married him."

"Y-yes." She blinks and for all her strength so far, she cracks for just an instant. Her eyes swell, tears beginning their forma-tion, but then she tilts her head up and stares into the lightbulb to dry them.

There's so much pain in her gaze and while I ache to reach for her, I don't.

"They were married two years ago. Stefano came around for a while before then. He was very charming and Mom was smit-ten. They wed, and we moved into his mansion. I learned who he was; I don't even know if Mom knew before the wedding."

"I never heard about him getting remarried." Stefano hid

this from all of us. He—My thoughts cut off before I get too deep in solving this that I miss more of what Della has to say.

She snorts lightly, still staring down at her hands. "Yeah, well, I'm sure he knew what he was doing. Life was weird with him. I was given a lot of the things that go along with an elite lifestyle, but he was very paranoid. My outside time was limited. He warned me of you and your family. Said if I strayed too far, you'd kill me."

"Fucker."

I don't think she's even heard me, still lost in the past. "Then Mom died last year in a car accident. I had nowhere else to go. You have no idea how many times I've wanted to leave, but I need his money. I wouldn't have made enough on my own to care for myself and—Anyway, he played on my needs. Said I could stay in the house in exchange for doing whatever he asked of me. For the past year, he made me clean the house. This was the first big thing he's requested."

Fuck. De Falco's a motherfucking douche for playing on a person's loss like that. There's a statement she started though: *"I wouldn't have made enough on my own to care for myself and —"* coupled with the fact she agreed to attend the party.

He's holding something over her head.

"What aren't you telling me, Della?"

My question breaks her, and I wish I knew exactly which part did it. Her eyes swell with tears that she doesn't hide this time, her hand coming up to cover her mouth. Despite the cuffs constraining her, she pulls herself as far away as possible, shaking her head back and forth wildly.

"Tell me, Della."

"I-I can't, Nico. This, I can't. Not without insurance. You say I'm not in a place to request anything, and I get it, but I can't..." Her breaths come out shallow, like she's struggling to catch her breath. Panic to the point of near hyperventilation. "I won't. Kill me first."

"What do you want?" I ask carefully.

"Safety," she whispers. "Not for me, but for my sister."

"Ariella," I recall the name she mentioned in that house. "Honestly, I thought you made that up. She's real then?"

Through a mask of tears, Della glances at me. The sight of her so broken makes my stomach flip. These aren't tears from being brought to the edge multiple times. They're not even tears because *I* harmed her. These are unbreakable tears: real and raw. Emotional. The ones that make me want to take her in my arms and forget she's my enemy.

"She's real." Della wipes her face. "Promise me, Nico. Not my life, but hers. She didn't live with me after Mom died, so she's completely innocent. Has nothing to do with my actions. She knows nothing, I promise." Della pauses, her eyes meeting mine, more naked and honest than I've yet to ever see. "Promise me. *Please.* I won't—I can't tell you anything until I know she's going to be safe."

She mentioned this after arriving back in Montreal, that she did all this for another person. Her sister. I'm an idiot for not piecing this together sooner. She even asked me if I'd do the same, to protect someone close to me, and I think about Rafael, my parents, Aurora, and even Hawke, and yes, I would. I'd betray anyone to keep them protected.

Which is why I lift my right hand and mark an X right over my heart, over my family's tattoo. She's seen it before, knows the significance. "I promise, Della. I won't touch your sister."

"No one will." Her finger points toward me, her eyes narrowing. "That's the promise I need from you, Nico. Not you, not your family, your staff, your soldiers, anyone in your employ, or those you manipulate."

Years with Stefano certainly has taught her much about this life—to cover her ass before accepting a man's word, to outline all the possibilities.

"I promise, Della. I will not have a hand in harming your sister, nor will anyone I employ, convince, or otherwise. No commands. No secret messages. Nothing that will hurt her."

She stares at me. Her nostrils flare with her deep breaths and weighted thoughts. Almost-visible debate rolls heavy through her mind.

Then she releases the longest breath I've ever seen someone take, becoming a whole other person.

Stronger. Resilient. A queen in control amongst a room full of death.

"She's all I've ever cared about. She's the reason I've done all this and I won't have her dragged down because of my errors." Della pauses, her throat moving into a swallow and then she launches into the remaining piece. "Mom died in a car accident...and Ariella was in the vehicle with her. Ariella survived, but she saw *everything*. She *saw* Mom's—" Della stops, a sob interrupting her speech. "She's never spoken about that day, but worse, she stopped talking entirely. The doctors diagnosed her with selective mutism as a trauma response. Her brain stopped allowing her to speak, so she can't offer up any of the details of that day. Selective, because I'm the only one she'll speak to. Even then," her expression pinches, "it's not the same. *She's* not the same."

I move before levelheadedness can stop me. I cup her cheeks with both my hands, using my thumbs to wipe away the stray tears. If I could go back in time and protect her family from that accident, I would, to save her today's pain.

"Cry if you need to, *petite souris.*"

I smooth my thumb over her lip, hating that I'm so confused by this little scrap of a woman. I shouldn't be

THE HUNT IN ELUSION

holding her tenderly. Not when she's behind my near-death experience.

"A-afterwards," she continues, "Stefano decided she was useless to him, but I guess he found a way to still use her. She was sent away, put into care, in exchange for my submission. I would do whatever he asked of me for her."

Whatever a man asks of a sexy woman like Della...My thoughts flash murderous. My next actions won't care whether she's innocent or guilty, but they will be decided by her answer.

"Did he...?"

She shakes her head. "No, not like that. Like I said, it wasn't much. House cleaner until the party gave him the opportunity. I agreed to the party, but I tried to get out of the rest when I learned of his true plans." She peeks up through wet eyelashes and rests her palm over mine. "Nico, believe me when I say I didn't want to. Even before really knowing you, I didn't, but I had to. He promised freedom for me and Ariella, and a million dollars. With that money, we could get away from him."

"The bag."

She nods glumly. "I hated taking that money. You think it was easy for me to walk away from you that day, but it wasn't at all. You have no idea how many times I almost admitted everything to you before then. I figured begging for forgiveness would be better."

I don't respond to any of that. I can't. Not yet. She's guilty of her crimes against me, but for the best plausible reason.

"Where's your sister?"

"Still in care. Until I had proof of your death, I wasn't risking her life by taking her on the run with me."

Her entire life for the past year has been spent living for her sister, whether it was inside De Falco's mansion, doing his bidding, or escaping from me. Everything she has said is admirable.

Villainy comes in many strange forms.

And so does loyalty.

She betrayed me for her sibling. But I'd do the same for mine.

32
DELLA

Nico's hands fall away from my face, leaving a sense of abandonment. I shouldn't relish his touch as much as I do, but if these are my final days before death, I may as well enjoy it in any way possible. He pulls a key from his slacks. Hope flares in my chest and it's met when he unlocks my wrist from the cuff.

I roll my wrists, revelling in the sensation of having both of them freed again. It feels strange to have complete use of my hands, but it's a welcome change.

Nico steps aside and gestures toward the staircase. "Walk."

Like out of here?

I don't dare question and stride past him, heading to the stairs. I don't think this is a con, knowing what I do about Nico. He wouldn't do that to me after revealing what I have. I think.

At the top of the stairs, Nico squeezes by me. His body brushes mine, making my own heat with desires I shouldn't be having. He leads the way down the length of the house and toward the staircase he last brought me up during better times.

It makes the severity of what I've done all more striking. Every step I take seems to weigh me down with regret and eventually, I'm steps behind Nico.

My hands curl and uncurl, warmth from an insulated house finally penetrating two days of a permanent chill. I hadn't realized exactly how cold the basement is until finally leaving it.

At the top of the staircase, we pass a large, decorative mirror. The reflection makes me pause. Nico in his standard suit and shiny shoes. His hair is brushed and even the injuries on his face are more healed than two days ago; the swelling in his cheek is nearly gone. And then there's me. My shoes are dirty from the basement, my clothes marred with days' old grime, first from travel and then from living on a floor that has seen more death than I can ever imagine.

Nico stands to the side, silently observing me watching us in the mirror. His expression remains flat, but in his eyes, I see a new emotion.

Pity.

For some reason, that pisses me off. I don't need to be *pitied* because I understand *I* did what has landed me in his bad graces. And I don't regret it for a moment. Not if it meant keeping Ariella cared for.

We continue walking until stopping at his bedroom door. A troubling knot tightens in my stomach, as I don't know what to think about all of this. Maybe his plan is to strangle me and leave me dead in his bed, so he can revel in my death.

Nico pushes his door open and stands aside. "Go in."

I do, pausing right inside the doorway. He follows me in and snaps the lock shut on his door, confining us both in the room.

"For now, you will stay in here."

"Your room." I skim the familiar space, eyes pausing on the large bed, recalling when he brought me here the other night under much different circumstances. "Why? What are you going to do with me?"

"First, you will shower." He leads me into the bathroom, reaching inside to switch on the shower. "You stink of death. Strip and clean yourself."

I expect him to stay and observe me with those soulful eyes as I dutifully follow his command, but instead, he exits the room, leaving me to wonder why this disappoints me.

Shaking off all the thoughts I shouldn't be having, I immediately get out of the dirty clothing, tossing them to the side and hoping I don't have to wear them again. When I move beneath the spray, I release an inhuman, ungodly loud moan as the steaming hot water stings in the most gratifying way possible, and sears my skin with its cleansing magic. Considering my last shower was at the hotel in Edmonton, this shower is everything good I need right now.

I tilt my head back, delighting in the water sluicing down my chest, between my breasts, and trailing the length of my body. I reach for Nico's shampoo bottle and pour a healthy amount into my hand. I don't know when the next time he'll allow me to clean myself, so I'll make this the best damned shower I've ever had.

I soap up my hair and then rinse it out before adding the conditioner. I grab a loofah and the same body soap he used on me the other day, and get to scrubbing days' old grime and sweat.

So lost in the heavenly feel, I don't hear him enter, nor sense him at all. Not until large hands clasp my hips and he pulls me backwards, letting me feel him—*all* of him. His bare legs lining up with mine, his hard abs against my back, and his cock brushing the curve of my ass.

I stop breathing, half frightened and partially hopeful at what he'll do next. He flicks wet ropes of hair off my shoulder, trailing his lips over the skin there, sucking up the water droplets as he goes. I shiver, leaning back into his touch. My head drops to the side, welcoming more of his touch. I shouldn't be enjoying this as much as I am, when so much of my future is still unknown, but for a moment, I'm transported back to days ago.

"Don't stop washing on my account, *petite souris.*"

With him at my back stalking my every move, I finish cleaning myself. When the loofah disappears between my legs, he lets out a low sound. I want to turn around and face him, but with his intense gaze raking over every inch of my back, I feel like I'll lose a piece of myself if I do.

When I replace the loofah and I'm completely rinsed of suds, my curiosity rises to the top; the need to know his reasoning. "Why are you being so nice to me all of a sudden?"

"I don't like dirty rats. Not suitable for my plans."

Rat again. The nickname switches often, and I wonder if he even realizes when he does it.

Despite the water on my face, my lips feel more chapped than ever and my tongue darts out to wet them. "Plans?"

"Do you remember what I said to you on the plane?"

"You said a lot of things."

"The part about being able to do whatever the fuck I want with you now."

Keeping my attention on the tile in front of my face, I'm careful with my next words. "Well, if I'm up here and you're insisting I get clean, I don't think you're planning to kill me."

"No," he purrs. He caresses the space between my ear and shoulder, his finger languidly dragging over the skin. Every pass feels like a threat; the reminder that he's now my real villain. "I've decided to keep you, Della. To use you in all the ways you've used me."

"For how long?" Nico didn't chase me across the country

and lock me in a basement, only to keep me as his personal whore. This isn't his plan.

He chuckles and the warmth of his breath passes right over my shoulder, trickling over the skin covering my heart. *"Tu es intelligente, petite souris."*

"I'm smart because I know what men in this life are like. You're all trained in the art of double meanings. You didn't chase me across a country to keep me chained to your bed. So how long am I safe from death?"

Finally finding the strength, I turn, placing my back against the tile. If he's deciding my fate, he'll do it to my face. His hand drops to his side, but I lift my own, resting it over the taut skin of his chest, tracing the many tattoos, including his most valuable one, etched over his heart, freely exploring him. Beneath my palm, he goes still, except for the beat of his heart, which feels like it speeds up. His silent exposure in how my touch affects him.

One hand moves up to cup his cheek, my thumb caressing over the faded bruise, which is nearly gone. "You've healed."

The green of his eyes glimmer as they lock on mine. "Do you care?"

"Yes," I reply with conviction. "Whether you believe me or not is irrelevant, but I felt sick every day I was gone, unsure if you were alive or not. If you were being harmed." Rolling my lips together, I take my shot, aware he'll deny the truth. "I think you do believe me. I think learning I did it for Ariella's life has changed something in you or else you wouldn't have brought me up here." I press into the hard lines of his body, feeling his cock jumping to life against my leg. "I think you're confused, Nico, and 'keeping me' is your answer. You think you need to be my villain and you're mad about the betrayal, but you also empathize with me."

"Empathize," he repeats, his tone dropping to frosty

temperatures, shattering the bubble I've managed to build around us.

Nico jerks his head away from my hand and backs me into the wall, crowding me. His arms come up on either side of my head, his lips inches from mine as he tips his head down. I place my palms on his chest, feeling the hard planes of his body—his heart, which reveals the truth he's determined to hide from me.

That I'm correct.

"That's what you think, Della, but you want to know what I think? I think your loyalty changes based on who'll provide you the best chance of survival, and right now, you're trying to appeal to the human side of me. Sweetheart, that side doesn't exist." His hand darts to my face and he grabs my jaw in a firm hold, squeezing my chin to the point of pain, but I won't show him that. "The first time you were here, you fucked your way to freedom. This time, you'll work for your life. Every time you disobey, I'll give you an injury comparable to one I received from your stepfather."

He's lying.

The man who chained me to a chair and left me alone for two days before bringing me to his own bedroom to be cleaned will not harm me in the ways he's talking about, but Nico needs to feel in control right now, and for my own chance at freedom, I'll let him have it.

Nico reaches between my legs, swiping two fingers through my core. My betraying body responds to his touch and my thighs inch apart.

"Even your body has switched loyalties," he murmurs. "Show me how loyal you can be, Della. Get on your knees."

I ignore him. I reach behind us and switch off the shower. I'm playing with fire, with his control. But if I wasn't able to— if he didn't want to test me—I'd still be cuffed to a chair two floors beneath us.

"You never answered the question of how long I'll be here," I say, exiting the shower and reaching for a towel hanging up on a hook on the nearest wall. I wrap my body in a fuzzy cloud and peek over my shoulder, catching a very enraged underboss standing abandoned in the shower. "At some point, you'll need to make a decision about me, Nico. Personal whore won't fly for long."

Then I exit the bathroom.

Three.

Two...

One—

Right on time, Nico stomps from the bathroom behind me, water droplets flying from his body as he rushes across the room toward me. He didn't bother with a towel, meaning every gleaming inch of his god-like body is on show.

My hair is practically ripped from my head, wrenching a pained cry from my throat as my body jerks back, knocking into his. His other hand snatches the towel from my weakened grip, tossing it to the floor. His hand curls, wrapping my wet strands around his fist, and he walks us backwards, toward his bed.

"Nico..."

"Shut your fucking mouth, Della, before I fill it with something to keep you quiet."

He drops me unceremoniously onto the bed, flipping me over. With his hand still gripping my hair, he shoves my face into the blankets. I push back, using my hands to get leverage and lift my head, but he snatches both my wrists into his other hand and locks them behind my body.

"You forget, *petite souris.*" He growls, bending over my body. His hardening cock slips in the space between my ass. "You forget your place. You think because I took you from the basement, you mean something to me? You think you're winning? That you'll be free?"

He releases my hair to reach between my legs and sends a sharp slap to my pussy. My betraying body responds, my insides flushing with a swarm of heat that makes it impossible to feign disinterest in his touch.

"You are nothing here. You're a lying whore who snuck her way into my bed to secure her own freedom. You think I care you were doing it for the good of your family?" He scoffs, his fingers stroking where he just hit. Two fingers slip inside my core, spreading as they push inside me. "I've decided to keep you alive *for now* because you feel so fucking good on my cock and it's be such a shame to discard a tight cunt that takes me so well."

"Nico..." Only this time, I don't know if I'm trying to deny him, or asking him to continue.

"Listen to you, fucking begging for it." Releasing my hands, he readjusts my legs, propping my ass up. His weight disappears from my back and his cock slips lower, at the entrance to my pussy. "I should deny you, Della, since you disobeyed me in the shower when I nicely asked you to get on your knees."

His cock slams inside me, burying deep in one thrust. I scream into the bed, muffled by the blankets. Nico's cock slides halfway out of me before seating himself again. He grabs my hair, arching my body backwards as he drives into me with an unforgiving speed. He's punishing me, regaining the control he felt slipping away when I ignored him. His sounds become animalistic. Fingers dig painfully into my hip, but I hardly feel it with the pleasure rippling my insides.

"Nico," I gasp. "Nico, this is—" I can't finish. Words can't form in my head long enough to speak a complete sentence.

"I know, Della," he says softer than before. "I'm giving you what you need, aren't I? What you certainly don't deserve. I should pull out now."

"I missed this," I softly admit before I can stop my own mouth from betraying me.

Digging my hands into the blankets, I thrust backwards, meeting him halfway. His grip on my hip gets heavier, but he doesn't stop me from participating.

"Don't play games. Stop fucking lying."

"Not a game. The moment I walked away from you, I missed this. Missed you."

I don't know if it was what I said, or something else, but with the hold he has on my hair, he propels me up onto my knees. One hand comes around my front and he strums my clit while hammering into me. I reach a hand around his neck, holding him tight to me.

The heat builds through my core quickly and my nails dig into his neck, seeking reprieve. My cries get louder, until the intensity of my release slams through my core, my pussy milking him through my orgasm. I trigger his own, and with his head in my neck, he growls, warmth flooding my insides.

We're silent afterwards, only our heavy breaths filling the silence. After a long moment, he lifts his head, taking my lips in a bruising kiss that makes my head go lighter than it already is.

Silent questions swirl around the room. What does this mean and where do we go from here?

His head drops against mine, a low, pained growl rumbling from his chest. "What the fuck do I do with you, Della?"

"Whatever you want."

"I get the sense that what I want isn't an option."

"Do you still want me on my knees?"

"Yes." He pauses. "No. I don't know. I should hand you over to Flynn to end your life. I also want to lock you in this room and degrade you to the point you understand just how badly you fucked up. But then I want to worship you and spread you out on my bed, where I can ensure you never leave again."

Shuffling forward, I break our connection and his cock slips from my contented body. I turn around, facing him, finding a Nico I've yet to be introduced to. Vulnerable. Pained. Troubled.

Resting my hand over his Corsetti tattoo, I show him how much I understand his position. This tattoo is representative of the promises he made to his family when he took his oaths, when he became their leader. He needs to do what's right for their safety.

But I won't go easily.

33
NICO

Della Lambert continues to force me into making mistakes I'll never come back from.

I shouldn't have brought her to my bedroom.

I shouldn't have entered the shower with her.

I shouldn't have taunted her with being kept.

I shouldn't have allowed her to somehow control the interaction.

I shouldn't have fucked her.

And I certainly shouldn't have let my vulnerability creep up by murmuring my troubling debate out loud: *"What the fuck do I do with you, Della?"*

Della is a danger. To me. To the family. To my fucking sanity.

To my heart.

I should return her to the basement, lock the door, and throw away the key until I figure out which course of action to take.

I jerk away, forcing her to drop her hand from where it was resting right over my heart, over my Corsetti tattoo. It's like

Della can fucking read me or something. She understands the precariousness of this situation and still offers me her sympathy, even though it's *her* life on the line.

Any other person, whoever even just *thought* of deceiving me or my family would be dead almost instantly, but Della...it's impossible to destroy a person who was only doing it for her sister. She's protective of her family, but now I need to be for mine as well, and somehow, there is no easy answer to this.

I'm drowning. Dragged to the depths by an aquamarine gaze, enchanting smirk, and survivor's soul.

From the first moment I met Della, I knew she was different. She didn't paw me like other women. She gave chase, made me go to her. But I see now that was only the surface of who Della Lambert is. She literally survived the loss of her mother, the illness of her sister, and continued to live, and work for, a man who then wanted little to do with her. She integrated herself into a crime family to ensure a better future for her and her sister.

I firmly believe Della has told me everything she knows, but I don't think that's all there is to this. It's too coincidental that De Falco happened to have stepdaughters at his disposal for such an occasion. He took a big risk sending Della to me. That wasn't planned suddenly.

Coincidences don't exist.

Without a word, I head for my closet, quickly dressing in one of my many suits. I grab a plain tee on my way out and toss it to her.

"Wear this. I'm burning your clothes."

She slips the shirt over her head and seats herself in the middle of my large bed, watching me through bold eyes. Her legs fold and her hands rest in her lap, like she's waiting for me to command her.

Instead, I give her my back. "I'll send up food," I call behind me. "Do not even attempt to leave this room or you won't like what happens."

I slip from the room and text Dario to come stand guard. I don't completely trust her to not try to breakout. Then, as I head to my office, I text everyone to meet me.

The sooner a rational decision can be made, the sooner I get rid of her.

~

Rafael, Rosen, Father, and Mother are situated in my office, each with varying degrees of interest as they watch me rock lightly in my office chair. I mindlessly scrape a letter opener beneath my fingernails, mentally reciting this conversation and how to reveal everything.

Rafael leans against a nearby wall, his lips pulled into a smirk as he observes our parents from where they each claim a seat in front of me. It's no wonder my mother's here too, since Father's been very clear about her role. She might avoid the crime and business dealings directly, but she's always been aware of what's going on.

Perhaps I'm more like him than he realizes. I want a woman who'd fit in with my family, who'll participate in the dealings and decision-making, who won't run scared by the thought of blood.

Someone like Della.

"Why is that traitor still alive?" Father growls, yanking me from my musings. "She should be dead for what she did to you." He sits on the edge of the chair, always ready for action.

An unnatural wave of protectiveness overcomes me and the letter opener in my hand feels very fragile as I tighten my grip, the blade beginning to cut into my fingers. I swallow it down before I end up fighting my own father, managing to clamp down the emotion through gritted teeth and a fury burning in my sternum.

"Because she was only trying to earn her freedom for her and her sister." I cut my eyes to my brother adding, "The same any of us would do for each other." I pause before telling them, "Two years ago, Stefano De Falco got remarried. He hid it well, obviously, since none of our intel ever learned of this. Della and her sister were his new wife's children. A year ago, there was an accident, which her mother and sister were involved in."

"Oh!" Mother interjects, her mouth forming an O. "That poor girl," she correctly deduces.

"Remarried," Father repeats, musing as he rubs at his chin. His gaze seems to be going through me, to the past as he attempts to recount that timeframe. "That's...alarming."

"Her mother perished in the accident. Her sister lived, but there were medical complications." I pause, opting to skip over the details of what happened with Ariella. "Della claims that he stuck her sister into care and, knowing she wouldn't be able to afford it herself, De Falco used the opportunity as leverage. In exchange for any tasks of his choosing, he would continue funding the medical expenses."

"What has she been doing this whole time then, if that was a year ago?" Rafael asks.

Father scoffs, shaking his head roughly. "Training. Planning our demise."

"Cleaning," I snap, shooting a cold look toward him. "She's been staff in his house until the party. He got her dressed up and sent her here to meet me. She came under the guise of gathering information, but afterwards, learned he had another plan, involving her getting close to me."

"And the bitch agreed."

Beneath the desk, my hands curl in fists. Blood pounds in

my ears until the only thing I hear is Father's easy breaths, until the thought of ending those breaths cloud my mind.

"He fucking offered her what he knew she wanted. A million dollars and freedom. With the money, she could afford to help her sister. They could go anywhere and begin a new life. *That's* why she did it."

I stop talking, waiting for their responses. Rafael merely grunts, crossing his arms as he watches on. Mother absently rubs at her neck, her eyes staring off into the large window behind me. Rosen remains silent, observing.

Father snarls. "You're defending her, son. You care for this girl too much. You're beginning to lose your wits."

"Fuck off," I snap. Finally, the rage boils over. My hand flicks, hurling the letter opener through the air, inches above his head. It misses him purposely, but is enough for my threat to be an effective warning. "She did what any one of us would have done. She was trapped and found a way out for herself and her family. She *survived*. I can't despise her for that." *No matter how hard I've tried.*

Father jumps to his feet, the red in his face expanding toward his neckline. His finger juts toward me. "I don't care if she was saving the motherfucking prime minister. She acted *against* us; therefore, she is an enemy and deserves nothing less than death."

That protectiveness returns and I won't let him keep talking how he is. I jump to my feet and reach over, snatching his dress shirt in my hand as I wrench him closer until his body jerks into my chest, aware that I'm roughing up my own father, and worse, my Boss; an act that could earn me death.

"Stop. Talking."

What normally would result in him shoving back, doesn't. Instead, I think he finally gets how serious I am, since his hands lift toward me, palms up.

With his submission, I release him with a jerk and retake my seat, my point now made. "Moving on. Don't you think it's awfully interesting that after many years of being alone, De Falco remarries a woman with two adult daughters, keeps the marriage a secret from society, and then his new wife is conveniently dead in an accident one year later?"

"Coincidences don't exist." Father echoes my previous thoughts.

Drumming my fingers along the edge of the desk, I murmur, "Exactly."

"So De Falco planned everything, you're saying." Rafael ambles closer. "Right down to the accident?"

"That's insane," Mother chimes in, her gaze whipping between Rafael and me, until finally shifting to Father. "But plausible," she whispers. "Enzo, we need to tell them. This has gotten bigger than just us, if he's targeting our children."

I still, sharing a confused look with my brother and then Rosen, who remains across the room, as Father lifts to his feet and wanders toward the other side. He sighs, and when he stops pacing, he seems a decade older. Hunched shoulders and a drawn expression look back at me.

"You've always wondered why De Falco spends so much effort on us. He despises us—your mother and me, but it's more than a power trip. Stefano's first wife, Giana Costa, got pregnant a year before her wedding to De Falco, but after giving birth, her family put the child up for adoption in hopes to hide the fact she was no longer an innocent. After marrying De Falco, she admitted the pregnancy to him and requested they find the girl."

Costa. An Italian crime family from overseas. We have no dealings with them, so it's a name I only hear occasionally in passing.

"We had more resources though, so De Falco requested we help find her. We did. You'd know her as Rozelyn De Falco."

"Why would you agree to that?" Rafael voices the question rising in my own mind.

Father looks at Mother, who answers this time, "The Costas have a deep history and a lot of influence in Europe, where we had no dealings or connections. At the time, I was pregnant with your brother," her hand rests on her stomach, "Hawke."

Raf's eyes dart to me and we share an identical look of caution. They don't know about my visit to Hawke, but what if what they tell us changes the importance of his location?

"In exchange for finding Giana's daughter, there was to be a union between Rozelyn and Hawke. We thought it wise to gain a connection to Costa, and De Falco's request created a prime opportunity."

"Fuck." I blow out a breath, reclining in my chair as I piece together the rest. Hawke's no longer with us, which means, no marriage occurred.

"The deal was made, but a lot changed in fifteen years. Giana passed away and De Falco wasn't right after that." Father pauses, his expression scrunching as he searches for appropriate words. "He became messy. Started making stupid decisions. The Costas cut him off, claiming they wanted nothing to do with Rozelyn and Yasmine, despite them being Giana's daughters. Then everything with Hawke occurred, and the marriage deal was voided."

"You didn't attempt to switch prizes?" Rafael hooks a thumb toward me, amusement slipping into his expression again. "You replaced Hawke's heirdom with Nico, so why not the engagement?"

"Like I said," Father continues, "De Falco became distraught. Dangerous. Breaking that union was probably the only benefit to what happened with Hawke. De Falco didn't like losing the connection to us though, and he swore up and down about getting revenge." Father shrugs half-heartedly. "Since then, it's been weak attacks."

They kept this from us—me—this entire time. Heat flashes through my neck and down my spine, but I remain firm in my seat, trying to determine how best to navigate the issue my parents posed.

"Wait." Rafael holds up a hand, coming to stand between our parents. "Wait, so let me get this straight: once upon a time, you helped Stefano De Falco and his wife track down a child in exchange for a marriage union, which got broken when Hawke left. Since then, De Falco's hated you for ending a fruitful match. So he marries a nobody with two daughters, all with the plan to murder the mother and utilize the daughters to infiltrate us." His eyes dart back and forth, slowly shaking his head, but before either of our parents respond to his summary, he whistles and his shock shatters for another easy smile. "Fuck, guys, you really know how to start wars. First, with New York when you," he points to Father, "sliced the neck of Franco Rossi, and then with Leo Bellini when you kidnapped his daughter." His attention slides to Mother, who was once the kidnapped daughter.

"This is what this life is about, son." Father turns, retaking his seat. Directly to me, he speaks, "Power. Family. Connections. And the price they sometimes have."

"All that's good and great, but what are you planning on doing with Della?" Mother asks me, twisting her hands together on her lap. "If she's no longer in the basement, where have you put her?"

"My room."

Rafael smirks at the same time Father sputters, his mouth falling open. "You put the snake right in your room? Son, have I taught you *nothing*?"

"She won't go anywhere." Not if she knows what's best for her.

Mother casts dark eyes toward her husband. "Like father, like son. Enzo, he's clearly learned more from you than you believe." Her dry tone is tinged with amusement at the memory of their own past.

Throughout their back and forth, my mind's been running, trying to come up with a plan that will benefit us all in the end. One in which Della can walk away free with her sister, and we get De Falco's head on a plate.

"De Falco went into hiding," I start, "but we need to draw him out. Della is the only opportunity we have, since we have no idea where his own daughters are." My soldiers have been outside their property for days, since I woke up, but no one's spotted any De Falco there.

"I doubt he cares for her," Rafael muses, his head tilting to the side. "After all, he offered her up as bait."

"He's scrambling though. Desperate. He had me in hand but lost, and if he truly despises us that much, he won't forgo another opportunity to retaliate. If he believes Della's willing to help him—if we stretch the truth a little bit, that I want her dead and she's seeking safety—he might."

Mother's expression pinches as she shares a similar expression with Father. "That's risky, Nico. De Falco might not be the wisest, but he's not that dumb."

"No," Father agrees, his gaze locking on a place faraway, "but we have nothing else. Any opportunity is a chance we need to take."

"You need to get Della to agree," Rafael points out, his fingers cocked toward me.

"Leave that to me," I tell them. "Della's a runner. It'll take little effort to convince her. For now, find me anything you can on the accident that killed her mother."

"On it," Rafael chimes. He glances back at Rosen and tips his head to the door. "Rosen, help me. Your skills are needed."

I stand, silently dismissing my family as I stride by all of them, heading for the door.

"What will you be doing?" My father calls after me.

"I'm going to talk to her sister."

34
DELLA

He's a fucking liar.

He told me food would be sent up. I have no way of tracking the time, but it's definitely been more than a few minutes. There's nothing to do in this room other than lie in the centre of his ridiculously comfortable bed and stare at the ceiling and imagine that I'm here for better reasons.

By the time I hear the door open, I don't bother to sit up. Instead, I roll my head to the side until I have the door in sight.

Nico enters, bracing a food tray in one hand and shutting the door with the other. He glances up as he enters and I notice how different he seems than when he left me earlier. More... tired. The skin between his eyes is wrinkled, his eyes slightly unfocused even as they look toward the bed.

I sit up slowly as he approaches and silently rests the tray on the bed. I try not to salivate over the crispy BLT, but considering I spent two days only slurping the soup they brought to the basement, a sandwich is heaven-sent.

"Hi," I say finally to break the rigidness in the air.

Still wordless, he pushes the tray toward me.

"Finally." I roll my eyes, trying to egg him into saying something.

Instead, he simply watches on and motions to the tray again.

Got it. Eat. Maybe then, he'll remember how to talk.

I lift the crispy bread and sink my teeth into it, taking the largest, un-ladylike bite possible, moaning as I chew the fresh, crisp lettuce, hot bacon, and juicy tomato.

I take another mouthful before mumbling, "Gonna sit at some point or just going to stand there and watch me eat like a creeper?"

Finally, I seem to snap something in him and find at least a fraction of the old Nico. With two fingers, he tilts my face up. "Is it so bad to enjoy taking care of you?"

Butterflies take flight in my stomach, soaring straight into my throat, making it impossible to formulate a proper response.

"If you really want to show your gratitude, I need to know where your sister is located."

Of. Fucking. Course.

As fast as those butterflies flew, they now die, dropping like a massive weight to the base of my stomach. "That's not happening."

I place the rest of the sandwich back onto the plate and roll from the bed, getting to my feet, an uncomfortable energy struggling to allow me to say put.

"Is that what all this is?" I gesture to the bed, then the bathroom. "The shower. Letting me stay here. Food. It's a bribe?"

His jaw tics, but in a deadly calm voice he replies, "You realize how easy my men can track down her location, right? Ariella Lambert wouldn't be hard to find. Yet, I'm here, asking you instead."

"Demanding, you mean."

Nico shrugs a shoulder, hardly blinking at the obvious difference. "See it how you wish to. I'm here on an act of goodwill."

"No." Not even a question. Ariella will *not* be dragged into this. "No, Nico. Kill me if you must, but do not look for her. She has nothing to do with this. You fucking promised me already."

"And I keep my promises." His hand lifts, making an X over his heart. *"Unisciti a leale. Muori leale.* You know I don't take those words lightly. I'm still honouring my earlier agreement."

For as much as Nico might falsify a lot, he won't go against his oaths. My muscles untense by a fraction. "Why do you want to know?"

"She might have information I need."

That wasn't what I expected. What could Ariella know that I wouldn't?

"Like what?"

"I can't yet say, in case I'm wrong."

He seems honest, but these words are nearly impossible to speak. To allow Nico inside that part of my life completely, opens me up and leaves me vulnerable. What if this is some giant ploy and he'll use her against me, the same way Stefano has been?

I think I need to trust him though because, for all his threats, he hasn't harmed me. I touch my throat. Well, not in a lasting way anyway.

Shoving aside years of self-preservation, I sigh so heavy, I feel the breath travel to my feet. "She's in the Douglas Mental Health University Institute. It's located on LaSalle Boulevard. Front desk has only cleared Stefano and me to visit." Not that Stefano ever has.

"It won't be an issue." Nico crosses the room and tilts my

face again, looking deep into my eyes. "I won't hurt her, Della. I only need to ask her a few questions."

Before I can fully comprehend what's happening, he swoops down and takes my mouth in a simple but longing kiss.

Then he's gone. The interaction leaves my stomach in a weird state that doesn't allow for any more food, so I move the tray to the floor by the door before returning to the bed to continue my previous activity of doing nothing. Only now, instead of wondering about my own life, I'm focused on Nico's bizarre behaviour and wondering what he possibly could need to speak to Ariella about.

In the midst of imagining their conversation, the door opens again and I shoot straight to my feet. There's no way he's back already, considering he only left minutes ago. Or am I losing it and hours have passed?

It's not Nico. Rather, a woman who shares many of his features, including that impassive expression as she studies me. Compared to her immaculate pantsuit and mile-high heels, I'm nearly naked in only one of her son's shirts. The differences are striking and as she pads over the thick carpet toward me, I try to tug the shirt down as far as possible, even folding my legs in a way to have less of my thighs revealed.

"Della," she greets with a perfect smile. "Lovely to meet you, considering how quickly my son dragged you from the office the other day when my husband and I arrived to speak with him. My name is Caterina Corsetti."

Is she seeking an apology? I don't reply.

Her knowing eyes scan the bed before painted lips curl in a half-smile and she slowly shakes her head. "He's exactly like his father, you know. Well," she pauses, her smirk expanding, "I guess there are differences. When his father locked me up, he cuffed me to his bed, but Nico has left you free."

I have no idea what she's talking about, but I do say, "Seems like you got the better outlook then since I was cuffed to a chair that's seen more blood than I have in my body."

Her lips twitch. "Hm. My son was right about you."

Instead of explaining, she gives me her back, slowly pacing toward the far window.

I scramble from the bed to stand, following for a single step before halting myself from going farther. "What did he say?"

"It's what he didn't say that was so loud, my dear." Facing the window, she pushes her hands into her pockets and continues, "He told us what you did and why. You're a fighter. You never back down."

Is this going somewhere pleasant or has she come to do what Nico couldn't?

Midnight hair flies around her shoulders as she peeks behind her and winks. "It's a good quality, Della. Very admirable."

This doesn't seem to be going south, so I stroll a few paces forward and ask, "You don't hate me?"

"Maybe if I lost my son I would, but I see this as an opportunity." Caterina faces the window again, only this time, I'm close enough to catch the glint in her eyes through the reflection. "You do what you must for family, Della. Not enough people would do what you had."

"She's my sister," I argue, the urge to shout tampered only by the unrest running through my body.

"Precisely. Like I said, I respect the decisions you made. It's a part of this life unfortunately. Women in crime families don't always get the happily-ever-afters we once dreamed of. We're not Cinderella, who married the prince after a single night, or even Sleeping Beauty, who was saved by the first man she met."

"You don't feel you have a happy ending?"

She spins again, facing me and leaning against the glass. "Oh, I do, but it wasn't instant. Fairy tales depict the prince only being the good guy, but sometimes, it's the villain who becomes that for us. My younger sister once made a point to me before I wed Lorenzo, and even all these years later, I constantly hear her in my mind. 'Princes might not exist in this life, but what if you can make him into one?' Sometimes we must take what we have and learn to love it."

Where is she going with this? "I'm not like you though. I'm not a woman from a crime family. I'm not Stefano's biological child."

She stares at me for a beat, her tongue skirting beneath her front lip. "Hm," she finally responds. "Aren't you though? You might be De Falco's daughter by marriage, but that union has made you one of us. Traditionally, that's how all our connections occur in this life—through marriage. You might not have been the one to say 'I do,' but you were connected to this life regardless."

I guess. "Does it matter though? I don't get the point in all this. Just because I'm one of you, as you claim, when it comes down to it, Nico won't care."

She snorts, and it's an action I wouldn't put with a woman who appears so immaculate. "My son will come to realize what you both already feel."

What I feel? "Excuse me?"

She winks and pushes off the glass, striding by me without another look in my direction. "Good luck, Della. I hope we get to have another conversation like this in the future. I have faith you'll make it through. Nico's a determined man, who needs a resilient woman by his side, not some simpering girl, no matter what my husband says."

"Wait—what?"

The door opens and closes quickly and she's gone through

it, exiting in a silent way, exactly how Nico had earlier. It's tempting to chase after her and demand a further explanation of her odd statements, but I almost don't want to know the answer.

Instead, I spend the remainder of my time alone, analyzing her words.

35
NICO

It's amusing for Della to think I wouldn't be able to get through the front doors of the medical centre, since I'm not cleared for visitation. Money talks, but more so, my name does. The entire city bows to me, so it's with little battle I get past the front desk and head for Ariella's room.

A doctor struggles to keep up with my long strides. They were very insistent to send a medical professional into the room with me. Something about their duty to protect and ensure I don't do Ariella more harm than good.

Whatever. I suspect if Ariella's willing to talk with me, this doctor won't be hanging around for long.

I knock on the door indicated by the front desk and wait, listening for the footsteps on the other side. The door swings open, revealing a woman who shares many of Della's features, except the most striking difference is Ariella's bold red hair, tied up in a messy bun.

Identical blue eyes flick up and down my form and the only sign of her surprise is her eyes, which widen in the smallest fraction. She maintains a great poker face though and steps aside, allowing the wolf straight into her den.

Interesting.

I step inside and the doctor follows me right in, shutting the door behind us. She positions herself against the door and very pointedly stares at me, but I pay her no heed as I scan the small hospital room.

They've allowed her to make it her own, with decorations on the wall and a standard bed. A TV sits on a stand at the end of the bed, and in the far corner, by the large window showing a large grassy lawn, is a small table set. Stacks of notebooks sit on it with a few pencils. On top, a music book. I study some of the décor, noting they're song lyrics.

"Hello, Ariella. Please sit and I'll explain who I am."

Undoing the buttons of my coat, I drop into the small chair, hoisting one leg over the other, looking like a picture of ease meant to calm her. Not that she conveys if she's nervous.

Ariella's brows lift a fraction, but she follows my request and takes the opposite chair.

I manage a pleasant smile. "Thanks. My name is Nico. I'm a friend of your sister and I'm here on behalf of her. She's okay," I rush to add, realizing how differently Ariella could take that statement. "She's told me about your diagnosis and I don't expect you to verbally respond, but I do hope you can answer a few questions about your stepfather."

The smile growing at the mention of her sister instantly fades as she stiffens right up, her eyes darting to the doctor and back. After a moment, she jerks her chin toward the doctor.

The woman obviously understands what that means, since her mouth opens and shuts a few times before she gives up and in a snappy tone says, "I'll be right outside this door." I think it's more of a warning for me, but I pay her no attention. As expected, the mention of De Falco entices Ariella's responses. This is positive.

"Two years ago, your mother married him," I recite facts. "Then last year...I'm sorry for your loss, Ariella. I can't imagine how it feels to lose a parent, especially how you did."

Her eyes flit outside and it's the only sign she gives that this conversation bothers her.

"Did you like that new life as a De Falco?"

Ariella lifts to her feet and paces to a nightstand beside her bed. There she retrieves a small whiteboard and blue marker before returning to the table. She rests it on the table and uncaps the pen.

This is more progress than I believed I'd get, considering who her sister is; I expected their similarities to include a fantastic skill of evading answering.

She doesn't write anything though, instead reaching behind her and grasping a book from the window ledge. She lays it in front of me and opens the front flap. Pages and pages of photos stare back at me.

The first one has two young children smiling into the camera. Ariella and Della presumably. She flips the page quickly, but I lock that image in my head. Ariella continues turning pages until finally stopping and twisting the book around, so I can view it properly. She points to a few particular photos on the page.

Wedding pictures.

A much older version of Della and Ariella stands front and centre, smiling into the camera, dressed in a puffy white dress. At her side is De Falco, and the sight of him has my blood boiling.

Ariella then points to another photo. Again, the wedding couple stands in the middle, but this time, four others are at their sides. Beside De Falco are his daughters, teenagers at the time this was taken. Beside the woman are younger versions of her daughters.

Della's hair is in flawless curls and her pink bridesmaid dress clings to her form. She's smiling into the camera, so blindly unaware of what will become of her life soon.

Beside her is Ariella. Her red hair hangs freely around her body, a contrast to the grass-green dress she wears. Unlike Della's bright smile, Ariella's expression is flat. Her eyes, hard and locked on the man at her mother's side.

I glance up toward the real version seated across from me. Already, she's jotting on the whiteboard.

Stefano isn't a good man. I knew it back then. I asked Mom not to marry him. So no, I didn't like my new life.

"She didn't listen."

Ariella nods, her eyes partially rolling in agreement.

"Did you know who he was? His family?" I ask, gauging her knowledge.

Yes. I also know who you are. Corsetti. You're a dangerous man.

"Yet you wanted to be alone with me." I tip my head toward the door, indicating the doctor she kicked out.

I don't want others to hear our conversation. This remains between us.

"I agree. I won't hurt you," I add, aiming for a bit of reassurance.

I know. You're not like Stefano.

"We're from the same lifestyle though."
Her lips purse briefly and writes,

But you're not the same.

Interesting. I think this is going where I half-expected it to.
"Can you explain?"

She turns the board around to face her again. Instead of writing though, her arm freezes, the marker balanced between her fingers. She stares at it, unmoving, until finally her rough swallow is the only sign she's still present.

I wait. Even as impatience begins eating at me and I drop my leg back to the floor, readjusting two more times as my eyes drill into that whiteboard, willing her to begin writing.

Then she lays the marker down and I open my mouth to protest and—

"Ke—" She swallows, wetting her lips, and I go still, trying to not push her. "Keep—" She stops again, her jaw clenching as she breathes sharply. "Keep my sister safe."

Words spoken so softly, practically whispered. Raspy through a voice not used nearly enough, stuttered with the struggle to push through her condition. I'd miss her talking if I wasn't on the literal edge of my seat, attuned to everything.

"You're talking."

Ariella shuts her eyes briefly, taking in a sharp inhale. She swallows again twice, before opening her eyes—identical to the look Della gives me.

"If you're here, it's gotten bad." She pauses, her gaze sliding to the window, becoming shadowed with the past. "From the beginning, something felt off about Stefano. Keep Della safe. That's all I ask. I know what she's been enduring for me."

Being in this life means liars are frequent, and I've gotten skilled at picking them out. Just like how I knew there was more to Della, there's more to what Ariella's saying. It's in her eyes. The stillness in her form as she speaks.

"What else do you know, Ariella? There's something else you're not saying."

"You get my words today, Nico, for her. Please protect her."

Leaning forward, my tone drops to near desperation, hoping she'll admit what she's hiding. "Why? What am I protecting her from?"

Ariella meets my eyes and shrugs, her lips pressing together, still remaining silent. There's more to Ariella and Della's past though, and I vow to discover it. If not from Ariella, then I'll find De Falco and will get the truth, even if I need to pry it from him one letter at a time.

I've put Rafael on the task of learning as much about their mother's accident, and it's Ariella's silence that tells me I'm on the right path.

Deeming the conversation over, Ariella takes both the whiteboard and photobook from the table and replaces them on the shelf. She tucks in her chair and then pointedly looks toward the door.

Goodbye, she silently says.

Only this is just the beginning.

36
DELLA

By the time I feel Nico slide into bed behind me, the sun has long dipped and made way for the moon, which has been my companion as I've lain here all night, gazing out the large window. His muscled arm wraps around my waist and he yanks me to his bare chest. I shouldn't enjoy the feeling of his tender touch as much as I do, since so much is still unknown, but I sigh, easing my body into his.

He fists the material of his shirt I'm wearing. "Why are you still dressed?"

"You told me to."

"Well, now I'm telling you to remove it."

Instead of giving me the space to do it myself, he grasps the neck and rips the shirt down the centre, pushing the sides over my shoulders without breaking his hold on me. Soft lips trail the length of my neck, while his warm hands cup my breasts, fingers strumming my nipples.

He rocks into my back, pushing his already hard cock into me. I move my body against his, getting swept up into the physical emotions he entices from me.

"I want you, Della, and you're going to allow me inside your pretty pussy."

"Yes." *Without question too because I'm an idiot.*

My legs widen and I prop one over his hip. He turns my head, taking my lips in a rough kiss as his fingers stroke my pussy, silently requesting my body to accept him. His tongue spears my mouth at the same time his fingers slip inside me.

"But first," he murmurs against my lips, "I'm fucking famished because I've missed supper."

He rolls us both, taking me with him as he readjusts on his back. Instead of facing him though, he flips me until I'm poised on my knees, one on either side of his body. He backs me up until the fervour of his breaths blows over my dripping pussy, inches from his mouth. His own cock stands in front of my face, begging me to touch it.

But...like this?

"Take me in your mouth, *petite souris*. Prepare me for your needy pussy while I eat my dinner."

At the same time? I have to suck him through the mind-numbing pleasure I know he's about to deliver?

Large hands encompass my thighs, and with strength my own can't compete with, he shoves me down until his tongue spears my pussy. I fist the sheets beside his legs, the pleasure almost instantly coursing through my insides.

I manage to circle the base of his cock with my hand, and reaching forward, wrap my lips around him tightly, sinking down to take him inside me a few inches. I've never had my mouth on a man before, and I don't really know how to tell him that, especially now. My lips stretch wide to accommodate him, but once the head of his cock hits the back of my throat, and I gag, I have to pull back a few inches.

But precisely when the shame hits me, when the anxiety I'm

doing this wrong becomes prevalent, he groans, his teeth nipping my sensitive clit in response.

"Good girl. Your mouth feels nearly as good as your cunt."

Using the momentary break, I release him and admit, "I've never...done...this." It's easy to confess when I can't see his face.

I feel him still beneath me. His legs go stiff for a second before relaxing again.

"You're doing great, Della. One day soon, I'll relish in teaching you, but for now, simply explore. You won't do anything wrong."

Ending the conversation, his mouth covers my core, his tongue dipping back inside. Keeping my lips tight, I take him into my mouth, again getting him as far down as I can before my gag reflex kicks in and I drag my mouth up. I do this a few times, and while I don't know if I'm doing it correctly, I also recognize I'm not doing it wrong, based on his reactions.

Every time my lips slide down his length, he pinches my clit with his teeth, making the pleasure near blinding. I rock my hips on his face as he moves in and out of me, both of us fucking each other in tandem.

"Use your tongue," he instructs into the skin of my leg.

At the same time? I suck him, noting how he takes up so much of my mouth, I don't see how I could possibly use my tongue too. Instead, I press it into his underside, giving it a flick right at the base of his head.

His responding groan is louder, so I do it again. And again.

And again, until my own orgasm rises to the top and working him and focusing on myself becomes an impossible task that neither my body nor my mind can handle.

"Nico, I'm going to..."

"Tell me what you need," he mumbles into my pussy, the motion of his words scraping his facial scruff against the sensitive skin there.

"To come."

"Do traitors get to come though?"

"They do if you wish to eat."

He chuckles, making a vibrating sound over my core. He covers me with his mouth again, and this time, when the orgasm rises to the top, he doesn't pull back. I swallow his cock, trying to remember everything he's already told me to do as pleasure wracks my body. My muscles quiver, my strength quickly diminishing.

Long after my hips stop rocking and the orgasm finishes pouring from me, he flips us over again until I'm on my back.

"Fucking delicious, Della. But I'm not quite done with you."

In a single thrust, he enters me. I cry into the room, the feeling of being so full, it's overwhelming. My insides are constricted tight from the recent orgasm.

"I shouldn't want this," he says suddenly. "I shouldn't want you. Show me how grateful you are to still be holding onto your life."

"You won't kill me. You would have done it by now."

The green of his eyes darken, nearly to the colour of a forest at nighttime. They glint, almost angry, before the darkness fades, flickering back into a bright light that is unable to deny the truth of my words.

He takes my jaw in his hand and claims my mouth in a harsh kiss as his hips hammer, driving his cock in and out of me at a speed I can't quite comprehend.

We're messy. We're an intensity I've never felt before.

Underboss and nobody.

Captor and captive.

Somewhere between my orgasm and our kiss, I realize I don't care how this ends. I don't care if my head ends up on his mantle or he throws me out of his house, because I have *this*—this memory to preserve.

Nico Corsetti in all his honesty, in all his benevolence. I found Nico Corsetti's unyielding heart.

"I'm going to come, my little whore, and you're going to take my cum. You're going to let me fill you up so you forever have a reminder of where I've been."

Forever.

"Yes."

His cock slams into me a final time before my insides are consumed with a claiming warmth. His head drops into the curve of my neck, his teeth scraping the skin there as his thrusts slow.

Eventually, his cock slides from my sated body and he pulls my face to his. I expect fire—because that's how it frequently is with Nico—but I get gentle instead. After a long moment, he releases me altogether and rolls to his side of the bed, swiping a hand harshly down his face.

He remains upright, his legs bent and his arms dangling over them. His expression in some form of mental torture he isn't sharing with me. After using the bathroom, I return to find him in the same position.

Nico seems to have ended the ability to be civil, for he doesn't even glance at me. I roll over and give him my back, tucking the pillow beneath my head.

Long after I've shut my eyes, but still while sleep hasn't claimed me, I hear him murmur, "Why can't I help but be obsessed with you, Della? Whether or not I empathize, and even forgive your previous transgressions, where do we go from here? Where *could* we go?"

He must assume I'm asleep because I don't think he's talking to me. What he's saying seems too private.

"I don't even know what I'm saying. You're fucking danger-

THE HUNT IN ELUSION

ous. I'm in the middle of needing to get you out of my life forever and restraining you to my bed until you give me your complete submission."

After Stefano, I told myself I would never submit to a man again. I would never let anyone else control me and my life. *I would always be in charge of my own destiny.*

But with Nico...I think it's different.

37
NICO

When the morning sun threatens to pierce through the curtain, I get up, leaving Della curled up asleep in my bed. She looks at peace and so comfortable in my bed, and I dislike the feeling in my chest that it gives me.

After getting dressed for the day, I head back to her side of the bed and fix the blanket, so her entire shoulder is covered. She rolls deeper into the pillow, her mouth falling open a fraction.

Della will help me lure De Falco out of hiding and then she can be free.

And I can forget about her because I have a family to run, and if Father gets his way, a marriage soon as well.

Marriage. A bride. A woman who'll sleep in the exact spot Della is right now. A boring, simpering, trained princess from this lifestyle, who'll attempt to be the "perfect" mafia wife, rather than what I want. What I need. What I crave. What I consider as perfection.

Someone fiery, who'll challenge me at every turn. Someone

who wants to integrate into this life in ways more than simply spending money and hosting parties. Someone with a fucking personality behind her.

Someone like Della. Like *my* Della.

She's not yours.

Soon, she'll be the world's. She and Ariella, out there, finally unimpeded from their stepfather's influence.

Shaking every single one of those thoughts from my head, I leave the room, aware our newest guest will be arriving momentarily. Once settling her, I'll have all the ammo I'll need to convince Della of her final task.

At the bottom of the stairs, I find Rafael walking opposite from the foyer. He madly gestures behind him, blanching. "Um, excuse me, who is that fucking *goddess* who was just taken upstairs?"

"Oh, she's arrived early." I slap him on the chest in appreciation as I turn around to return to the second floor. "Excuse me, Raf."

He hurriedly rushes after me. "No, Nico, you don't get to leave without explaining yourself. Why is it, every time I turn around, a sexy woman is inside this house? Wait," his steps falter, "did Father finally do it? Is this the future Mrs. Corsetti?"

That name gives me pause, my hand tightening around the banister while I try to scrub it from my mind. "No," I reply, snippier than I mean to. "That would be Ariella. Della's sister."

At the top of the stairs, I approach the wing opposite of my own, where some of the other rooms are kept, including the one I've gifted to Ariella for the time being.

Rafael pushes into my back, still trying to garner my attention. "*That's* her sister? She's hot."

"And off-limits." My gaze cuts to him, to show him how serious I am. "Don't go there."

Rafael shrugs. "She entered looking a bit timid anyway. You know I like mine feistier."

I roll my eyes, thankful for that much at least. Rafael wouldn't be able to handle a woman who won't respond to him. She'd break him within the week.

He continues following me as I stop in front of the room I've instructed the staff to put her in. The door is open, the morning sun pouring through from the window opposite of us. The glow catches in the red of Ariella's hair, making it more striking, as she stands by the bed, rooting through an open suitcase.

I knock lightly to announce my arrival before possibly frightening her. "Feel free to unpack, Ariella. Welcome to my home."

She glances up, showing no sign of any disquiet. She gives me a curt nod, before returning to her task. Instead of hanging around, I back away, letting her have her peace, wondering when the last time she was inside a regular house was. Has De Falco ever brought her home for holidays, or will this be the first time in a year Della's gotten to live with her sister? I get the sense De Falco wouldn't have done anything kind for them, if it didn't advance his motives in any way.

"Talkative," Rafael remarks as he trails behind me.

"She's mute," I explain, keeping my voice low so she doesn't hear.

"Ah." He lifts his hands in a submissive sign. "Yeah, she's safe then. You know I prefer my women loud, if you know what I mean." He waggles his brows as he reaches the top of the staircase.

Before he can take a step though, I call after him, "Any leads on the accident?" I need the certainty. Both Lambert siblings deserve the complete truth concerning their mother's death.

"None." Previous amusement melts away for a flat, determined expression. "It's buried well, but we're looking."

"Thanks."

I stalk down the hallway and return to my bedroom to wake my sleeping captive. With Ariella here, everything is in place.

I find Della in the same spot I left her earlier. She's sprawled on her stomach now, the blanket positioned halfway down her body. The slim stream of sunlight that peeks between the curtains slices across her back.

I approach, trailing the tips of my fingers up and down her spine, enticing her to gradually awaken. After a moment, she moves, rotating her shoulders and a sleeping gasp whips between her lips as she becomes more aware.

Grasping the blanket, I tug it down, my fingers chasing every inch of skin that is revealed. She moans, moving her hips in tandem with my touch, and spreads her legs when my fingers dip low between her ass, finding her sweet hole.

"Always so available for me," I murmur, stroking her clit and plunging my finger slightly inside her entrance. "No matter how much I hate you, your cunt can't deny my touch."

Into the pillow, she mumbles, "Seems like you don't hate me that much."

"Enjoying your pussy has nothing to do with my emotions toward you."

Gathering her juices, I shift my hand, pushing my fingers between the curve of her ass, finding that tight ring of muscle, which makes her stiffen, her head jerking up from the pillow.

"There are things in life we want but can't always get." I rotate her ring, teasing her, simply reminding her of how easy it'd be to take this part of her too. "Things we can steal but are so much more enjoyable once we work for it. What's something you want in life, Della?"

Pure set-up, and she responds with the very answer I expect

her to: "I want to be happy. I want a nice life for Ariella and me, like we had before Mom married Stefano. I want her to get the medical care she needs while being at home with me."

"And where's home?"

"Anywhere that isn't Stefano's house. Anywhere we can find a smidge of happiness."

I remove my hand from her ass, catching the moment her spine decompresses, and she untenses. Della rolls over, sitting up in the same motion.

"What if, with a little bit of hard work, I can promise you that? Freedom for you and your sister. No more fear. No more running. You and she can go wherever you want, do whatever you want."

I expect her to argue a little bit, to question my meaning, to even point out that I've essentially guaranteed her life.

Instead, without a beat, she demands, "What do you need?"

"Depends how far you'd go to get it."

"Anything," she breathes, a new hope lighting up her expression. She shifts onto her knees, her hands scrunching in the blankets, as though to conceal her true emotions from me.

Backing away, I gesture toward the closet. "Dress and we'll talk. I've had a few articles of clothing bought for you. I first want to show you how seriously I take my promises."

Della slides from the bed, but instead of going to the closet, she stops in front of me. "What happened yesterday when you went to see my sister?"

"Dress," I repeat, side-stepping her and walking toward the door. I position myself there, crossing my arms to wait her out.

She disappears into the closet for a couple of minutes before returning in jeans and a plain tee, and while she looks so *normal*, my sternum hurts, pained by how natural and stunning she is. As gorgeous as the first time I ever saw her, when she was adorned as a sinful princess meant to tempt me to my death.

Silently, I lead her from my bedroom, down the wing, and into the accompanying one, heading for the room I've placed Ariella in. Della glances at the other, empty rooms, false understanding brightening her expression.

"What's this? My own room? I'm honoured, Nico."

"Not happening," I reply, my voice graver than I mean it to be. Until she marches her luscious ass off my property, it'll be only my bed she sleeps in.

"Then what..." Her question trails off when I stop in front of Ariella's room.

Della stares past me, her mouth falling open in pure glee. Her body does this bouncy thing, an elated but impatient energy flinging her through the room and straight into her sister's arms.

Leaning on the doorframe with my arms crossed over my chest, I watch as the sisters reunite, wrapping their arms around one another. Della whoops, her face glowing red in her excitement as she pulls back but doesn't release Ariella. Her flustered happiness shoots a burning through my body, making my throat dry with impossible desires—to make Della this joyful all the time.

Seeing them has me wondering about Aurora's impending return in mere weeks. Will she be excited to be reunited with us, or will she be distant? Likely the latter, and I wouldn't blame her. No one would be able to approach a family who abandoned them with any sense of excitement or glee, only cold reservations.

"Oh my God, you're here!" Then with the blink of an eye, all that excitement catches up to Della, likely recalling where she is, and she repeats, "You're here." Her tone is sluggish as her gaze drifts back to me. Her eyes harden, her shoulders lowering a fraction. A mix of anger and pain flashes through her expression because she lightly coughs, clearing her throat, and releases her sister with a barely-there smile that doesn't meet her eyes.

Ariella glances at me with a pinched, apologetic look to which I shrug at. Della's reaction was expected, given the fierce protective feelings she holds for her sister.

Della stomps out of the room, grasping the knob on her way past the door and yanking it shut behind her. It slams with her exit, before she whirls on me, finger jabbing into my chest. She doesn't have the tough effect she's going for though.

"What the fuck is wrong with you, Corsetti? You said she wouldn't be harmed. Bringing her here, into the motherfucking crime world, is *not* keeping her safe."

Making a show of it, I glance at the finger she's prodding me with before swatting it away easily. The moment her contact breaks, I snatch the same wrist, lifting her arm above both our heads and backing her into the nearest wall. She goes without a fight, her focus not on the hold I have her in, but rather still on the person in the room beside us.

"I should be insulted, *petite souris*. This place is probably the safest for either of you. You think anyone can get by the men I have stationed here?"

"You know that's not what I meant." Her mouth flattens, her nose flaring with her deep, exasperated breath. "I kept her away from this life as much as I could and you brought her right into it."

"Sweetheart," I bare my teeth, leaning closer to her, "I didn't do fuck all. She's De Falco's stepdaughter, as you are, so put the blame elsewhere. *I* didn't bring her into this life because she's already fucking here."

In a smaller voice, she argues, "You took her away from her medical care."

I sigh heavily. "Once again, I should be hurt that you believe I would have so little consideration for her. The family's private doctor has received all her records, *with her consent*," I enforce, insisting on Ariella's agreement to her relocation here. "He will be seeing her until you—" *Until you leave.* I don't finish my sentence, instead asserting, "You continue to forget who's boss here, Della. I made a vow regarding her safety, and this is me keeping it. Do you honestly think she's in more danger here than that medical centre?"

"No," she finally concedes.

"Good." I drop her wrist but don't back away, continuing to keep her pinned to the wall with the force of my body. "You play with fire when it'd still be so easy for me to end this. There's a house full of people who'd love to see your head on a spike, but I've chosen to keep you alive out of generosity."

She levels her stare with mine, her brow hiking in defiance. "I'm alive because of your dick."

Ignoring the taunt, I return to previous subjects. "I did you a favour. 'Thank you' are the words you should be saying to me. Everything you did for De Falco was for her, and I've gotten her out of there and into a better place to live for now."

She narrows her eyes. "I could have done that. I have the money, remember?"

"Except you found yourself on the run."

"I'm still not free though, am I? Now, she isn't either."

Close but not quite, ma petite souris. "*She's* free. You're not. She's here, that way when you do what I need and release you, a step can be saved having to retrieve her."

"You're the fucking same then," she snaps. "You're Stefano two-point-oh, eh. Using my sister to bribe me into doing what you want?"

My hand twitches in need to show her all the ways I'm very different from De Falco, but comprehending the concept behind her words, I reply, "Yes. Same deal, Della. You help lure De Falco out and I'll send you and your sister on your way. An extra two million will be deposited in your bank. My jet will take you both anywhere you want to go. You can walk away and forget all about this. That's my offer."

"That or death, right? That's not much of a deal."

I shrug. "It's your reality so come to terms with it."

"And how am I supposed to, as you say, lure him out?"

I push away from the wall, breaking the spell bonding us together. "Speak with your sister," I instruct, "then come find me and we'll discuss the details."

I spin on my heel and stalk away. The future's in Della's hands now and I know the exact path she'll take to get there.

38
DELLA

When Nico disappears down the stairs and I feel as though I have some semblance of control on my sanity, I enter Ariella's new room. She glances up from her suitcase, and then peeks past my shoulder, presumably searching for Nico.

That pisses me off. Slamming the door behind me to ensure he doesn't encroach on my time with my sister, I grumble, "He's gone. You're safe."

Ariella rolls her eyes and shakes her head, silently berating me, telling me my assumptions were incorrect. She thinks she's safe here; she trusts him.

I've learned the hard way to never trust a made man. They all only crave one thing—to get ahead. Without the care of how they harm other lives.

"You don't know these people, Ari. They're worse than Stefano."

The lie makes my throat dry, the truth trying to push through. Nico is not worse than Stefano. They exist on different planes of humanity. But Ariella's protection is what matters most and if she believes they're not decent people, then she won't be getting comfortable here. With Nico's pending proposition, we won't be here for much longer anyway.

Ariella rolls her eyes again, but this time, opts to verbalize her disagreement too. "He's protecting you. He cares for you."

"Okay." My responding laugh comes straight from the base of my stomach. "Right. I'm sorry that the medical centre has sheltered you so much you see it like that. He hates me." Pausing, I add in a quieter voice, "For good reason though. I did something that could have nearly cost him his life, and now, I'm paying the price."

Ariella's brows lift, but they seem to be less in shock and more a reaction of doubt. "He doesn't hate you."

"Then look again. I betrayed him. Nico despises me for that. It's why I'm here. It's why you're here."

Ariella's lips purse and she glances away, toward the large window overlooking the back of the Corsetti property. In the distance, the forest Nico and I once spoke about in a moment of utter fantasy sits bright against the green grass.

"I'm here because he told me you and I would be going somewhere soon. Offered me a nicer place than the centre. Told me he'd protect me from Stefano. I've been there for so long," she sighs, "I said yes without question."

That's what he was counting on, I bet. Bring her here, dangle her in front of me, and force my hand.

"What did he tell you about Stefano?" I ask, mentally readying to murder him if he spoke out of line.

Ariella tips her head in her typical expression of thoughtfulness. She always does it when her mind goes elsewhere. It's one of her quirks that I love about her. Eventually, she blinks, returning to the present.

"Stefano isn't a good man, Della." She approaches the window, laying her hand over the glass as she continues to speak, talking more than I've heard from her in a long time. "Nico didn't say anything."

Her reflection in the glass shows a woman with soft, sad, heavy eyes. Eyes of someone carrying deep secrets.

"I know."

"You truly don't," she murmurs, nearly at a level I wouldn't be able to hear her. "One day you will though."

What does Ariella know that I don't? What did Stefano *do* to her? Murderous rage enflames every nerve in my body, forcing me to stalk toward her, the need to know too strong.

"Did he do something to you? Has he—what does that mean, Ari?"

She sighs heavier than earlier, and her entire body decompresses. Those sad eyes shift into pure exhaustion. Her hand lifts, her palm resting on the window, right over where her heart would be in the reflective version of herself.

"It's not worth your own emotional well-being to know. You've carried so much of the burden for me, Della, but this is mine to shoulder. Go to Nico. He's waiting on you."

That doesn't—

"Ari—"

Her hand swats the air, her silent *Go!* extremely loud. In the reflection, her eyes cast toward me, hardening. Determined.

I've kept many secrets from her over the years, and while the drive to know is so strong, I have to respect her decisions for now.

"I'll see you later then," I mumble and exit the room, more confused than ever.

Leisurely, I make my way toward Nico's office as I replay the conversation with Ariella over and over in my mind. So much of it doesn't make any sense. More questions pop up in my head, but the most discerning ones relate to the fact that she knows something. The same something I suspect I've tried to hide from her, to protect her from.

"You've carried so much of the burden for me, Della, but this is mine to shoulder."

Ariella, what does that mean?

Outside Nico's office, I pause at the booming voice coming through the thick, panelled door.

"Nico, you need to end this soon. The longer that girl remains here, unpunished, the more people will question your decisions. Alliances will be harder to obtain if other families see you as weak."

They're talking about me.

And alliances? Alliances with who?

Careful to not make any noise and signal my arrival, I press against the wall beside the door, listening for Nico's response.

"You were the one who created this problem, Father. Just like the Rossis, I'm trying to clean up your mess."

"Careful, boy," his father growls. "Do this quicker. Don't forget, your sister comes home soon and the threat of De Falco, accompanied with her re-entry into this life, won't make for an easy mix."

His sister? Nico and Rafael have another sibling?

"Aurora will be safe. Rosen is going to be her bodyguard until the wedding."

Wedding? What wedding?

"Well, that's something then," his father concedes. "That doesn't solve the issue of your own legacy though. When we first hosted the party, you requested time. That you had found a woman and were determined to seek her out again. You asked me to hold off any potential deals until you saw this through." He pauses, his voice lowering to a volume I must strain to hear. "Son, you have to admit it's time to move on. You found her again—or she found you; however, you wish to see this, but she's not who you thought."

Me. They must be talking about me.

Nico held off on making a union for himself until finding me?

A storm of unrest and jealousy battles within me, making my veins icy.

A giant pregnant pause fills the area and I hold my breath in case Nico replies and I miss it. But it's silent. Not even the sound of them shifting from beyond the door.

And then— "You're right, Father. Let me get Della out of here and I'll entertain any match you present. After all, it's what's best for this legacy. For the future. Securing the line to ensure we prosper many years more."

Weight drops into the base of my stomach. But it doesn't stop there. Oh, no—it rips through my stomach and smashes straight to my feet, and even through, making a giant hole in the ground I can only hope to be swallowed up in.

I don't know why this upsets me. Nico and I were fire and ice from the beginning. Not meant to survive each other. Not meant to burn the world together, nor freeze those in our path who'll do us harm.

We're nothing. A trick. A deception. The ultimate hunt for us both until one of us fell into the trap we each laid. Until one of us lost.

I still can't determine which one of us that was. In my game, I won, but in his, I've lost.

And, as fire and ice frequently do, we'll separate soon. Once Nico gives me the direction as to how I can earn my freedom, I'll do so and will be taking Ariella with me and disappearing from everything involving mob life. Then he can be free to continue his job, which sounds to involve producing children with the intent of continuing his criminal organization.

The door opens suddenly and I skitter back a few steps, feigning as though I'm just arriving. I toss my hand toward my chest in fake surprise as Lorenzo Corsetti trudges by me, his hard, knowing gaze glowering at me.

I press myself to the nearest wall, so he can have the maximum amount of space to get around me, and finally, once his back is to me, I hasten into Nico's office, seeing him as the safer option of the two.

"Close the door and come here."

I shut the door, but I remain by it, keeping my expression neutral when I give my own command. "So, let's get on with this thing. What's your grand plan?"

Shadows encompass his face, and even from a distance, I catch the moment he snaps. The second his jaw ticks and his teeth slam together. There's an air of authority around him, strengthened only by his powerful poise as he straightens in his chair, glowering at me.

Well, he can be angry all he wants. He's already made it beyond apparent that he's prepared to move past all this. Past me.

"Get over here, Della."

"Why should I? Tell me what you need to, so we can move on. You're ready to, and so am I. You obviously have weddings to plan and baby making to do." I don't mean for it to come out as petty as it does, and curse myself for hinting toward any jealousy I'm currently trying to taper down.

His tongue darts over his teeth once as realization breaks his glower. "You overheard the conversation I had with my father."

"He speaks loudly. It'd be impossible not to. You're all so ready to get rid of me, so let's make it happen. You have a future being mapped out. May as well get to it."

Nico stands, and while I expect him to command me to approach, he instead comes to me. His steps are controlled, a hunter's gait as he stalks forward. His lips curl in that delicious smirk I've come to love as he stops a mere inch in front of me, the toe of his shoes in line with mine.

"What if I'm not ready to be done with you quite yet? Then what? We can postpone this plan indefinitely."

"Your father will have me murdered by tomorrow if you hold off any longer. Besides," I sniff, lifting my chin a fraction, "*I'm* ready to get out of here, so why stall any longer than we have to? You want to see Stefano gone, and I'd love it if the fucker rots in hell."

"You're saying we can make magic together then." Nico places a hand on either side of my body, his behaviour shifting to indicate the double meaning in his words.

I press my palm into his chest, feeling his hardened planes. But it's safer to have distance between us.

"I'm saying, I've come to your office to hear your plan, exactly as you've instructed me to."

He grunts lightly, leaning down until his head is aligned with mine. His eyes flicker with a sense of playfulness that I turn my head against. He makes another noise, this one more appreciatively, and then he's kissing up the side of my neck, his lips and tongue making soft nips that I feel all over my body.

"You know what I think?" he murmurs into the skin behind my ear. "I think you're jealous. I think you dislike hearing that another woman will soon be replacing you in my bed. She'll be the one to wear my ring, to take my cock until I fill her up with the future heir. She'll be the one I hunt through the woods." He pauses, and it's in that three-second silence, my heart shatters with the thought of his fantasy played out with someone else. "She'll be my good girl."

Jealousy. A stupid concept, which is *exactly* what I feel. It tightens every muscle in my body, while igniting a flame inside my chest. The strength of it courses through my arms, giving me the force to slam both hands into his body, trying to throw him off me.

He shows no sign I've even touched him as he continues his emotional and mental onslaught. "She'll be who I kiss, *petite souris*. She'll be the one to take my cock down her throat and whose pussy I'll eat for dessert each night. And maybe," his voice lowers to the closest thing a human purring can sound like, "if you're good, I'll sometimes picture you in her place. When I have her on her knees, her cunt ready and dripping for me, you're who'll I'll picture sinking my cock into."

"Fuck off," I grit, shoving into him again. The burn of jealousy cools, leaving only nausea in its place.

"Admit it, Della. You want this to end. You want to move on. Say the words. Tell me how hearing all that makes you feel."

He wants the *truth*? After the emotional abuse he tossed my way, he believes he deserves to know how I feel?

Fuck him.

Fuck him because the truth slips out before logic can tie it down.

"Yes, okay, it fucking pisses me off. But this is what life is—a giant disappointment. You and I were never meant to be, so it doesn't matter. I was a con shoved in your face and you fell for it. You deserve someone who your parents pick out for you. So tell me your plan for Stefano so we can—"

I don't get an opportunity to finish.

He swallows my ramble with his lips.

39
NICO

This was supposed to be a straightforward conversation. Emotionless. Transactional.

But then she didn't obey me and I saw the crack in her exterior. A crack I'm determined to rip wide open until she gives me the final pieces of herself I've yet to claim.

I don't know why I'm bothering though. If Della's happy to walk away now, why am I digging for the emotions she's trying to hide after overhearing my conversation with Father?

My stance on a future bride still stands, but I said what I had to, to get him out of my office, aware Della would be arriving soon. I never would have thought it'd provide such an opportunity as this one.

After her admittance of jealousy, and when my own hunger is too great to ignore, I claim her mouth. I shouldn't though. We need to be following Della's advice to make a plan to deal with De Falco, so she can get on with her life.

I shouldn't be kissing her.

My hands shouldn't be going around her waist until I hoist her up, cupping her ass as I walk us toward my desk and deposit her on top. The hands that are clenched in my shirt don't release me right away, and I smirk, as once again, her actions do not align with her denying claims.

"Maybe I'll take my future wife right here on this desk for our first time."

Her kiss gets rougher, her teeth nipping my lip in anger. She grabs my shirt with one hand, while her other pushes against my shoulder. Her body is in the midst of its own battle to determine if she wants to hate me or fuck me.

While she continues her battle, my hands glide up the back of her shirt until shifting to the front, cupping her full breasts in my palms. I tug down the cups of her bra until her pointed nipples are revealed.

"Maybe I'll lick her nipples until she comes."

I shouldn't be teasing her in such a way, but her responses are too addicting to ignore. She continues to balance her jealousy with the pain my words bring her. I see it in her gaze, no matter how many times she looks away and fights the urge to reveal those parts of her. I'm hurting her.

Maybe it's self-sabotage, but that's why I'm doing it. If Della hates me, she'll leave without looking back, giving both her and me the break we'll need after this. I know without a doubt, no woman will be what Della is for me, but that's the reality of what's happened.

She wants out.

And I want her to have it.

"You're an asshole," she murmurs against my lips. Her back arches into my touch.

As fucking much as I'm dying to give her what she craves one last time, since this might be our final chance, I release her, returning my hands back to my side and stepping from between her legs.

Heartbreak ripples over her expression, and before I turn

away I catch how her hands lift from the desk, reaching for me, before quickly falling back to her side.

"What's De Falco's biggest weakness?" I ask, turning until my back is to her.

"His paranoia."

Close. "His pride," I counter. "I learned why De Falco hates my family so much, and it goes right back to my parents. Disloyalty is certainly a theme with him."

"What happened?"

"Doesn't matter. He's been planning to come for my family for some time, it seems, and although he's had his shot, I doubt he'd turn down an opportunity to try again."

I hear her slide from the desk. She scoffs, enticing me to face her again. "So, what? You want to repeat what we've already gone through? He's not the wisest, but he's also not an idiot."

Ignoring her opinions, I explain, "De Falco will jump at a chance to get me in his grasp again. His mansion is empty, and you've been on the run. You will return home. You will contact him, wait him out, whatever it takes. You will pretend to fear the threat I bring to you. You will present an offer to him: that you wish to return to his side and take me down. He will come home, or direct you to him, and my men will attack on sight."

Her brows scrunch and she barks out a single laugh. "That's the stupidest plan I've ever heard. Stefano will not believe I want to return to him. Even *if* he does, do you not think he'd find it suspicious? Or worse, he'll deny me because I'm of no use to him now. The ploy's up; you know who I am."

Crossing my arms, my expression replicates her own. "What's it matter? You do this and you're free, regardless of whether or not I succeed."

She seems to contemplate that with pursed lips and a narrowed gaze before shrugging one shoulder. "True. Your funeral, I guess." She turns, heading for the door, deeming this conversation over. Her ass shakes as she walks, and I bite down on my urge to throw her to the floor and claim it. "Can't believe you're an underboss of this organization and *that's* the best you come up with."

Maybe. But it's an opportunity. At this point, we have nothing, so an attempt is better than nothing.

At the door, she peeks over her shoulder. "Well. You coming? Sounds like we need to get started."

∾

Later, after the sun has gone down, a group of Rafael's regiment are gathered in the foyer of my home. Rafael is by my side, tucking his Glock into the waistband of his jeans. He grins, way too fucking excited by the prospect of this entire thing.

On my other side, Della stands, firm and unblinking as a circle of ten killers observe her. She's dressed the same, in jeans and a tee, only I've made her toss on one of my hoodies. Until I'm ready to send her inside, the hood will cover her form and identifiable blonde hair, in case anyone spots us encroaching on De Falco's grounds.

She watches me, waiting for my orders, as do the men. Some shift in spot, readjusting their weapons as they wait restlessly.

"Rafael, Rosen, Della, and I will be in the first vehicle." I nod to Rosen, where he stands directly across from me. "The rest of you in the other two. We will drive to the De Falco property lines, but will not approach. If he sees us all there, he will not return home. Hang back while we," I gesture to my mini-platoon, "deposit Della at the front door before hiding. Only approach when signalled. Understand?"

I scan the group, catching all their nods of agreement. Some rumble, the enthusiasm of potential kills making them eager.

Rosen strides past me and out the door, to where the SUVs wait. Rafael shoots a crooked smile at Della before following him out. Men stream all around us until it's only Della and me left in the house.

I grasp her hand, keeping her tight to my side for as long as I can, until it's time for me to release her.

"Let's go."

40
DELLA

It's curious how a house could seem so different now than what it was two weeks ago. Stefano's house—my home for a while—was familiar for a long time. Not exactly comfortable, but as safe as I could be. It was stable, even after Mom's death, as at the very least, it was where I laid my head to rest each night.

Now, as Rosen drives the SUV toward the De Falco mansion, it looks so different. Desolate. Cold. Nothing like the glorious castle Mom once sold this place off as being. As though even the memories of her walking the large property with Ariella and me at her side have disappeared with Stefano's absence.

I lean forward to get a better view as the vehicle drives forward. It puts my face by Nico's arm, where it's resting on the centre console from his spot in the passenger seat. Beside me, Rafael whistles.

"Not so impressive, is it?"

"No," I agree. Not like the Corsetti mansion.

The vehicle slows to a stop halfway down the long road

THE HUNT IN ELUSION

leading to the house. Rosen pulls over, shutting off the car, and the three men leap from the car at the same time. Nico yanks open the back door and reaches in for me, lifting me by my hips easily from the tall SUV.

Somewhere behind us, the rest of his men wait nearby for the call. I can't see where they've pulled over, and as I scan the property, I realize I can't see much of anything. The lights Stefano used to have lit have been shut off, basking the property in complete darkness.

"We're going on foot from here," Nico explains.

Rosen takes the lead, his gun poised in the air as he walks forward. His knees are slightly bent, his arms firm, ready to shoot if necessary. To my left, Rafael's in a similar position, his gun also out but angled toward the ground. His expression is grim, his eyes locked in the distance, squinting and searching. It's the most serious I've yet to see him be.

To my right, Nico has his gun partially poised. He stands closer to me than his brother though, and while he also keeps his attention up and toward the property, I catch him glancing at me every minute.

No one speaks. We walk at a hurried pace, with only the rocks underfoot giving our approach away.

When we finally arrive at the front door, my stomach is in my throat. Rafael and Rosen both pause on the step, letting Nico and me past, to the door. They stand guard on either side, guns up, scanning the area.

Nico pulls my phone from my pocket, where he was certain to tuck it earlier today. "He'll recognize your number and will more likely answer," he had explained.

He slides the cell between numb fingers. "Call him from this. Say what we talked about earlier. We'll be hiding nearby because he must think you're alone here. Try to get him to come here, since we'll have the advantage, but I'll also accept a location."

He stops talking and cups my cheek, his thumb caressing the skin beneath my eye. He presses a barely-there kiss to my forehead, his nearness giving me the opportunity to breathe in his scent. Firm emotions pass through his expression, but then he blinks, and it's gone.

Gripping the phone to my chest, I nod. One phone call. One conversation. Then this ends.

"All right."

Rosen tests the knob, his eyes darting to mine when finding it unlocked. My response is a shrug, since I have no answer to the question also swirling through my head. Why would Stefano leave his house unlocked?

Unless he's not planning on returning.

Rosen enters the house slowly, his gun darting in every direction, a flashlight I hadn't realized he had in his other, pointing to every corner in the dark house. It lights up part of the foyer only, the attached hallways still dark.

Rafael enters the house next and calls, "All clear."

Nico gestures for me to enter and I immediately go for the nearby wall, to the light switch I know that's there. The chandelier above turns on, bathing the foyer in light, and Rosen shuts the flashlight off, tucking it back into a pocket in his cargo pants. I study the staircase, leading to a dark upstairs, unable to see the details of the first-floor railing that allows for a view into the foyer. In fact, the chandelier makes it more difficult. I feel the need to go turn on every light in the house, but I don't plan on this taking long. In and out, ideally.

"This is where we leave you, Della." Nico signals something, and as fast as they all entered with me, they exit, leaving me alone.

Fuck. This place is...spooky. Haunting. Nothing like what

Mom first brought me to two years ago. A feeling of dread has me going cold as I reposition the phone and unlock it, fingers dialling the familiar number and tapping the camera option. Perhaps if he sees me in his house, he'll believe my words.

He won't answer. This will go south before it begins. Nico and his stupid pl—

"Stepdaughter."

Oh my God.

There are no words to describe the turbulent feeling of seeing the man who brought my life so much happiness. The man who accepted me, who I hoped would be a father for me, who laughed as I ran excitedly through these halls, amazed at my new bedroom, which was bigger than the old apartment I grew up in.

But with that happiness, there is also a sense of hell that now is indescribable. He forced my hand, made me get close to a person, who simply shares the last name of the people he feels wronged him once. He's a villain. He *used* my sister's condition to gain my submission.

This must work.

"Stefano." Steeling myself, I manage, "I'm home."

"Yes. I recognize my own house."

"I want to come back. To you."

His brows lift, his mouth twitching. "Is that so? The last impression you left me with said you were eager to be free of me. That was the point in all this, right?"

"I suppose what I thought I wanted and what I truly do is different." The longer this conversation goes on, the worse the nerves get, tightening around my heart and squeezing any courage from me. I must hang on though, and ensure he doesn't see through my lies. "Corsetti is dangerous, but I know where he is. He's after me, and I see now how stupid I was to leave you. Let me come home and we can finish this together."

Every word I speak, Stefano nods, as though accepting what I'm telling him. With every gesture of faith, a new layer of accomplishment shields the fear. But then the nods don't end when I've finished speaking.

And he smiles.

We've lost.

I recognize that smile. He doesn't give it frequently, but I know it. It's the smile he gave when learning I gained Nico's attention. The one he gave me when he said he'd fund Ariella's medical care.

It's his *I've won* grin.

The phone nearly slips from my hand, but I hold tight and firm, hoping I'm merely misreading the moment. Until he says otherwise, I'll continue the lies.

"Stefano—"

"Della, I've already beaten you."

The screen goes black.

Over the sound of my heartbeat—the sound of impenetrable fear—of utter terror for myself, for Ariella, for Nico, and for his family, I don't hear the steps until it's too late. When they emerge from the shadows of the nearby hallway.

A sharp point knicks into my back, right through Nico's thick sweater, cutting off my freedom. My life.

"Ni—"

A leather gloved hand slaps over my mouth, muffling the rest of my scream. "You're fucking dead, slut," an unfamiliar voice growls in my ear.

No! I hurl my body to the ground, trying to break his hold, but the man's other hand manages to hold me upright, his arm becoming an impenetrable band around my waist. The knife digs into my throat and I tilt my head, trying to keep the sharp blade away from my skin.

My half-scream was enough, and the front door crashes

open, Nico barreling through. His gun circles the area, until finding us in the middle of the foyer, and I don't recognize the man I see in front of me.

Death. An anger settles over him, darker than even when I left him in the basement to die. He levels the gun, his attention completely on the unknown man at my back. For the quickest second—I'd miss it if I wasn't so attuned to him—Nico glances at me. It's the little bit of ease, of comfort I need from him to make it through this moment.

"You shoot, I cut," the man threatens. "Don't test my speed, Corsetti."

In the same second, Rafael and Rosen appear behind Nico. Rafael angles his gun on the man, alongside his brother, but Rosen scans the dark areas of the house again. He moves past us slowly, heading for the staircase, and I want to yell after him not to. We missed this guy's presence, and if Stefano knew we were here, who else has he hidden throughout this place?

The man whistles, stopping Rosen in his tracks. "You honestly think Stefano only sent me? If any one of you move, the snipers will take you out."

I try to tip my head farther back, to get away from the blade and scan the dark upstairs, seeking the red light that will give the weapons away. Rosen pauses on the bottom step, his hands coming up in submission.

Nico hasn't looked away from the guy yet, but the frustration is becoming apparent. His arms get tenser. Muscles in his cheek twitch, and I long to reassure him.

"As for you—" The blade digs in a small fraction more, enough to spark a sharp gasp from me. "Stefano's changed his mind about your freedom, traitor. He's had me tracking you since the moment you left that basement."

From the side, a shadow moves. Death flies across the room, barrelling into me and the threat, knocking us both to the ground. Instinct drives me to my feet, skittering backwards and away from the fight breaking out.

Nico manages to get to his feet and has his gun drawn on my almost-kidnapper, the trigger pulled before anyone can take a second breath. The knife in the man's hand clangs to the ground with an easing noise of relief.

Except fucking war breaks out then.

Nico's murder activates a handful of men—of soldiers we didn't spot—who sprint down the stairs, shooting blindly into the dim lighting. More ring out from above, and my arms curl over my head, pulling my hood up too, as though it could provide any protection.

"Fuck!" I don't even know who shouted that. Maybe it was me. I can't know, as the terror, the threat of death, becomes more apparent than anything.

Rosen and Rafael circle me, shooting back at the men descending on us. I spot Rosen tap something on his shoulder, and I can only hope it's like in the movies and he's just called for all those backup soldiers. Nico rushes across the room again and shoves me to the door.

"Go, Della!"

He wants me to leave?

"Get out of here!"

I can't leave him. But I also can't fight. I have nothing.

"Retreat!" Rosen yells, pushing his body back into mine and forcing my feet to move. "Nico, we can't win. Not until backup arrives." He reaches for Rafael, grabbing him by his sweater, and somehow manages to shove him through the doorway with me.

Nico's back is to all of us, as gunshots continue to fly throughout the house. Measured steps slowly bring him toward us, and with every one, I feel my heart manage a whole other beat.

Rafael grasps my wrist and begins tugging me down the staircase, but it's in the final seconds—the new angle being one step down provides—that I catch it.

The sniper trained on Nico. The red light angled right at his chest.

I don't think.

Don't consider how I could also be killed.

I rip my sleeve away from Rafael, whose grip isn't firm enough to hold me. He yells out after me, but I get by him, past Rosen, who's shooting up toward the second floor, and throw myself right back into the house's darkness.

41
NICO

Very few things in life surprise me.

Della Lambert is the surprise I never saw coming.

When other women fawned over me, Della ran the opposite way.

When I had my enemies identified, Della became one too, unbeknownst to me.

When I believed her to be heartless, she was simply protecting her family.

And when her small, lithe body slams into me from behind, the suddenness of her actions is such a surprise, my muscles don't have the opportunity to lock themselves and prevent the fall.

I land on my side. The pain shooting up my arm becomes secondary to the realization Della is on top of me, wide open to be killed. At the same time, a bullet whizzes by, inches away from where I last stood.

Della saved me.

Wrapping my arms around her, the only thing on my mind

284

is keeping her safe and getting her out of here alive. I tuck her into my side and dart away as Rosen and Rafael cover us, distracting the shooters.

The moment my boot hits the front step, my soldiers are there. They attack the house as Rosen and Rafael follow behind me, and all four of us run into the evening night and back down the road.

~

I shut my bedroom door where I've left Della with her sister and Dr. Shappo, who's checking her injuries over. I can't count how many instances she could have been shot, and then there's the blade the fucker had at her throat.

Every time I blink, it's all I see. The fear in her large fucking, soulful eyes. The hope that it wasn't the last time she'd look at me with them.

The moment I heard her scream from outside of the house, the game changed. It wasn't about De Falco anymore. I placed Della in harm's way and almost paid the price of that stupid decision.

A knife. A blade. A fucking *four-inch* blade is what nearly took *ma petite souris* from me. If he reacted a second later, her throat could have been sliced, and I would be presently deep in DeFalco's guts as I rip them out in fucking repentance.

The need to be by her side and care for her, to make sure she's safe and uninjured, nearly takes me back to my room, but I still turn away, sticking to the original plan.

As soon as Della wishes to, she's free to go, past transgressions no longer mattering. Two million dollars was deposited the moment we pulled away from the house earlier. She did as I asked her to, even if we didn't succeed.

In my office, I find Rafael and Rosen both seated, nursing a bottle of scotch between them as they wait for my arrival to debrief. I snatch the third glass they pre-poured for me and down it in one gulp, dropping into my office chair. Exhaustion —mental, emotional, and physical—tears at my body, but this night isn't done yet and I feel like I might still have a mountain to climb.

I study the two men in front of me, both of whom I trust nearly more than anyone in my life. A bandage is wrapped around Rosen's arm in two places and Rafael looks unscathed, thankfully.

"You know she saved you, brother. That rifle was on you and the girl didn't even hesitate. Ripped from my hold and threw herself right into the line of fire."

I know. I certainly don't need him to remind me. Stefano De Falco has a lot to pay for, but nearly taking Della from me, not just once but twice, will make his death slow and painful.

As Underboss, I'm used to people trying to protect me. My soldiers protect me out of loyalty. My family out of love.

But Della?

"I know," I reply curtly.

My brother's eyebrows shoot into his hairline as I obviously don't grant him the response he was hoping for. "That's it? You have nothing else to say regarding the fact she nearly died protecting you?"

My jaws snap together. Hearing it detailed yet again is sending my mind into a slow agony.

Rosen speaks up. "She's a badass, boss. Mad respect after that. Actions speak louder than words, you know, and I'm pretty sure that woman just screamed."

I shoot a scathing glare his way. "Both of you leave. I'm not in the mood to do this now if you're only going to focus on that one fact."

They share a look before Rosen stands, taking his half-empty glass with him.

"Night," he calls out behind him.

My brother hangs back, waiting until Rosen closes the door behind him before asking, "And Della?"

"She's leaving. Tonight. Tomorrow. She's done."

He shakes his head, his expression pinched. "You're a fucking moron, brother."

When he finally leaves, an air of aggravation lingers, but I can't care about what he thinks. He doesn't realize how tedious this role is. How every step is so carefully monitored. How Della has made her wishes known, and I'm not it.

Moments after my brother leaves, the doorknob twists again. I reach for the nearest thing to me, which happens to be his empty glass, ready to chuck it at him if he's returned only to give me hell.

Instead of Rafael, it's the very woman who's weaseled her way into my head and refuses to leave, no matter how much anguish I toss at her.

She shuts the door behind her and pads toward me. Her neck has a small bandage on it and I refill my glass only to down that one too, to taper the hint of red creeping over my vision at the sight of her injury. She stops on the other side of my desk, wisely keeping the furniture between us.

"Figured you would be in here," she murmurs, her eyes flicking around my frame.

"How are you?"

"Alive, thanks to you."

"I can say the same." It comes out rougher than I mean it to. With the subject opened though, I can't ignore the fact she very nearly gave up her life for me. Slamming my glass onto the desk's surface with a *thud* neither of us pay attention to, I stand, pressing my hands into the wood as I lean closer to her. "You nearly got yourself killed today, Della."

Her lips part, her whisper almost silent. "You would have been shot. I couldn't watch you die."

Why? I must know her reasoning. I need to hear her *say* it— say the words I feel she will. I have to know, even if it changes nothing.

"Why?"

"Nico." She leans away, twisting her face, her hair blocking her from my view. "Nico, no."

No. It's more than a simple no though. *No, I won't tell you. No, because it'll change shit.* So many reasons for denying me.

"Della," I growl, a tenseness working through my shoulders.

She flicks her hair off her face and returns my look, the fierceness I love about her returning. "Same question for you then. You leapt right into the house, saving me, killing him."

"I couldn't watch you be harmed."

"Why?"

We end up in a stare-down, neither of us willing to fill in the gaps of what we both know but won't admit. Of the electricity sparking between us. Of the unspoken promises of more.

We can't keep doing this. This either ends *now* and she gets the fuck away from me before I refuse to ever let her go or...

Shoving away from the desk, I complete the precarious pace to the side, stopping inches from where she stands.

"I know why *I* did it, Della. I saved you because the thought of witnessing a single drop of your blood was more than my sanity could handle. Because even after *fucking everything*, you're all I see when I shut my eyes. All I smell. All I think about." I take a small step nearer, so small she doesn't realize I've done it. "I couldn't watch you die because I'd lose my fucking mind, slaughtering everyone around me until I had De Falco in my grip, so I could make him pay one drop of blood at a time. One scream at a time. Dragging it out to be the most excruciating pain he'll ever know. *That's* why." Another step. "So, tell me, Della, why did you do it?"

She gulps so loud, I can practically hear it. Her eyes cut to the side and back. To the floor and back. To my chest, to her hands, to anywhere but my eyes.

"We can't do this, Nico," she murmurs. "Our lives are so different. I betrayed you. Everyone hates me. We were thrown together after an unfortunate circumstance. We were two souls who never even should have been in the same room together. You have decisions to make to better your role here, and I'm not it."

I take another step, lining our bodies up together. Our hearts hammer against one another. When she tips her head up to look me in the eyes, our breaths mingle and heat, empowered by her unspoken words.

Ignoring her entire tirade, I demand again, "Why did you save me, Della?"

She shakes her head. "Nico..."

"Tell me."

"Nico." She shuts her eyes, her lips folding together with the deepest breath I've ever seen her take, and when she opens her eyes again, I spot the truth. The vulnerability in the ocean blue of her eyes. The fact she'll stop lying.

"Because some-fucking-how, despite every single reason I shouldn't, I've fallen so hard for you."

I smash my lips to hers, wrenching her body against mine. I feel her *everywhere*. Feel the moment she realizes she's lost.

That she's mine.

That I'm hers.

She pushes me away. "We can't though."

Okay, Della, let's play and for real this time.

I release her, backing away one step. Two. Three. Far

enough to ensure I can't grab onto her and cheat for the next part.

"Run."

She blinks, eyes blank, mind working to catch what I demanded. "What?"

"You think we can't be this, so run away. Get the fuck out of my house and far away. But," I pause, letting the weight of that word hang over her head before I grant her the rest, "if I catch you, that's it. You're mine and I'll never let you go."

She doesn't move. The hesitation tells me everything. She doesn't know what to do—listen to logic or to her heart—but it's too late to make this a civil debate. Her hesitation—her secret desires—have woken this part of me.

The need to hunt.

To chase.

To fuck.

Then, as if my own house is on my side, the clock rings.

Midnight.

How fitting.

The stakes have just increased.

"Tick, tock, *petite souris*. You have until the clock stops chiming to escape this house. If I catch you before the final strike..." I trail off, my earlier threat filling in the gap. *"Run."*

Della runs.

She flies out the door, slamming it shut behind her, as though that'll slow me down. I take a moment to roll up my sleeves as I slowly walk across the room. The more time she has to run away, the more confident she'll feel.

That's when she'll fuck up.

And when I catch her, I'll claim her pussy, her mind, and her fucking heart.

42
DELLA

ing dong!

    My feet take off before my mind does. Unknowns swirl around me as I throw myself from his office, slamming the door roughly behind me and bolting down the hall.

The unknown of where to go. Of what's happening. Of what will happen if he catches me. Of whether or not I *want* to get away. Of what letting him catch me will mean.

When I reach the end of the hallway, the crashing of his office door echoes far behind me.

Shit.

He's coming.

Arms, heart, and blood pumping, I turn the corner, knowing at the end is the front door. I can make it there with plenty of time to spare before the massive clock stops its midnight chimes.

Ding dong!

Freedom is *right there*.

One hallway. One sprint. One doorway.

That's all there is between freedom and me. From getting away from Nico.

Nico, who makes my heart physically hurt when I'm thinking about the fact I'm hurrying away, but I saw what he was actually telling me inside his office, and I know the realities of this life. Nico is an underboss with an important role here. His family would never allow him to be with an outsider, especially one who betrayed them all and nearly got him killed. Twice.

"*Petite souris.*"

Shit!

I push into a faster run, my legs eating up as much of the carpeted flooring as I can.

Ding dong!

Almost there...Then Nico will have to let me go and I can take Ariella away from here and it'll just be her and me and I can care for her.

I stop.

That's all I ever do. Care for others. Work for others. Run away when I need to feel safe. What would happen if I were to do something for myself? What if running away is the opposite of what I need? What happens if I listen to Nico and say fuck everything else?

What happens if I let my heart decide what it wants?

It wants Nico.

I think I need to find out and do this for myself.

I turn, doubling back, and heading for *the* hallway. The hallway he found me inside that first night. Nico won't think to check here because he'll assume I've left the house.

I make it to the hallway, hooking my hand around the corner as I dash down it, heading straight to the end, where the small greenhouse is located. I shove open the glass door, almost banging it into the house's side in my hurry. I dive into the garden, scanning the fountain, and then the greenery, searching for somewhere, anywhere, I can hide.

Ding dong!

When I spot a bush of the ideal size, I lunge toward it, falling on my hands and knees. The grass is cool from the night time chill and my breath comes out in short pants as I settle down and wait.

Ding dong!

The garden's door opens and shuts, announcing his arrival.

Ding dong!

"Petite souris."

Ding dong!

The chimes end.

It's over.

Who's won? I didn't get out of the house before the chimes finished, but he hasn't caught me either, because I changed the game in a way neither of us expected.

I stayed.

And if the game changed, it means the rules have too.

"Oh, Della, you really should have gotten away from me while you had the chance."

Prickles zip their way through my body, awakening every one of my senses. My ears pick up on the lowest of sounds as small pebbles roll out of the way as their boss walks through the space. The energy in the garden visibly shifts, taking either his or my side. My pussy clenches with awareness of how close he is, mere feet away. Like how a hunter can sense his prey, I, the prey, can sense the hunter. The danger he exudes. The fright he rouses in my nerves.

It'd be so simple to stand and allow him to take me right here, where it all began, but I'm not a quitter. My body might be silently begging for him to claim me this instant, but he and I are not finished yet. The game still must be won; the new, unspoken rules must be followed.

"We're past midnight. When I find you, you're fucking mine."

He doesn't sound like the Nico I've come to know. He's no longer in control of himself, no longer sane. He's animalistic. Wild. Free.

To my left, the other door leading to back of the house, stretching into the massive property with the forest beyond. *Perfect.*

I push to my feet, my hands helping propel me forward, and I take off into the darkness. I don't glance behind me. Don't think. Just run.

With a last-minute thought, I reach into my back pocket and take my phone, tossing it behind me. It'll likely break upon landing on the cement, but my point will be made.

Find me.

Nico curses and his feet pound after me, eating up much of the grass I've left behind. He'll catch me in a second with his current pace, but if he sees where I'm headed, he'll let the game conclude how we're both longing for it to.

I don't peek behind me, knowing the moment I do, I'll lose my way, and he'll be on me. Pumping my limbs as fast as I can, I'm now halfway to the forest.

"Scurry into the woods, *petite souris*. That's it. You forget who owns these lands."

It's getting more and more difficult to go on, my breathlessness feeling like my lungs are breaking. My sides burn, the need to stop and catch my breath, accompanied with the exhaustion from this emotionally draining day, slow me down exponentially, but I don't stop—won't stop—not for anything. If only to win. If only to show him, despite our history, I can give him what he wants. Me and only me. There's no one his family will propose that will be his equal.

Because if I take this leap, he must agree to follow me down.

Finally at the treeline, my hand hooks around a trunk as I make a sharp right, and then another right and another, then a left, twisting and weaving between the trees so fast, making my direction choices last-minute. Only when I feel like I've gotten far enough away, do I stop. Pausing behind a tree with my hand on my speeding heart, feeling the evidence of what Nico does to me.

Crack.

He's here.

Aware he'll likely hear me, I bolt, shoving away from the tree trunk and farther into the darkness. The trees are thicker here, and less and less moonlight streams though, meaning I've lost the advantage of sight.

"Oh, Della," he croons.

I freeze, trying to locate the direction of his voice. It echoes through the forest, being masked by gentle winds and flickering leaves.

Shit.

"Petite souris."

Shit! His voice is much closer now. It caresses over my skin, enticing me toward him, while the urge to continue running, to continue this game of chase, has me walking forward, eyes darting through the darkness, straining to pick up on any indicative shapes.

Crack!

I freeze. He's nearby...

I dash off. Darting through the woods, aware I'm no longer even trying to be quiet. My steps crack over the forest floor, praying to maintain my footing, so I don't end up breaking anything. I sprint as fast as I possibly can, hearing nothing indicative of him catching up to me.

A flash of moonlight casts over the forest floor, lighting up my next turn and—

My body flies forward as two arms wrap around my waist, flinging me over his shoulder, my ass in the air, which he sends a sharp swat to.

"Caught you."

"Nico!"

He stalks through the woods, and I'll admit, I'm quite disappointed that he's not taking me right on the forest floor.

"When I fuck you, when I claim you as mine, I want to see you come on my cock," he explains. "Which means today, I'm not taking you in the woods. I long to see what the moonlight on your skin looks like. The stars above, dimmer than the ones I'll be making you see."

"I can walk." I wiggle my legs, moving my body this way and that until he realizes how annoying I can be, to the point he'll place me on my feet.

A firm smack lands on my ass again, and I wiggle for an entirely different reason now, gasping as my pussy aches for relief. I squirm, trying to press his shoulder into that one particular part between my legs that'll give me what I need.

Instead, I'm thrown right way up again as Nico swings me to my back the moment we break from the woods and re-enter the moonlight. He pushes me down, climbing overtop me, his hard cock pressing into the base of my stomach through my pants.

Nico spreads my legs, yanking my jeans down my legs in the same action. Then he grabs the material of my shirt and rips it from the base to the collar, shoving the shirt halves aside. He reaches between my breasts and snaps the piece of my bra holding it all together, also discarding that article of clothing.

I expect my panties to follow, but instead, he lowers himself down my body, pressing his nose right between my legs, breathing in the scent of my pussy.

"You know what gave you away? How I found you so easily? The smell of this hot, aching pussy, calling to me." With only the use of his teeth, he takes the edge of my panties in his mouth.

Once again, I expect one thing—that he'll tug them down my legs—but his head jerks roughly to the side and—*Rip!*

"H-how?"

Nico lifts his head, my blue panties dangling from his teeth. Around the material, his mouth curls in a delicious smirk and he drops them on the ground beside my hip.

"Around me, your cunt will never be covered again. I want you always primed and ready to take me. To smell your cunt beckoning me at any time of the day."

"Yes," I hiss, because Nico makes me want to agree to anything.

His fingers swipe over my clit, making me whimper. He roughly forces my legs aside, shouldering himself between them. His nose tickles my core as he breathes me in.

"You can never escape again, Della. I have your scent memorized."

I don't want to.

His fingers push inside me. Two, which he pumps a few times, my pussy growing wetter with every thrust until I'm stretched and he's able to add a third.

"It's so...much..."

If there's any part of me still restrained, I release it to the sky. The moonlight encompasses my body, takes me over, brings me to a new level with Nico. My hands fist the grass, my head being thrown back and forth as a ravenous need climbs my throat.

"Nico..."

"What, baby?"

"I need..."

"What do you need?" His fingers curl inside me, pressing right on the button that makes me—

He straightens his fingers, pulling them out halfway. "Tell me, Della."

"I need to come, Nico."

His fingers flex again, this time harder, stronger, before easing them again. He leans over me, lining his face up with mine. "And you need to remember who you now belong to. Who controls you. Who allows you to come."

"Nico." It comes out wanting, lined with a heavy beg.

Nico leans over me, his fingers slowly pumping in and out of my core. He licks his way down my body, his teeth unforgiving as he lays claiming nips to my neck, my breasts, my stomach, pausing only when he's above my pussy. His bites don't hurt because my skin is made to take his claims.

"You're only allowed to come when I've had my taste. You teased me with this wet cunt, running through my halls, hiding in a garden, and your biggest error yet: believing you can evade a hunter in his own territory. It's only fair I get to eat what you've been offering."

"Yes." It ends on a hiss.

His tongue licks from my ass to my clit, taking his time to circle me once, twice, as his fingers, still inside me, continue their slow, agonizing pumps, drawing my orgasm out slowly. My hips rock with his, but he presses his free hand into my stomach, pinning me still.

"This won't be gentle," is the only warning I get, mumbled against my inner thigh.

His fingers hammer inside me, his tongue skating up and down my clit. The orgasm rises to the top, and it won't be held back this time. Not by him. Not by a command.

His teeth nip my clit at the same time he presses on my G-spot and I feel my insides constrict around his fingers, trying to bring him inside me. White spots rob my vision, pleasure wracking my every sense. His touch is all I feel. His breaths all I hear.

With a final lick, he pulls back, chuckling. "You have no fucking idea how striking you are right now, soaked in your desire, wrought out beneath the moonlight." Nico leans over me, pressing a rough kiss to my mouth. His tongue tangles with mine, sharing the taste he's drawn from me. "But I'm still starving. Get on your hands and knees."

43
NICO

I can't recall the last time I actually chased a woman like this. And not through my halls, as I had the first time I met Della, but a real chase. A hunt. A time for my inner beast to finally be unleashed how he craves. For him to stalk the woman he desires. To not be gentle.

Della obeys me without question, turning over, putting that perfect ass in the air as she repositions onto her hands and knees. I groan. I want to claim her there. Claim her *everywhere*.

I will. Tonight. By the end of this, she'll understand what it means to be mine.

I send a quick slap to her ass, revelling in how it blooms red with the impact before the colour fades, taunting me with the urge to do that again and again until the red becomes permanent.

"Play with yourself, Della. Show me how you fuck yourself."

Again, she obeys me, her hand going between her legs as she rubs that dripping pussy. I nearly dive for another taste, but I must be inside her soon before I go mad.

Besides, there's always later, or tomorrow, and the next day. I'll spend the rest of our lives savouring Della as dessert each night. I'll chain her to my fucking kitchen table until she comprehends that being mine means allowing me to eat whenever I'm hungry.

I strip my clothes, tossing them to the side. The midnight air washes over my body, energizing me beneath its light. I fist myself, rubbing the bead of precum on the head of my cock around as I observe Della stroking her slit, rocking on her own hand.

She peeks behind her shoulder, her eyes glowing bright when she sees I'm naked and ready. It's that look that does me in. Her own hunger, her own urges, begging me to satisfy them.

With my hand at the base of her neck, I shove her down until she's moaning into the cool grass. It puts her body at an angle with her ass in the air.

Nudging her hand away, I replace her fingers with my cock and plunge into her, thrusting unforgivingly. The beast inside me roars his approval as she cries into the ground, her nails scraping it as she does.

I'm taking her as mine. Marking her. Ensuring no one even *considers* harming an inch of her perfect body, knowing the price they'd pay as I wreak havoc in revenge would be too great and impossible to survive.

Fisting her hair, I arch her back, throwing her face to the stars as I push in all the way, her wet pussy taking my cock so easily, so greedily. I hammer roughly in and out of her, my own orgasm rising to the top much quicker than I'd prefer.

Her pussy milks me as she cries out, the sound becoming strained with the angle her throat is at. She comes, her orgasm soaking her pussy.

I reach between her legs, swiping my finger through the

evidence of desire before placing it between her ass, gently poking that tight ring of muscle.

"I'm going to put my finger in here, Della, and I promise, you'll love it."

Nerves in her shoulder stiffen, her arms going rigid.

"Just my finger," I reassure her. "One day, your ass will know the feel of my cock as well. There is not an inch of you I won't be owning.

My beautiful girl moans, her nerves loosening again. She doesn't try to end this. Simply accepts it—accepts me.

I pull my cock most of the way out of her until only my head is inside her. I gather more of her wetness onto my finger before finding the ring of muscle again and spreading it there. I circle the area, trying to ease her.

"Deep breath, Della."

She obeys, sucking in a gulp of the night air and releasing it after a long beat.

"Good girl."

My finger pushes through muscle at the same time I sink an inch back in her pussy. Gradually, I add more of my finger, and for every fraction her ass takes me, I reclaim her cunt too, trying to associate the sensations with each other, to ease any possible discomforts.

I want quick and animalistic, but with my finger in her ass for the first time, I refuse to hurt her or make her fear me in any way.

"You okay?"

"P-perfect," she pants, rocking her hips lightly, gasping as she moves herself over my finger. "Fucking perfect, Nico. So full."

That's all I needed to hear. I hammer in and out of her tight cunt, while keeping my finger in her other hole, letting her get accustomed to the sensation. I release her hair to send sharp slaps to her swollen clit. She gasps into the night air, her moans increasing in volume, uninhibited by the outdoors, where no one can hear her.

"You take me so well, Della," I praise her. But I also need to know: "Tell me..." I hike my breath, trying to hold enough air inside to finish my question, "tell me what you actually wanted to admit to me inside."

"T-that in the middle...of how fucked-up everything is...I love you."

Love.

"Say it again." I pump faster, feeling my orgasm right on the edge. My abs clench tight, pleasure working up and down my spine.

"I love you." She gasps, another orgasm quickly approaching. She'll hold off, so we can come together though.

"Again."

"I love you, Nico."

"Again."

"I fucking love you!" Her final word ends on a screech, as she bellows it into the air, her cry, her orgasm being swallowed up by nature.

As her pussy clenches around my cock, draining me, my cock jerks a final time, shoving my cum so far deep down inside her, she'll feel it tomorrow. I paint her insides white—my exact shade—so every fucker out there knows I'm the only one who'll own her cunt.

After a moment, her own energy subsides, and her arms and knees give out, her body slumping to the ground. The movement has my finger sliding from her ass, but still, I follow her down with my own body, lying on top of her and pressing her into the cool ground. Grasping her jaw, I force her head to the side, where I take her mouth in a claiming kiss.

"This is crazy," she whispers when I pull back. "What did we do, Nico?"

Doubt. Worry. It creeps up quickly, but I don't want her there.

Wrapping a hand around her thigh I lift it, sliding my hand between her legs, so I can pet her exhausted pussy. She's drenched, a mixture of her own desire and my cum dripping onto the grass. Gathering it, I push it back inside her.

"Can't let this get away. After all, how will people know who owns your pussy if my cum continues to fall out?"

"Nico," she says, her tone deepening with doubt again.

"When you didn't leave the house, you realize what you did, right?"

She lifts her head, jerking her chin toward the mansion across the yard. "Technically, I did. The moment I made it to the garden, I was outside, and the bells hadn't finished chiming by that point. You never said it had to be the front door."

Shit. She's right. Kind of.

"Well, you also never left my property."

"So we both lose?"

"No, Della."

I remove my hand from between her legs and help her stand, finding my shirt nearby and dressing her in it before slipping on my pants. It's a shame to cover up her skin that is decorated in my claiming nips, but if anyone catches us entering the house, at least her body will be concealed.

I take her hand and begin leading her across the yard, toward the mansion.

"No, Della," I start again. "We both win."

~

THE HUNT IN ELUSION

Once my cock had her outside, I woke her up three more times throughout the night. Once with my cock pushing inside her, once with my fingers playing with her clit, and once by sinking my tongue in her core. She's a taste I'll never get my fill of. A feeling I'll never tire of.

By the time morning comes, we share a much-needed shower. She's silent through it, her gaze often faraway, but the silence is also pleasant, as I now have to ensure my parents won't despise their future daughter-in-law.

If I'm not considering their reaction, I'm thinking about last night. For all the progress Della and I have made, we still don't know where De Falco, nor where his daughters, are located. Him being ahead of us makes me feel a fear I never imagined I would before.

I'm sitting on the edge of the bed when she leans over me from behind, placing her chin on my shoulder. "We should talk, Nico."

Reaching around, I grasp her hips and pull her on my lap, resting her over my cock. We're both still wet from the shower and undressed, so I adjust her, placing her legs around my waist. If we talk too long, she might just find me buried inside her.

"So talk."

"Yesterday, you were pleased to be getting rid of me. You agreed with you father about needing a union for your family." She glances down. "I'm not it."

Fury licks up my spine because, once again, she's fucking running, and not in the pleasant way. Did she not understand what last night meant?

"Della—"

She holds up her hand, pausing my pending argument. "No, I *want* to be. That's why I stayed." Her palm cups my shoulder as she presses her forehead to mine, her ocean eyes threatening to drown me. "I meant what I said yesterday when I said I love you. But I'm worried that you'll regret this in a year."

Snatching her left hand, I take it, pressing it over my heart —over my tattoo. "One day soon, I will be making oaths to you that mean more to me than the ones I for my family, and I fucking mean that." Finding her fourth finger, I caress it. "By the end of the day, you will have my ring on this finger. I gave you an opportunity to run from me and you didn't take it, which means you deal with the consequences."

Her mouth breaks into a large, pleased smile that shadows over her anxiety, and it makes me feel pretty fucking happy that I can garner such a response from her. Whatever's in her head, though, quickly darkens that happiness again.

"Nico, we've known each other for, like, less than two weeks. We know so little about one another. Your family hates me and for good reason. I provide no connections to you and—"

I place my hand over her mouth, effectively silencing her. "Let me handle my family. Fuck the connections. As for the speed of our unconventional relationship, most unions in this life are arranged, which means the couple meets one another *maybe* twice, if they're lucky, before the wedding. If that eases you. I've found what I want, so there's no point in denying it. We'll get to know everything about one another in time. Any other concerns?"

"Stefano," she mumbles around my hand, reminding me to lower it.

"We'll worry about that together. He is an issue, yes, and I'll have men scouring this fucking country searching for him, but for now, he won't ruin us."

"One more thing then." She pulls her lip into her mouth, chewing on it until I free it from her teeth, stroking my thumb over the delicate skin.

"What, *ma petite souris*?"

"Because I'm not from this life, I don't know how to *be* in it. I've gone to school, I worked, I helped Mom. I'm *normal*. When we moved into Stefano's house and he had me quit my job, at first it was nice. I mean, what person wouldn't enjoy not having to work, but still getting to enjoy a lavish lifestyle? But after a while, I got bored." Her eyes search mine. "Don't you get it, Nico? I can't be your mother. I can't simply sit around and shop. I have no clue what your organization even does, but more so, maybe I could be involved. Maybe I could, I don't know..." She rests her palm over my tattoo. "Take the oaths. Perhaps it'll even help your family accept me more."

Oh. Oh. "Della..." Regret weighs down my tone. I don't want to ever deny her a wish, but this request is a bit much. "Della, I understand you, but that's not how this works. I can't even fathom inducting you and allowing you to do what my men do. For one, you're not trained, and two—"

This time, she slaps a hand over my mouth. "Excuse me," her brows lift, "but who was it that rushed inside a house full of snipers to save your ass?"

I shudder. "Please don't remind me. Witnessing it once was enough to make me sick for a lifetime." Hooking my arm around her and my hand at her neck, I lock her into a position she's unable to move from. "I can't even think about losing you like that again, but I understand your wants and I'm sure we can find you a job to do. Something safe, where I can keep you protected, but you'll never be in the dark." We have many businesses acting as legal fronts; I'm sure I can make her a manager of one of them, as long as there's soldiers around protecting her.

Her mouth folds into a frown, but she doesn't persist with the argument, seeming to consider what I say. After a while, she nods, murmuring, "Okay, but I could still take the oaths and promise myself to your family."

"You will be." I stroke her left hand again. "A man's oaths are to the organization. A woman's to her husband. Your loyalty will accompany your *I do*."

Her nose wrinkles and she tries to jerk away from my unyielding hold. "Wow, can there be rules more sexist than those?"

Della must be the only woman in the mob to ever demand to be inducted. Even Mother, who has always been involved in the politics and not kept from the truths, knew she could only be *so* involved.

"According to my father, my mother once made a similar request. Nothing to the extent you're at, but she also wanted to know about the business dealings. Growing up, they were an influence on me, and I always knew I'd want a wife who could stand by my side and not shy away from the difficult truths of this life." Brushing a chunk of her hair away from her face, I pointedly look her in the eye. "You're that woman, Della. I'll never hide anything from you, but I can't formally induct you. I'm sorry."

Della smiles gently and leans forward to press a kiss to my lips. "Thank you, Nico. I get it. I'll accept it, even if I'm not letting this topic go. Give me a job and I'll be satisfied."

"I'd be disappointed if you did drop the subject." She wouldn't be Della if she didn't persist. "Now," taking her in my hand, I rub her against me, and my cock responds, waking to life, "I'm not quite ready to leave this room yet."

44
DELLA

"Y ou're not in there with him?" Ariella jerks her head toward her door, indicating that somewhere within this house, Nico is informing his family of our engagement. Which I imagine won't be a pleasant conversation.

Based on what I overheard his father talking about when he was in Nico's office yesterday, I'll bet my life he's less than thrilled. His mother is kind of a question mark for me. She must support her husband and want what's best for this family, but reflecting on the conversation we had the other day, I get the sense she also just wants Nico to be happy.

Rafael is also another one I question. When I betrayed Nico, he rightfully didn't exactly like me, but recent experiences make it seem like he's too chill of a person to care about things like arranged marriages and whether or not Nico is making the best choice for them all.

As for anyone else who'll have an opinion, I realize, I don't *know* any of his family members. One of many facets of Nico Corsetti unknown to me.

I shrug, glancing at my sister again from where she reclines against her bed, a large notepad propped against her knees. "I almost was, but he didn't want me around in case his father's a complete dick about it. His words, not mine. Either way, it gave me a chance to talk to you."

She looks up from her music composing, an activity I've only seen evidence of when she was at the centre, but haven't observed in a long time. Her brows wrinkle as she silently asks me what about.

"Do you think it's weird for me to agree to marry him so soon?"

"He loves you," she immediately murmurs. "And you love him, so no, I don't think you chose wrong. Love sometimes sneaks up in the most random of places."

The wistfulness in her tone nearly has me inquiring further. Ariella has never given the impression of exactly being interested in romance.

I reach across the bed, laying my hand over top of hers. "I'm worried about you now, Ari. I mean, Stefano might have had you in a centre, but now you're here. I always hoped it'd just be you and me out there, fending for ourselves, and I don't want you to feel trapped with me. Whatever you want, I'm sure Nico could help us ensure you get it."

Her lips purse and she rolls her eyes, gently shaking her head. She tugs her hand away and rests it on top of mine instead. "You got us a new chance at a family. I can't hate that. There's nowhere I want to be more than here, with you. Dr. Shappo will be seeing me and he's setting up a therapist to visit me regularly. We both knew the centre wasn't a requirement. That's why I was so reluctant to do anything there. It wasn't a *bad* place, but I wasn't happy, Della."

"This is a whole new life though. I don't think it'll be like how it was with Stefano. The Corsettis are the real deal. I think." I reflect on the grandness of the party I snuck into, and something tells me those events are the norm for them.

"Because life was *so* good before now." Wrinkling her nose, she chuckles lightheartedly. "I think it'll be a welcome change. Anything's better than living in a hospital. Now, go away," she jerks her chin toward the door, "I'm writing a song."

~

"**H**ow's your sister settling in?" Nico asks later that day when he *finally* emerges from his office. Exhaustion lines his eyes, but he doesn't say anything about what happened with his family. I won't be able to go on for the rest of the day without knowing, so instead of answering his question, I ask, "How did your conversation go?"

"We'll chat later. How's your sister settling in?"

Does he think that eases me? Biting my lip, I mumble, "She's good. Happy. I think she's already liking it more. Told me about her set-up with your doctor and that they're finding her a therapist."

Nico nods and slides by me, walking down the length of the hallway, leaving me to trail after him. "I've instructed Dr. Shappo to find the best in the area. Once he does, her care will be completely in her control. And yours, if she wants it to be. With Dr. Shappo's professional advice, of course. She won't be forced into anything, Della. I don't know the complete circumstances of her diagnosis, but if one day, she finds herself done with therapy and no longer wants it, then so be it. Nothing's mandatory here."

My steps pause, even though he continues walking. A new wave of admiration comes over me. I've left the details of Ariella's situation very limited, and for all Nico's need for control, and what his role demands of him, he's not taking control of her care.

He's not being Stefano.

"T-thank you."

He glances behind him, stopping at only spotting me farther away. With a crooked smile and a hand outstretched toward me, he says, "I should be ashamed you'd think I'd be a dick about this."

I slowly pad toward him, catching up. "Well, no, it's not that. It's just...I don't know."

With my hand enveloped in his, he wraps an arm around my waist and leads me to the front door. "Your sister was tossed into care, but from everything you've said, it seems a bit much for her condition. She's been treated like a nobody for over a year, when she's fully capable, minus speech."

"Exactly." How can he know so much without me having told him all that? "Did you read her file?"

"No."

"Dr. Shappo tell you?"

"No. Doctor-patient confidentiality and all that. He only has orders to unless she consents or if it's too important to hide from me."

Oh. Once again, he's doing it. Somehow, giving up his need for control, and for that, I love him even more.

"Pretty obvious, I think. De Falco only put her into the centre to get rid of her. Not because it was mandatory for her condition."

"Exactly," I repeat, more muted than earlier.

Nico leads me outside, to his car waiting out front. No one's around, but this is the first I know of him leaving the house, so I figure he's had staff bring it out earlier. He opens the passenger door and gestures for me to get in.

"We going somewhere?" I ask the obvious as I slide in, settling into the soft leather.

When he gets in and starts the car, the smooth rev of the engine indicating a highly expensive car rumbling beneath me. Then he finally answers, "We're going to look at some options. You want a job and not to sit around all day in the house, and I respect that. I have a list of tasks I've approved you to do, and it's up to you to pick."

I swear, he makes me love him a bit more each time he does something thoughtful.

45
NICO

That night in bed, Della is curled up in my arms, her hand resting over my abs. Her fourth finger is still bare, despite my morning claim that she'd be wearing my ring by now. She's too special for a plain, diamond ring, so I'll find something that suits her perfectly first.

Today was long. Between my parents—mainly Father—and going around from business to business with Della. It took a lot of strength for me to gather the list I had, since every one of our places are not as safe as I'd like them to be if Della's within them. She mentioned waitressing in the past, but my patience won't last the moment some drunk fucker touches her at one of our bars, so she's settled for managerial work at one of the clubs, working behind the scenes with a bodyguard around her at all times. My only stipulation: she starts after the wedding.

Her nails trace invisible circles around the hard planes of my chest and it's in this moment, I don't think there can be a better form of contentment than this.

"Nico," she murmurs into the skin of my chest, "you never

told me about the conversation with your family today. How did that go?"

Mentally, I groan at her insistence to remove that ease I felt moments ago. Aloud, I sigh. "My mother seems almost excited about it. Kept saying how she wants us both to be happy. Don't be surprised when she drags you and Ariella out to lunch soon. She seems pretty focused on welcoming you both."

She tips her head until her eyes can meet mine. "I appreciate that, and I think Ariella will too. Your brother?"

"Rafael's easy-going. He muttered something about knowing the moment you leapt into the De Falco mansion to knock me out of the way. You impressed him that day. As for my father..." Mentally, I erase quite a few of the curse words he threw up and down my office during his tirade, until Mother calmed him down. "He came around eventually."

Della pushes into a sitting position, staring down with a knowing expression. "Try that again, Nico, because I know what bullshit that is."

"It's true. My mother helped a lot with that though. He needs to get over what happened, and it'll take time." I shrug it off because for all Father's negativity, I know he'll eventually accept her. "Don't be surprised if he spends a lot of time ignoring you. You did gain some respect when I said you requested being inducted formally."

"I doubt he and I have much in common anyway." She glances at her hands and back, her lip curling beneath teeth, telling me she has more questions but struggles for a way to ask.

I sit up, pushing into the wall of pillows at my back. Then I reach for her, tugging her onto my lap where I can force her to look at me head-on.

"Ask what you want to know."

"I feel like there's so much."

"Ask what's clearly bothering you right now."

"You won't get mad?" There's nothing this woman can possibly ask me that'll anger me, so when I shake my head, she says, "There's you and Rafael, but I heard you mention a sister."

Ah. Somehow, I knew this conversation would eventually come up, and while I'm fine with sharing it, it's disconcerting to admit such things, when few people in the world know.

"Part of being a leader means to make the hard decisions," I start. "It means to make the choices we might not want to, but we do it for the family. *Everything* is for the family. *Unisciti a leale. Muori leale,*" he recites. "Whether that be an arranged marriage, a business trade...or separating a family. Of four siblings, I'm the second-born son and Raf is the third."

"Four?" Wide eyes slide to the side and I can nearly see the thoughts turning in her head as she calculates. "Wait, if you're the second-born son, then how are you—"

"Underboss?" I finish. "This isn't an easy story, Della, and it's not one many people know. There's four of us, and in order: Hawke, myself, Rafael, and my sister, Aurora." I pause, letting her digest the names. "I'll skip the details for your own sake, but Hawke, older by nearly a year, was kidnapped as a teenager. Taken by a group of men who felt Father owed them things. They used Hawke to try to appeal to my father's transactional side. It didn't work, of course, and the men didn't survive for long."

Her mouth slips open.

"Hawke should be in my position right now. He already hated so much of this life, thought it was too greedy, but what happened to him was the last straw. He left us, walked away from the life entirely, even knowing the oaths we take," I rest my hand over my tattoo, "could mean death by turning away. He hadn't officially taken them yet, and I think that's one of the only things saving him."

"Can you blame him for leaving?"

"Not in the slightest." When my muscles feel weaker and my hands slide from her hips, emotions getting heavy, I realize I've never told this story before. Anyone privy to the details were there and included in some way. "It sucks because even to this day, I miss him."

"So you've never seen him since then?"

I pause, preparing for another truth no one outside Rafael knows. "I'm trusting you with all my secrets, *petite souris*. I found him after a long time looking, but he wanted nothing to do with me. Recently, he reached out for help, which I happily gave, but that was it after that. No one knows this, Della. Not my parents. It'd break their hearts if they learned I had contact with their oldest and never said anything to them."

She lays her hand over my heart and nods a single time, silently promising.

"After Hawke left, my parents got extremely worried. About all of us, but especially my little sister, Aurora. She was only a young child then—six—and worse, a girl. It made them very anxious. So, they shipped her off to a private school in Toronto. It's sequestered, home to only select kids from prominent families, those who want their children safe and away from danger."

Della's brows lift. "There's enough families who abandon their children that there's an entire school for them?"

"It's not really a school. More like a house. Very small. Very elite. You'd be surprised what some families will do in a world like ours. Aurora's been there since they sent her off."

"Wow. You mean, she's *never* been back? Not even holidays?"

As she talks, I shake my head. "My parents debated it a few years ago, but at the time, she was so close to finishing school, they decided to keep her there. She's twenty now and she'll be coming home in a few weeks. It's time for her to reclaim her place as a Corsetti."

Della, ever fucking knowing, just says, "You mean, it's *convenient* for her to return now because you've set up a marriage deal."

"That's part of it, yes." I swipe a hand around her neck, propelling her face to mine, locking her in place. "Now's not the time to discuss those details, but we will, if you wish to know. I'll explain the history between our family and the one Aurora is engaged to, and it'll all make sense."

"I doubt that," she murmurs wryly, her lips pressing together. "Thank you for telling me all that though, Nico. I get the difficulties in sharing family secrets sometimes."

"They're your family now too," I say fiercely, meaning every word.

Della seems to take what I say seriously; she manages to pull away, her hand rubbing at her lips, eyes faraway, as though deep in thought. She slides from my lap and crosses her legs before she speaks.

"There's going to be a lot of newness in this family then. Me, your sister, my sister. A lot of learning. I wonder if there's some way to help Aurora get integrated easier."

"As kids, we're often thrown right in, honestly, and that's my plan with her. We'll throw her a welcome-home party and will invite all the prominent Montreal and surrounding areas' families."

She nods, as though expecting that response. "What if," she starts slowly, "we do that, but the focus isn't on her? You haven't commented on how long our engagement will be, but what if we make it shorter and use the engagement party and wedding as ways to acclimate her into society? Maybe she'll be comfortable if the attention isn't completely on her."

I stare at my bride-to-be, wondering how I managed to

snag one so fucking smart. "I'll invite her fiancé and this can be an opportunity for them to meet before their own engagement."

Della rolls her eyes. "Geez, I can see how I'm assisting your matchmaking skills."

I wink. "Because we know each other that well, *petite souris.*"

She lifts to her knees and shuffles to my side, pressing a single kiss to the side of my mouth. With a wicked grin, warning me she's not done yet, she adds, "Well, the ideas don't stop. Invite Hawke to the wedding."

Her suggestion rolls through my mind over and over until it formulates a different sentence, one that makes more sense.

"Della. No."

"I'm serious. How good would it be to have all the Corsettis back together again? Aurora, and if Hawke were to visit, your parents would be so happy."

Growling, I roll over and slide from the bed. I stalk to the large window across from it, giving her my back as I press a palm to the pane, staring into the dark outdoors, the forest I chased her in and beyond.

"It's not that easy. I get why you think it is, but I know my brother. He'd never agree. Between our union and my sister's, I can't stress about Hawke's return either." Especially if he were to bring his girl.

Tempting though. Picturing Hawke here, amongst all our family makes my heart clench with a new tightness, different than anything I've felt. More welcoming. Pleasant.

But it's not that easy.

Della's soft steps bring her to my side, and she wraps her arms around my waist, resting her head against the middle of my back. With my free hand, I rest it over her arms, silently conveying I'm not upset with her.

319

"I'm sorry, Nico, I get it. It was just an idea. Come back to bed?"

I carry her bridal-style back to the warmth the bed provides, tucking her against my large form. Both of us silent in our thoughts. Even after she falls asleep, I'm still staring at the moon through the window, picturing Hawke somewhere else, staring at the same one.

46
DELLA

The day after our conversation about his family, Nico texts me and asks me to go to the ballroom, where we first met when he spotted me rushing through the crowd. After leaving Ariella eating breakfast, I head across the main floor to the large, wide-open room.

A chandelier grander than anything I've probably ever seen before lights up the space. Old-fashioned paintings hang on one wall, while the others are adorned with filigree in the wall paint. I wonder how old this mansion is, and how many generations of Corsettis have walked these halls.

When his footsteps echo through the room, I turn around, the mid-length dress twirling around my legs. Nico's mossy eyes devour me as he approaches, promising more to come later. He looks every bit a mobster in his slacks and white button-down with the sleeves rolled up. His collar is opened an extra button, revealing a bare, tattooed chest I ache to rub my hands over.

"Curious place for you to ask me to wait."

Nico reaches for my hand and lifts it above my head, twirling me around in the same movement.

"It's where we first met."

"I'd argue that would be the greenhouse. That's where we first spoke."

"You're wrong, *ma petite souris.*" Wrapping an arm around my waist, he turns us slowly enough that my feet manage to keep up. "This is the place where a party was held so a certain underboss could find a wife. Then this fascinating, gorgeous, compelling woman insisted on looking the other way. When everyone was endeavouring to gain his attention, she ran away. What she believed was avoidance was actually a call to him though, and he knew any woman who gave chase and wasn't on her knees begging for a scrap of attention, was a woman he was intrigued by."

My smile is tentative, uncertain, as he details our initial meeting, wondering where his points are headed.

"She used the crowds to elude him until he caught her."

Nico reaches for my arm, his long fingers wrapping like a bracelet around the wrist he had once managed to snag as I was pushing through a crowd of onlookers.

"And then, even when he had, she still managed to get away, disappearing through this house, forcing him to have to hunt her down." Lowering my arm again, he tilts my face up. "So, no, Della, the greenhouse isn't where we first met."

I glance between us, at our barely moving feet. "Is that why we're here? This is some punishment because I didn't stick around that night?"

"Quite the opposite actually. I believe in endings. Every beginning deserves an ending, but sometimes, for one beginning to get a happily-ever-after, it requires a redo. You, my sweet girl, are my new beginning, right here in the very place we first met."

It's then I realize that in the midst of Nico's conversation, he's brought us toward the side of the room, in the exact place he first grabbed my wrist and managed to stop me from running off. When he demanded my name and gazed at me with inquisitive, entrapping eyes.

Nico reaches into his pocket and pulls out a ring. The band is a thin gold, making the bright blue sapphire massive in comparison. It glints in the chandelier's light above us.

"I'm not asking because the other night you agreed to be my wife the moment you ran into the forest rather than away. But if you're to be an underboss's queen, you'll do it with my ring on your finger."

He takes my left hand and slides the ring over my skin. It's cold at first, but my skin quickly adjusts. My hand feels weighed down, but I know it'll get easier with time.

He grasps the back of my neck and forces my attention away from the ring, back on him.

"I never wanted a wife, Della. It's why you heard me say what I had to my father. It's why I attended the party. I knew my role though, and what had to be done. What this job requires of me. I didn't want someone permanently in my life because the thought of spending forever with a woman who simply wanted me for the lifestyle I could provide made me want to swallow a bullet. Then, you ran through this fucking room, dressed like a siren, and your spell worked." He caresses the skin around my eyes, and while I want to shut them and fall victim to his gentle touch, I can't look away. "I drowned in the deadly sea of your eyes. Even when you turned back into a pumpkin and your veil dropped, I didn't care. I couldn't stop looking at what was so obviously right in front of me." His forehead falls onto mine and there's not a place my body, heart, and soul doesn't feel him. "I love you, Della. And I'll fucking chase you forever if I need to."

My chest feels halfway between agony and relief, between death and life, between villain and hero. Because that's what

Nico will always be for me. The villain who held my life in his hands, while becoming the hero who saved me from myself.

Tipping my head, I kiss him, first gently, and then harder as he kisses me back.

"I love you too, Nico Corsetti."

"There's only one thing left then."

There can be so many "one things" still to discuss, and though I open my mouth to ask those questions, he manages to answer first.

He releases me, his demeanor instantly transforming. Even without knowing what he's about to say, my body does. It responds to his deadly stance—becomes the prey to his predator —and I pace backwards.

"Della."

"Yeah?"

"Run."

47
NICO

3 Weeks Later

The Corsettis line the front foyer, a united front. I stand in the centre with Della at my side, her hand gripped in my own. Beside her is Ariella. On my other side is Rafael, leaning on the nearest wall, his expression nonchalant, despite the situation we're finding ourselves in. Closest to the door, my parents wait. Father appears at ease, but his hands continue to flex every couple of seconds, indicating otherwise. Mother paces back and forth, occasionally leaning on her husband as she fights anxiety.

ROSEN

Two minutes away.

"They'll be here in a moment."

Moments pass. No one speaks. No one moves. The silence is tense, packed with an electrifying energy we all pretend to disregard.

Then a car pulls up, the sound of the tires on gravel

325

reaching us, even through the mansion's thick front doors. My parents gravitate closer to the door, Mother's hand reaching for the knob, before my father pulls her back, shaking his head when she glances at him.

"She'll come to us," I hear him whisper to her.

At my side, Della presses closer. Her hand strokes over my back, disappearing beneath the jacket. The gentle touch of her easing presence soothes my mind from the chaos that's about to occur.

More silence. I wish I could hear when they get out of the car. When Aurora approaches the house.

"I swear to fuck, they better be on the other side of this door! Because if they don't even have the fucking decency to meet me at the door—"

Rafael sniggers. "Oh, we're all so fucked."

My sister's screeches are silenced by the front door opening. Rosen steps in first, shooting me a look of complete exhaustion and aggravation, before stepping aside and holding the door open.

A girl—woman, I suppose—steps through the door. A snarl lines her lips, her very apparent rage rolling from her shoulders and making the entire foyer stifling with her hate.

Aurora Corsetti is home.

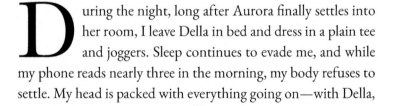

During the night, long after Aurora finally settles into her room, I leave Della in bed and dress in a plain tee and joggers. Sleep continues to evade me, and while my phone reads nearly three in the morning, my body refuses to settle. My head is packed with everything going on—with Della, Aurora, and De Falco.

With Hawke.

It's been three weeks since Della made the point about inviting Hawke, and for every reason I shouldn't, I come up with two more for why I should.

Inviting him won't change the fact that Hawke will *not* attend. He's made it extremely clear not wanting anything to do with us, and now that he has his own girl, he wouldn't bring her to a place he views as hell.

But what if he said yes?

What if Hawke agreed to come home?

It's that nagging voice driving me downstairs to my office. To my desk, where I pull out a pen and paper. To where I place the pen on the paper and write my request, detailing all the ways I'll ensure his visit would go smoothly.

Brother,

I know I promised you wouldn't hear from me again. That this family owes you their silence, and while I want to respect that, I suppose I'm not.

You see, like you, I found my forever. My queen. She's perfect. Challenges me like I'd never believe someone could. Hell, she even tried to have me killed. I think you'd like her.

We're getting married in two weeks.

I want you to come.

I want you to come, Hawke. You and Willow.

I know you're immediately saying no. You're thinking of your girl's safety, but I promise if anyone lifts a hand to either of you, I'll help you kill them myself. I won't have selfishness ruin my girl's day, nor your re-arrival.

I understand all the reasons you'll decide not to. I'll respect them too, but I needed to ask. Actually, my fiancée is who suggested this, so you see, she really does make me a better person.

I hope you come and see that for yourself.

Other things in the family have changed since you last were here, and while I understand you don't wish to know, I also should tell you, it's about Aurora. She could use you through this next little while.

I'm not above bribery.

Please come, brother.

-N.C.

When I'm done, I fold the letter up and slip it into the envelope, sealing it. I leave it on my desk until morning and retreat back to my bedroom.

In bed, I crawl behind Della, wrapping my arms around her waist and pulling her against my body. She mumbles something in her sleep before burying her head deeper into the pillow. Hair falls over her face, which I flick aside, pressing a longing kiss to the spot.

Despite the war with De Falco, she's also given me so much. Her. Her love. A future. A companion to be by my side.

Nothing else matters. Nothing else besides the fact that I've found my queen and we will rule this city, burning everyone in our wake.

Thank you for reading! Reviews are highly appreciated and so helpful to an author. Reviews for The Hunt in Elusion can be left on Goodreads, Bookbub, and Amazon.

The Craving in Slumber (Fractured Ever Afters #2) is a Sleeping Beauty inspired forbidden romance between Aurora and Rosen.

Lastly, want to see how Hawke reacts to receiving that letter? You can download the free bonus scene by visiting my website.

ALSO BY M.L. PHILPITT

ACKNOWLEDGMENTS

Thank you to my readers for going on this mafia romance adventure with me!

Lee Jacquot, despite the hecticness in both our lives, you're always here to talk over stuff, and I love you for it.

Megan, lady, how do you put up with me? Especially through this one. You know I appreciate you because I can't even list the items you've talked me down from when I was writing... editing... formatting... thinking... planning... this one. If it involved this book, you made me take three steps back and try again.

Colleen, thank you for being a wonderful beta and answering my billion questions.

Rebecca Barney from Fairest Reviews Editing Services gets huge thanks. Here's to the start of another series!

Thank you to The Next Step PR. Colleen, Jill, Megan, Anna, and of course, Kiki - you're all amazing. Thank you for everything you do. You're the best team to have!

Thank you to Cat Imb of TRC Designs for creating the best cover a mafia romance inspired by Cinderella can have.

Thank you to Karina (@id_rather.be.the.moon) and Cat Imb for double checking my French.

Thank you to all the bloggers, booktokers, and bookstagrammers who helped with the release of this book. Your help doesn't go unnoticed!

ABOUT THE AUTHOR

USA Today Bestselling author M.L. Philpitt writes both dark romance and paranormal romance. When she's not writing made-up realities, she's reading them. She lives in Canada with her four pets and survives life with coffee and an obsession with fictional characters, especially the morally grey kind. By day, she masks as a therapist, and is still waiting for her Hogwarts letter so she can be sorted into her Ravenclaw house.

Printed in Great Britain
by Amazon

34701272R00199